美国亚裔文学研究丛书

总主编　郭英剑

An Anthology of Korean American Literature
美国韩裔文学作品选

主编　郭英剑　宋晓涵　刘向辉

本研究受中国人民大学科学研究基金资助，系2017年度重大规划项目"美国亚裔文学研究"（编号：17XNLG10）阶段性成果。

中国人民大学出版社
·北京·

图书在版编目（CIP）数据

美国韩裔文学作品选：英文、汉文 / 郭英剑，宋晓涵，刘向辉主编 . -- 北京：中国人民大学出版社，2022.10
（美国亚裔文学研究丛书 / 郭英剑总主编）
ISBN 978-7-300-31088-6

Ⅰ.①美… Ⅱ.①郭… ②宋… ③刘… Ⅲ.①文学－作品综合集－美国－英、汉 Ⅳ.①I712.11

中国版本图书馆 CIP 数据核字（2022）第 184111 号

美国亚裔文学研究丛书
美国韩裔文学作品选
总主编　郭英剑
主　编　郭英剑　宋晓涵　刘向辉
Meiguo Hanyi Wenxue Zuopinxuan

出版发行	中国人民大学出版社			
社　　址	北京中关村大街 31 号		邮政编码	100080
电　　话	010-62511242（总编室）		010-62511770（质管部）	
	010-82501766（邮购部）		010-62514148（门市部）	
	010-62515195（发行公司）		010-62515275（盗版举报）	
网　　址	http://www.crup.com.cn			
经　　销	新华书店			
印　　刷	唐山玺诚印务有限公司			
规　　格	170 mm×240 mm　16 开本		版　次	2022 年 10 月第 1 版
印　　张	14.25		印　次	2022 年 10 月第 1 次印刷
字　　数	263 000		定　价	68.00 元

版权所有　　侵权必究　　印装差错　　负责调换

总 序

美国亚裔文学的历史、现状与未来

郭英剑

一、何谓"美国亚裔文学"?

"美国亚裔文学"(Asian American Literature),简言之,是指由美国社会中的亚裔群体作家所创作的文学。也有人称之为"亚裔美国文学"。

然而,"美国亚裔文学"这个由两个核心词汇——"美国亚裔"和"文学"——所组成的术语,远没有它看上去那么简单。说它极其复杂,一点也不为过。因此,要想对"美国亚裔文学"有基本的了解,就需要从其中的两个关键词入手。

首先,"美国亚裔"中的"亚裔",是指具有亚裔血统的美国人,但其所指并非一个单一的族裔,其组成包括美国来自亚洲各国(或者与亚洲各国有关联)的人员群体及其后裔,比如美国华裔(Chinese Americans)、日裔(Japanese Americans)、菲律宾裔(Filipino Americans)、韩裔(Korean Americans)、越南裔(Vietnamese Americans)、印度裔(Indian Americans)、泰国裔(Thai Americans)等等。

根据联合国的统计,亚洲总计有48个国家。因此,所谓"美国亚裔"自然包括在美国的所有这48个亚洲国家的后裔,或者有其血统的人员。由此所涉及的各国(以及地区)迥异的语言、不同的文化、独特的人生体验,以及群体交叉所产生的多样性,包括亚洲各国由于战争交恶所带给后裔及其有关人员的深刻影响,就构成了"美国亚裔"这一群体具有极端的复杂性。在美国统计局的定义中,美国亚裔是细分为"东亚"(East Asia)、"东南亚"(Southeast Asia)和南亚(South Asia)。[1] 当然,也正由于其复杂性,到现在有些亚洲国家在美国的后裔或者移民,尚未形成一个相对固定的族裔群体。

---

[1] 参见:Humes, Karen R, Jones, Nicholas A, Ramirez, Roberto R. (March 2011). "Overview of Race and Hispanic Origin: 2010" (PDF). United States Census Bureau. U.S. Department of Commerce.

其次，文学主要由作家创作而成，由于"美国亚裔"群体的复杂性，自然导致"美国亚裔"的"作家"群体同样处于极其复杂的状态，但也因此使这一群体的概念具有相当大的包容性。凡是身在美国的亚裔后裔、具有亚洲血统或者后来移民美国的亚裔作家，都可以称之为"美国亚裔作家"。

由于亚裔群体的语言众多，加上一些移民作家的母语并非英语，因此，"美国亚裔文学"一般指的是美国亚裔作家使用英语所创作的文学作品。但由于历史的原因，学术界也把最早进入美国时，亚裔用本国语言所创作的文学作品，无论是口头作品还是文字作品——比如19世纪中期，华人进入美国时遭到拘禁时所创作的诗句，也都纳入"美国亚裔文学"的范畴之内。同时，随着全球化时代的到来，各国之间的文学与文化交流日益加强，加之移民日渐增加，因此，也将部分发表时为亚洲各国语言，但后来被翻译成英语的文学作品，同样纳入"美国亚裔文学"的范畴。

最后，"美国亚裔"的划分，除了语言、历史、文化之外，还有一个地理的因素需要考虑。随着时间的推移与学术界研究【特别是离散研究（Diaspora Studies）】的进一步深化，"美国亚裔"中的"美国"（America），也不单单指"the United States"了。我们知道，由于全球化时代所带来的人口流动性的极度增加，国与国之间的界限有时候变得模糊起来，人们的身份也变得日益具有多样性和流动性。比如，由于经济全球化的原因，美国已不单单是一个地理概念上的美国。经济与文化的构成，造就了可口可乐、麦当劳等商业品牌，它们都已经变成了流动的美国的概念。这样的美国不断在"侵入"其他国家，并对其他国家产生了巨大的影响。当然，一个作家的流动性，也无形中扩大了"美国"的概念。比如，一个亚洲作家可能移民到美国，但一个美国亚裔作家也可能移民到其他国家。这样的流动性拓展了"美国亚裔"的定义与范畴。

为此，"美国亚裔文学"这一概念，有时候也包括一些身在美洲地区，但与美国有关联的作家，他们用英语进行创作或者被翻译成英语的文学作品，也会被纳入这一范畴之内。

应该指出的是，由于"亚裔"群体进入美国的时间早晚不同，加上"亚裔"群体的复杂性，那么，每一个"亚裔"群体，都有其独有的美国族裔特征，比如华裔与日裔有所不同，印度裔与日裔也有所不同。如此一来，正如一些学者所认为那样，各个族裔的特征最好应该分开来叙述和加以研究。[1]

---

[1] 参见: Chin, Frank, et al. 1991. "Preface" to *Aiiieeeee! An Anthology of Asian American Writers*. Edited by Frank China, Jeffery Paul Chan, Lawson Fusao Inada, and Shawn Wong. A Mentor Book. p.xi.

二、为何要研究"美国亚裔文学"？

虽然上文中提出，"美国亚裔"是个复杂而多元的群体，"美国亚裔文学"包含了极具多样化的亚裔群体作家，但是我们还是要把"美国亚裔文学"当作一个整体来进行研究。理由有三：

首先，"美国亚裔文学"与"美国亚裔作家"（Asian American Writers）最早出现时，即是作为一个统一的概念而提出的。1974年，赵健秀（Frank Chin）等学者出版了《哎咿！美国亚裔作家选集》。[1] 作为首部划时代的"美国亚裔作家"的文学作品选集，该书通过发现和挖掘此前50年中被遗忘的华裔、日裔与菲律宾裔中的重要作家，选取其代表性作品，进而提出要建立作为独立的研究领域的"美国亚裔文学"（Asian American Literature）。[2]

其次，在亚裔崛起的过程中，无论是亚裔的无心之为，还是美国主流社会与其他族裔的有意为之，亚裔都是作为一个整体被安置在一起的。因此，亚裔文学也是作为一个整体而存在的。近年来，我国的"美国华裔文学"研究成为美国文学研究学界的一个热点。但在美国，虽然有"美国华裔文学"（Chinese American Literature）的说法，但真正作为学科存在的，则是"美国亚裔文学"（Asian American Literature），甚至更多的则是"美国亚裔研究"（Asian American Studies）。

再次，1970年代之后，"美国亚裔文学"的发展在美国学术界逐渐成为研究的热点，引发了研究者的广泛关注，为此，包括耶鲁大学、哥伦比亚大学、布朗大学、宾夕法尼亚大学等常青藤盟校以及斯坦福大学、加州大学系统的伯克利分校、洛杉矶分校等美国众多高校，都设置了"美国亚裔研究"（Asian American Studies）专业，也设置了"美国亚裔学系"（Department of Asian American Studies）或者"亚裔研究中心"，开设了丰富多彩的亚裔文学与亚裔研究方面的课程。包括哈佛大学在内的众多高校也都陆续开设了众多的美国亚裔研究以及美国亚裔文学的课程，学术研究成果丰富多彩。

那么，我们需要提出的一个问题是，在中国语境下，研究"美国亚裔文学"的意义与价值究竟何在？我的看法如下：

第一，"美国亚裔文学"是"美国文学"的重要组成部分。不研究亚裔文学或者忽视甚至贬低亚裔文学，学术界对于美国文学的研究就是不完整的。如上文所说，亚裔文学的真正兴起是在20世纪六七十年代。美国六七十年代特殊的时

---

[1] Chin, Frank, Chan, Jeffery Paul, Inada, Lawson Fusao, et al. 1974. *Aiiieeeee! An Anthology of Asian-American Writers*. Howard University Press.

[2] 参见：Chin, Frank, et al. 1991. "Preface" to *Aiiieeeee! An Anthology of Asian American Writers*. Edited by Frank China, Jeffery Paul Chan, Lawson Fusao Inada, and Shawn Wong. A Mentor Book. pp.xi–xxii.

代背景极大促进了亚裔文学发展，自此，亚裔文学作品层出不穷，包括小说、戏剧、传记、短篇小说、诗歌等各种文学形式。在当下的美国，亚裔文学及其研究与亚裔的整体生存状态息息相关；种族、历史、人口以及政治诉求等因素促使被总称为"亚裔"的各个少数族裔联合发声，以期在美国政治领域和主流社会达到最大的影响力与辐射度。对此，学术界不能视而不见。

第二，我国现有的"美国华裔文学"研究，无法替代更不能取代"美国亚裔文学"研究。自从1980年代开始译介美国亚裔文学以来，我国国内的研究就主要集中在华裔文学领域，研究对象也仅为少数知名华裔作家及长篇小说创作领域。相较于当代国外亚裔文学研究的全面与广博，国内对于亚裔的其他族裔作家的作品关注太少。即使是那些亚裔文学的经典之作，如菲律宾裔作家卡罗斯·布鲁桑（Carlos Bulosan）的《美国在我心中》（*America Is in the Heart*，1946），日裔女作家山本久惠（Hisaye Yamamoto）的《第十七个音节及其他故事》（*Seventeen Syllables and Other Stories*，1949）、日裔约翰·冈田（John Okada）的《不－不仔》（*NO-NO Boy*，1959），以及如今在美国文学界如日中天的青年印度裔作家裘帕·拉希莉（Jhumpa Lahiri）的作品，专题研究均十分少见。即便是像华裔作家任璧莲（Gish Jen）这样已经受到学者很大关注和研究的作家，其长篇小说之外体裁的作品同样没有得到足够的重视，更遑论国内学术界对亚裔文学在诗歌、戏剧方面的研究了。换句话说，我国学术界对于整个"美国亚裔文学"的研究来说还很匮乏，属于亟待开发的领域。实际上，在我看来，不研究"美国亚裔文学"，也无法真正理解"美国华裔文学"。

第三，在中国"一带一路"倡议与中国文化走出去的今天，作为美国文学研究的新型增长点，大力开展"美国亚裔文学"研究，特别是研究中国的亚洲周边国家如韩国、日本、印度等国在美国移民状况的文学表现，以及与华裔在美国的文学再现，使之与美国和世界其他国家的"美国亚裔文学"保持同步发展，具有较大的理论意义与学术价值。

三、"美国亚裔文学"及其研究：历史与现状

历史上看，来自亚洲国家的移民进入美国，可以追溯到18世纪。但真正开始较大规模的移民则是到了19世纪中后期。然而，亚裔从进入美国一开始，就遭遇到了来自美国社会与官方的阻力与法律限制。从1880年代到1940年代这半个多世纪的岁月中，为了保护美国本土而出台的一系列移民法，都将亚洲各国人们排除在外，禁止他们当中的大部分人进入美国大陆地区。直到20世纪40-60年代移民法有所改革时，这种状况才有所改观。其中的改革措施之一就是取消了

国家配额。如此一来，亚洲移民人数才开始大规模上升。2010年的美国国家统计局分析显示，亚裔是美国社会移民人数增长最快的少数族裔。[1]

"美国亚裔"实际是个新兴词汇。这个词汇的创立与诞生实际上已经到了1960年代后期。在此之前，亚洲人或者具有亚洲血统者通常被称为"Oriental"（东方人）、"Asiatic"（亚洲人）和"Mongoloid"（蒙古人、黄种人）。[2] 美国历史学家市冈裕次（Yuji Ichioka）在1960年代末期，开创性地开始使用 Asian American 这个术语，[3] 从此，这一词汇开始被人普遍接受和广泛使用。

与此时间同步，"美国亚裔文学"在随后的1970年代作为一个文学类别开始出现并逐步产生影响。1974年，有两部著作几乎同时出版，都以美国亚裔命名。一部是《美国亚裔传统：散文与诗歌选集》，[4] 另外一部则是前面提到过的《哎咿！美国亚裔作家选集》。[5] 这两部著作，将过去长期被人遗忘的亚裔文学带到了聚光灯下，让人们仿佛看到了一种新的文学形式。其后，新的亚裔作家不断涌现，文学作品层出不穷。

最初亚裔文学的主要主题与主要内容为种族（race）、身份（identity）、亚洲文化传统、亚洲与美国或者西方国家之间的文化冲突，当然也少不了性别（sexuality）、社会性别（gender）、性别歧视、社会歧视等。后来，随着移民作家的大规模出现，离散文学的兴起，亚裔文学也开始关注移民、语言、家国、想象、全球化、劳工、战争、帝国主义、殖民主义等问题。

如果说，上述1974年的两部著作代表着亚裔文学进入美国文学的世界版图之中，那么，1982年著名美国亚裔研究专家金惠经（Elaine Kim）的《美国亚裔文学的创作及其社会语境》的出版，作为第一部学术著作，则代表着美国亚裔文学研究正式登上美国学术界的舞台。自此以后，不仅亚裔文学创作兴盛起来，而且亚裔文学研究也逐渐成为热点，成果不断推陈出新。

同时，人们对于如何界定"美国亚裔文学"等众多问题进行了深入的探讨，

---

[1] 参见：Wikipedia 依据 "U.S. Census Show Asians Are Fastest Growing Racial Group" (NPR.org) 所得出的数据统计。https://en.wikipedia.org/wiki/Asian_Americans。

[2] Mio, Jeffrey Scott, ed. 1999. *Key Words in Multicultural Interventions: A Dictionary*. ABC-Clio ebook. Greenwood Publishing Group. p.20.

[3] K. Connie Kang, "Yuji Ichioka, 66; Led Way in Studying Lives of Asian Americans," *Los Angeles Times*, September 7, 2002. Reproduced at ucla.edu by the Asian American Studies Center.

[4] Wand, David Hsin-fu, ed. 1974. *Asian American Heritage: An Anthology of Prose and Poetry*. New York: Pocket Books.

[5] Chin, Frank, Chan, Jeffery, Inada, Lawson, et al. 1974. *Aiiieeeee! An Anthology of Asian-American Writers*. Howard University Press.

[6] Kim, Elaine. 1982. *Asian American Literature: An Introduction to the Writings and Their Social Context*. Philadelphia: Temple University Press.

进一步推动了这一学科向前发展。相关问题包括：究竟谁可以说自己是美国亚裔（an Asian America）？这里的 America 是不是就是单指"美国"（the United States）？是否可以包括"美洲"（Americas）？如果亚裔作家所写的内容与亚裔无关，能否算是"亚裔文学"？如果不是亚裔作家，但所写内容与亚裔有关，能否算在"亚裔文学"之内？

总体上看，早期的亚裔文学研究专注于美国身份的建构，即界定亚裔文学的范畴，以及争取其在美国文化与美国文学中应得的席位，是 20 世纪七八十年代亚裔民权运动的前沿阵地。早期学者如赵健秀、徐忠雄（Shawn Wong）等为领军人物。随后出现的金惠经、张敬珏（King-Kok Cheung）、骆里山（Lisa Lowe）等人均成为了亚裔文学研究领域的权威学者，他/她们的著作影响并造就了第二代美国亚裔文学研究者。20 世纪 90 年代之后的亚裔文学研究逐渐淡化了早期研究中对于意识形态的侧重，开始向传统的学科分支、研究方法以及研究理论靠拢，研究视角多集中在学术马克思主义（academic Marxism）、后结构主义、后殖民、女权主义以及心理分析等。

进入 21 世纪以来，"美国亚裔文学"研究开始向多元化、全球化与跨学科方向发展。随着亚裔文学作品爆炸式的增长，来自阿富汗、印度、巴基斯坦、越南等族裔作家的作品开始受到关注，极大丰富与拓展了亚裔文学研究的领域。当代"美国亚裔文学"研究的视角与方法也不断创新，战争研究、帝国研究、跨国研究、视觉文化理论、空间理论、身体研究、环境理论等层出不穷。新的理论与常规性研究交叉进行，不但开创了新的研究领域，对于经典问题（例如身份建构）的研究也提供了新的解读方式与方法。

四、作为课题的"美国亚裔文学"研究及其丛书

"美国亚裔文学"研究，是由我担任课题负责人的 2017 年度中国人民大学科学研究基金重大规划项目。"美国亚裔文学研究丛书"，即是该项课题的结题成果。作为"美国亚裔文学"方面的系列丛书，将由文学史、文学作品选、文学评论集、学术论著等组成，由我担任该丛书的总主编。

"美国亚裔文学"研究在 2017 年 4 月立项。随后，该丛书的论证计划，得到了国内外专家的一致认可。2017 年 5 月 27 日，中国人民大学科学研究基金重大规划项目"美国亚裔文学研究"开题报告会暨"美国亚裔文学研究高端论坛"在中国人民大学隆重召开。参加此次会议的专家学者全部为美国亚裔文学研究领域中的顶尖学者，包括美国加州大学洛杉矶分校的张敬珏教授、南京大学海外教育学院前院长程爱民教授、南京大学海外教育学院院长赵文书教授、北京语言大学

应用外语学院院长陆薇教授、北京外国语大学潘志明教授、解放军外国语学院石平萍教授等。在此次会议上，我向与会专家介绍了该项目的基本情况、未来研究方向与预计出版成果。与会专家对该项目的设立给予高度评价，强调在当今时代加强"美国亚裔文学"研究的必要性，针对该项目的预计研究及其成果，也提出了一些很好的建议。

根据最初的计划，这套丛书将包括文学史 2 部：《美国亚裔文学史》和《美国华裔文学史》；文学选集 2 部：《美国亚裔文学作品选》和《美国华裔文学作品选》；批评文选 2 部：《美国亚裔文学评论集》和《美国华裔文学评论集》；访谈录 1 部：《美国亚裔作家访谈录》；学术论著 3 部，包括美国学者张敬珏教授的《静默留声》和《文心无界》。总计 10 部著作。

根据我的基本设想，《美国亚裔文学史》和《美国华裔文学史》的撰写，将力图体现研究者对美国亚裔文学的研究进入到了较为深入的阶段。由于文学史是建立在研究者对该研究领域发展变化的总体认识上，涉及文学流派、创作方式、文学与社会变化的关系、作家间的关联等各方面的问题，我们试图通过对亚裔文学发展进行总结和评价，旨在为当前亚裔文学和华裔文学的研究和推广做出一定贡献。

《美国亚裔文学作品选》和《美国华裔文学作品选》，除了记录、介绍等基本功能，还将在一定程度上发挥形成民族认同、促进意识形态整合等功能。作品选编是民族共同体想象性构建的重要途径，也是作为文学经典得以确立和修正的最基本方式之一。因此，这样的作品选编，也要对美国亚裔文学的研究起到重要的促进作用。

《美国亚裔文学评论集》和《美国华裔文学评论集》，将主要选编美国、中国以及世界上最有学术价值的学术论文，虽然有些可能因为版权问题而不得不舍弃，但我们努力使之成为中国学术界研究"美国亚裔文学"和"美国华裔文学"的重要参考书目。

《美国亚裔作家访谈录》、美国学者的著作汉译、中国学者的美国亚裔文学学术专著等，将力图促使中美两国学者之间的学术对话，特别是希望中国的"美国亚裔文学"研究，既在中国的美国文学研究界，也要在美国和世界上的美国文学研究界发出中国学者的声音。"一带一路"倡议的实施，使得文学研究的关注发生了转变，从过分关注西方话语，到逐步转向关注中国（亚洲）话语，我们的美国亚裔（华裔）文学研究，正是从全球化视角切入，思考美国亚裔（华裔）文学的世界性。

2018 年，我们按照原计划出版了《美国亚裔文学作品选》《美国华裔文学作品选》《美国亚裔文学评论集》《美国华裔文学评论集》。2022年上半年，我们出版了学术专著《文心无界——不拘性别、文类与形式的华美文学》。2022年下半年，还将出版《美国日裔文学作品选》《美国韩裔文学作品选》《美国越南裔文学作品选》《美国西亚裔文学作品选》《美国南亚裔文学作品选》等5部文学选集。

　　需要说明的是，这5部选集是在原有计划之外的产物。之所以在《美国亚裔文学作品选》之外又专门将其中最主要的国家与区域的文学作品结集出版，是因为在研究过程中我发现，现有的《美国亚裔文学作品选》已经无法涵盖丰富多彩的亚裔文学。更重要的是，无论是在国内还是在美国，像这样将美国亚裔按照国别与区域划分后的文学作品选全部是空白，国内外学术界对这些国别与区域的文学创作的整体关注也较少，可以说它们都属于亟待开垦的新研究领域。通过这5部选集，可以让国内对于美国亚裔文学有更为完整的了解。我也希望借此填补国内外在这个领域的空白。

　　等到丛书全部完成出版，将会成为一套由15部著作所组成的系列丛书。2018年的时候，我曾经把这套丛书界定为"国内第一套较为完整的美国亚裔文学方面的系列丛书"。现在，时隔4年之后，特别是在有了这新出版的5部选集之后，我可以说这套丛书将是"国内外第一套最为完整的美国亚裔文学方面的系列丛书"。

　　那么，我们为什么要对"美国亚裔文学"进行深入研究，并要编辑、撰写和翻译这套丛书呢？

　　首先，虽然"美国亚裔文学"在国外已有较大的影响，学术界也对此具有相当规模的研究，但在国内学术界，出于对"美国华裔文学"的偏爱与关注，"美国亚裔文学"相对还是一个较为陌生的领域。因此，本课题首次以"亚裔"集体的形式标示亚裔文学的存在，旨在介绍"美国亚裔文学"，推介具有族裔特色和代表性的作家作品。

　　其次，选择"美国亚裔文学"为研究对象，其中也有对"美国华裔文学"的研究，希望能够体现我们对全球化视野中华裔文学的关注，也体现试图融合亚裔、深入亚裔文学研究的学术自觉。同时，在多元化多种族的美国社会语境中，我们力主打破国内长久以来专注"美国华裔文学"研究的固有模式，转而关注包括华裔作家在内的亚裔作家所具有的世界性眼光。

　　最后，顺应美国亚裔文学发展的趋势，对美国亚裔文学的研究不仅是文学研究界的关注热点，还是我国外语与文学教育的关注焦点。我们希望为高校未来"美国亚裔文学"的课程教学，提供一套高水平的参考丛书。

五、"美国亚裔文学"及其研究的未来

如前所述,"美国亚裔文学"在20世纪70年代逐渐崛起后,使得亚裔文学从沉默走向了发声。到21世纪,亚裔文学呈现出多元化的发展特征,更重要的是,许多新生代作家开始崭露头角。单就这些新的亚裔作家群体,就有许多值得我们关注的话题。

2018年6月23日,"2018美国亚裔文学高端论坛——跨界:21世纪的美国亚裔文学"在中国人民大学隆重召开。参加会议的专家学者将近150人。

在此次会议上,我提出来:今天,为什么要研究美国亚裔文学?我们要研究什么?

正如我们在会议通知上所说,美国亚裔文学在一百多年的风雨沧桑中历经"沉默"、"觉醒"、走向"发声",见证了美国亚裔族群的沉浮兴衰。21世纪以来,美国亚裔文学在全球冷战思维升温和战火硝烟不断的时空背景下,不囿于狭隘的种族主义藩篱,以"众声合奏"与"兼容并蓄"之势构筑出一道跨洋、跨国、跨种族、跨语言、跨文化、跨媒介、跨学科的文学景观,呈现出鲜明的世界主义意识。为此,我们拟定了一些主要议题。包括:1. 美国亚裔文学中的跨洋书写;2. 美国亚裔文学中的跨国书写;3. 美国亚裔文学中的跨种族书写;4. 美国亚裔文学中的跨语言书写;5. 美国亚裔文学中的跨文化书写;6. 美国亚裔文学的翻译跨界研究;7. 美国亚裔文学的跨媒介研究;8. 美国亚裔文学的跨学科研究等。

2019年6月22日,"2019美国亚裔文学高端论坛"在中国人民大学举行,会议的主题是"战争与和平:美国亚裔文学研究中的生命书写"。那次会议,依旧有来自中国的近80所高校的150余位教师和硕博研究生参加我们的论坛。

2020年年初,全球疫情大暴发,我们的"2020美国亚裔文学高端论坛"一直往后推迟,直到2020年12月5日在延边大学举行,会议的主题是"疫情之思:变局中的美国亚裔文学"。因为疫情原因,我们劝阻了很多愿意来参会的学者,但即便如此,也有近百位来自各地的专家学者与研究生前来参会。

2021年6月26—27日,"相遇与融合:2021首届华文/华裔文学研讨会"在西北师范大学举行。这次会议是由我在延边大学的会议上提出倡议,得到了中国社会科学院文学所赵稀方教授的积极响应,由他和我一起联合发起并主办,由西北师范大学外国语学院承办。我们知道,长期以来,华裔文学和华文文学分属不同的学科和研究领域,其研究对象、传统和范式都有所不同,但血脉相承的天然联系终究会让两者相遇、走向融合。从时下的研究看,虽然两者的研究范式自成体系、独树一帜,但都面临着华裔作家用中文创作和华人作家用外文创作的新趋势,这给双方的学科发展与研究领域都带来了新的挑战,也带来了新的学科发

展机遇。我们都相信，在学科交叉融合已成为实现创新发展必然趋势的当下语境中，华裔/华文文学走到了相遇与融合的最佳时机。为此，我们倡议并搭建平台，希望两个领域的学者同台进行学术交流与对话，探讨文学研究的新发展，以求实现华裔文学和华文文学的跨界融通。

事实上，21世纪以来，亚裔群体、亚裔所面临的问题、亚裔研究都发生了巨大的变化。从过去较为单纯的亚裔走向了跨越太平洋（transpacific）；从过去的彰显美国身份（claiming America）到今天的批评美国身份（critiquing America）；过去单一的 America，现在变成了复数的 Americas，这些变化都值得引起我们的高度重视。由此所引发的诸多问题，也需要我们去认真对待。比如：如何在"21世纪"这个特殊的时间区间内去理解"美国亚裔文学"这一概念？有关"美国亚裔文学"的概念构建，是否本身就存在着作家的身份焦虑与书写的界限划分？如何把握"美国亚裔文学"的整体性与区域性？"亚裔"身份是否是作家在表达过程中去主动拥抱的归属之地？等等。

2021年年底，国家社会科学基金重大招标课题揭晓，我申请的"美国族裔文学中的文化共同体思想研究"喜获中标。这将进一步推动我目前所从事的美国亚裔文学研究，并在未来由现在的美国亚裔文学研究走向美国的整个族裔文学研究。

展望未来，"美国亚裔文学"呈现出更加生机勃勃的生命力，"美国亚裔文学"的研究也将迎来更加光明的前途。

2018年8月28日定稿于哈佛大学
2022年8月28日修改于北京

前言

"美国亚裔文学"研究，是由中国人民大学"杰出学者"特聘教授郭英剑先生担任课题负责人的2017年度中国人民大学科学研究基金重大规划项目。"美国亚裔文学研究丛书"，是该项课题的结题成果。由郭英剑教授担任该套丛书的总主编。这是国内第一套最为完整的"美国亚裔文学"方面的系列丛书，由文学史、文学作品选、文学评论集、学术论著等所组成。

所谓"美国韩裔文学"，是指由美国社会中的韩裔群体作家用英语创作的文学作品，发表时为亚洲语言之后被译作英语的文学作品也涵盖其中。此处的韩裔群体，不仅指在美国出生的韩国人，如苏珊·崔、凯瑟琳·钟等，还指在美国本土以外出生后来到美国的移民作家，如车学庆、金晏密等。

需要说明的是，就移民来源地而言，由于历史、政治等特殊原因，来自朝鲜的移民数量远低于来自韩国的人数，因此，我们选择了"美国韩裔"这一概念，而非"美国朝鲜裔"的界定方式。但是，由于韩国在1948年8月15日独立，朝鲜在1948年9月9日建国，而在此之前史称"朝鲜王朝"，因此，在述及此前的历史与人物时，还会使用"美国朝鲜裔"的说法。

"美国韩裔文学"无疑是"美国亚裔文学"版图中不可或缺的一部分，它在近百年的发展中突破重围、不断壮大。"美国韩裔文学"题材多样，既聚焦韩裔族群的家国历史与民族品质，又关注其他族裔乃至全球热点。现在，韩裔文学作品不仅通过对过往多重维度地审视，展现了一幅韩裔美国人在历史潮流中奋力创生的画卷，而且通过对现实的深切关怀，为当下社会发展与人类福祉提供借鉴。

今天的朝鲜人与韩国人到美国的第一次移民浪潮，早在两国建国之前就开始了，横跨20世纪初至20世纪50年代。此阶段的移民以"照片新娘"、流亡人士、劳工等为主，也夹杂着少数积极进步的知识分子。第二次大规模移民，则发生在朝鲜半岛战争期间，以"战争新娘"居多。之后的美国《1965年移民法案》放宽了人才引进条件，一大批教育水平较高、专业技能过硬的韩国人涌入美国，形成了第三次大规模的韩裔移民浪潮。这第三次移民浪潮迅速壮大了"美国韩裔文学",其发展势头迅猛,一大批高产的韩裔作家应运而生,代表作家包括加里·朴、宋凯西、玛丽·李和李昌来等。21世纪以来,李敏金、克里斯·麦金尼等新生代作家频出佳作,极大地丰富了美国韩裔文学的万花筒。

鉴于日益壮大的韩裔作家及其出色的文学作品,我们认为需要将"韩裔文学"单独列出,编写这部《美国韩裔文学作品选》,便于人们领略更多韩裔作家的风采。

《美国韩裔文学作品选》聚焦历史的沉淀与传承,精选了30位美国韩裔作家的作品,并以作家的出生年代为顺序进行编目排列。

《美国韩裔文学作品选》力图展示美国韩裔移民一个世纪以来的生存状况与奋斗历程,以折射出美国社会乃至世界风云变幻的局势,探讨韩裔文学中的身份认同、个体命运、家国往事、文化冲突、战争与和平等母题。本作品选力求全面创新,不仅选取了经典作家的传世之作与全新力作,还包含了诸多后起之秀(如70后扬·吉恩·李、卡西·朴·洪,80后保罗·尹)最近几年的获奖佳作,以彰显韩裔文学的历史演变与发展趋势,使读者纵向理解韩裔作家们深厚的功底与敏锐的感知力,进而更好地把握美国韩裔文学的最新动态与学术前沿。

除了深刻的思想性,美国韩裔文学作品还具有高超的艺术性。因此,在体裁选择上,我们尽可能多地选取不同类型的作品。本选集涉及长篇小说、短篇小说、诗歌、戏剧、故事吟唱剧、散文、传记几大文类,其中小说还进一步细化为科幻小说、悬疑小说、青少年小说等类别,力图全面呈现韩裔文学精湛的叙述技巧与艺术手法。

遗憾的是,由于篇幅所限,《美国韩裔文学作品选》中的部分作品只是节选片段,而且因为各种历史与现实的原因,一些优秀作家的作品仍未能囊括其中。但通过这些选文展现出的冰山一角,大家可以按图索骥,继续探寻韩裔文学的广袤空间。

无论如何,我们都希望《美国韩裔文学作品选》能够成为学术界研究"美国亚裔文学"特别是"美国韩裔文学"的重要参考书目。

编者
2022年8月28日

目 录

1. 姜镛讫 (Younghill Kang, 1898—1972) ·· 1
   East Goes West ··· 2
2. 白广善 (Mary Paik Lee, 1900—1995) ·· 8
   Quiet Odyssey: A Pioneer Korean Woman in America ················· 9
3. 玛格丽特·K. 帕伊 (Margaret K. Pai, 1914—) ······························· 13
   The Dreams of Two Yi-min ··· 14
4. 玄大卫 (David Hyun, 1917—2012) ··· 19
   I Work Sugarcane Fields ·· 20
5. 金兰英 (Ronyoung Kim, 1926—1987) ·· 23
   Clay Walls ··· 24
6. 金恩国 (Richard Eun Kook Kim, 1932—2009) ······························· 30
   The Martyred ··· 31
7. 崔淑烈 (Sook Nyul Choi, 1937—) ·· 38
   Year of Impossible Goodbyes ·· 39
8. 朴灿应 (Chan E. Park, 1951—) ··· 43
   In 1903, Pak Hŭngbo Went to Hawai'i ································· 44
9. 车学庆 (Theresa Hak Kyung Cha, 1951—1982) ····························· 51
   Dictee ··· 52
10. 加里·朴 (Gary Pak, 1952—) ·· 62
    A Ricepaper Airplane ··· 63
11. 宋凯西 (Cathy Song, 1955—) ··· 67
    Picture Bride ··· 68

　　　　All the Love in the World···69

12. 沃尔特·卢 (Walter K. Lew, 1955—)···72
　　　　Down from the Monastery···73
　　　　Mānoa Run···75

13. 金晏密 (Myung Mi Kim, 1957—)···77
　　　　Under Flag···78

14. 多恩·李 (Don Lee, 1959—)···81
　　　　The Price of Eggs in China···82

15. 崔东美 (Don Mee Choi, 1962—)···87
　　　　DMZ Colony···88

16. 玛丽·李 (Marie Myung-Ok Lee, 1964—)···90
　　　　Finding My Voice···91
　　　　The Evening Hero···97

17. 李昌来 (Chang-rae Lee, 1965—)··101
　　　　Native Speaker···102
　　　　A Gesture Life···107

18. 诺拉·奥卡佳·凯勒 (Nora Okja Keller, 1965—)···112
　　　　Fox Girl···113

19. 南希·金 (Nancy S. Kim, 1966—)···118
　　　　Like Wind Against Rock···119

20. 伦纳德·张 (Leonard Chang, 1968—)···124
　　　　Triplines···125

21. 李敏金 (Min Jin Lee, 1968—)··132
　　　　Pachinko···133

22. 娜美·文 (Nami Mun, 1968—)···137
　　　　Mr. McCommon···138

23. 苏吉·克沃克·金 (Suji Kwock Kim, 1968—)···145
　　　　The Chasm···146
　　　　Fragments of the Forgotten War···148

24. 苏珊·崔 (Susan Choi, 1969—) ·· 150
    The Foreign Student ·· 151
    Trust Exercise ·· 156

25. 帕蒂·金 (Patti Kim, 1970—) ·· 160
    A Cab Called Reliable ·· 161
    It's Girls Like You, Mickey ··· 167

26. 克里斯·麦金尼 (Chris McKinney, 1973—) ································· 170
    The Tattoo ··· 171
    Midnight, Water City ·· 174

27. 扬·吉恩·李 (Young Jean Lee, 1974—) ····································· 177
    Shipment ··· 178
    Lear ··· 181

28. 卡西·朴·洪 (Cathy Park Hong, 1976—) ··································· 186
    Minor Feelings: An Asian American Reckoning ················· 187

29. 凯瑟琳·钟 (Catherine Chung, 1979—) ····································· 194
    Forgotten Country ··· 195

30. 保罗·尹 (Paul Yoon, 1980—) ·· 200
    Run Me to Earth ··· 201

1 (Younghill Kang, 1898—1972) 姜镛讫

作者简介

姜镛讫(Younghill Kang, 1898—1972) 出生于朝鲜咸镜南道(South Hamgyong),是少数来自朝鲜半岛北部地区的作家、评论家、翻译家。姜镛讫幼年时便受到儒学熏陶,广泛吸纳儒家基本理念,奠定了其后期的文学创作与文学评论意旨。出于此原因,早期学界曾将其划归中国学者之列。姜镛讫十二岁时偷渡到日本求学,之后回到祖国,进入美国传教士创办的教会学校。1921年朝鲜内政动荡,姜镛讫离开家乡先后前往加拿大和美国求学,于1925年在波士顿大学(Boston University)获得理学学士学位,1927年在哈佛大学(Harvard University)获得英语教育学硕士学位。

姜镛讫是首位获得古根海姆奖学金(Guggenheim Scholarship)资助的亚洲人,担任过美国大都会艺术博物馆(Metropolitan Museum of Art)的策展人以及美国政府部门(U.S. Military Office of Publications, the Corps Office of Civil Information)的亚洲专家,参与编辑《大不列颠百科全书》(*Encyclopedia Britannica*)并多次在《纽约时报》(*The New York Times*)发表书评。姜镛讫荣誉等身,包括哈柏林·卡明斯基奖(Halperine Kaminsky Prize)、圣路易斯·魏斯纪念奖(Louis S. Weiss Memorial Prize)、高丽大学(Korea University)荣誉博士等。

虽然姜镛讫一生大都在异国他乡游学奔波,但他时刻挂念祖国,积极参加演讲并外译朝鲜文学作品以向世界宣传朝鲜,为美国亚裔文学的发展奠定了坚实的基础。姜镛讫最初用朝鲜语和日语写作,1928年在美国妻子的鼓励下改用英语创作。其自传体长篇小说《草堂》(*The Grass Roof*, 1931)以朝鲜三一运动为背景,

揭示了保守怀旧、不思变革的社会终将会被现代化所冲袭的规律。它的姊妹篇《从东方到西方》(*East Goes West*, 1937)则记述了主人公韩青坡(Chungpa Han)移居美国的涅槃之旅,身份的位移性与复杂性促使他在新奇与革新的环境中思考拯救母国的良方。

  选文摘自《从东方到西方》第一章。韩青坡在朝鲜"感觉正望着死亡,一个古老星球的死亡",于是踏上西行之旅。初到纽约后的他对一切都充满好奇,并在探索新世界的同时不断回溯反思故国往事。

作品选读

East Goes West

Book One
(excerpt)
By Younghill Kang

Life, like a dome of many-colored glass,
Stains the white radiance of eternity
Until Death tramples to fragments...

Shelley has said. It was my destiny to see the disjointing of a world. Upon my planet in lost time, the heyday of life passed by. Gently at first. Its attraction of gravity, the grip on its creatures maintained through its fervid bowels, its harmonious motion, weakened. Then the air grew thin, cooler and cooler. At last, what had been good breathing to the old was only strangling pandemonium to the newer generations....

  I know that as I grew up, I saw myself placed on a shivering pinnacle overlooking a wasteland that had no warmth, that was under an infernal twilight. I cried for the food for my growth, and there seemed no food. And I felt I was looking on death, the death of an ancient planet, a spiritual planet that had been my father's home. Until I thought to stay would be to try to live, a plant on the top of the Alps where the air is too cold, too stunting, and the wind too brutally cruel. In loathing of death, I hurtled forward, out into space, out toward a foreign body... and a younger culture drew me by natural gravity. I entered a new life like one born again. Here I wandered on soil as strange as Mars, seeking roots, roots for an exile's soul. This world, which had sucked me in by its onward, forward magnetism, must have that in it, too, to feed and anchor man in the old durability... for in me has always burned this Taoistic belief in the continuity of living and of time...

It was here... here in America for me to find... but where? This book is the record of my early search, and the arch of my projectile toward that goal.

From an old walled Korean city some thousand years old—Seoul—famous for poets and scholars, to New York. I did not come directly. But almost. A large steamer from the Orient landed me in Vancouver, Canada, and I traveled over three thousand miles across the American continent, a journey more than half as far as from Yokohama to Vancouver. At Halifax, straightway I took another liner. And this time for New York. It was in New York I felt I was destined really "to come out from the boat." The beginning of my new existence must be founded here. In Korea *to come out from the boat* is an idiom meaning *to be born*, as the word "pai" for "womb" is the same as "pai" for "boat"; and there is the story of a Korean humorist who had no money, but who needed to get across a river. On landing him on the other side, the ferryman asked for his money. But the Korean humorist said to the ferryman who too had just stepped out, "You wouldn't charge your brother, would you? We both came from the same boat." And so he traveled free. My only plea for a planet-ride among the white-skinned majority of this New World is the same facetious argument. I brought little money, and no prestige, as I entered a practical country with small respect for the dark side of the moon. I got in just in time, before the law against Oriental immigration was passed.

But New York, that magic city on rock yet ungrounded, nervous, flowing, million-hued as a dream, became, throughout the years I am recording, the vast mechanical incubator of me.

It was always of New York I dreamed—not Paris nor London nor Berlin nor Munich nor Vienna nor age-buried Rome. I was eighteen, green with youth, and there was some of the mystery of nature in my simple immediate response to what was for me just a name... like the dogged moth that directs its flight by some unfathomable law. But I said to myself, "I want neither dreams nor poetry, least of all tradition, never the full moon." Korea even in her shattered state had these. And beyond them stood waiting—death. I craved swiftness, unimpeded action, fluidity, the amorphous New. Out of action rises the dream, rises the poetry. Dream without motion is the only wasteland that can sustain nothing. So I came adoring the crescent, not the full harvest moon, with winter over the horizon and its waning to a husk.

"New York at last!" I heard from the passengers around me. And the information was not needed. In unearthly white and mauve, shadow of white, the city rose, like a dream dreamed overnight, new, remorselessly new, impossibly new... and yet there in all the arrogant pride of rejoiced materialism. These young, slim, stately things a thousand houses high (or so it seemed to me, coming from an architecture that had never defied the earth), a tower of Babel each one, not one tower of Babel but many, a city of Babel towers, casually, easily strewn end up against the skies—they stood at the brink, close crowded, the brink of America, these Giantesses, these Fates, which were not built for a king nor a ghost nor any man's religion, but were materialized by those hard, cold, magic words—opportunity, enterprise, prosperity, success—just business words out of world-wide commerce from a land rich in natural resources. Buildings that sprang white from the rock. No earth clung to their skirts. They leaped like Athene from the mind synthetically; they spurned the earth. And there was no monument to the Machine Age like America.

I could not have come farther from home than this New York. Our dwellings, low, weathered, mossed, abhorring the lifeless line—the definite, the finite, the aloof—loving rondures and an upward stroke, the tilt of a roof like a boat always aware of the elements in which it is swinging—most fittingly my home was set a hemisphere apart, so far over the globe that to have gone on would have meant to go nearer not farther. How far my little grass-roofed, hill-wrapped village from this gigantic rebellion which was New York! And New York's rebellion called to me excitedly, this savagery which piled great concrete block on concrete block, topping at the last moment as in an afterthought, with crowns as delicate as pinnacled ice; this lavishness which, without prayer, pillaged coal mines and waterfalls for light, festooning the great nature severed city with diamonds of frozen electrical phenomena—it fascinated me, the Asian man, and in it I saw not Milton's Satan, but the one of Blake.

I saw that Battery Park, if not a thing of earth, was yet a thing of dirt, as I walked about it trying to get my breath and decide what was the next step after coming from the sea. It was oddly dark and forlorn, like a little untidy room off-stage where actors might sit waiting for their cues. The shops about looked mean and low and dim. A solitary sailor stumbled past, showing neither the freedom and romance of the seas, nor the robust assurance of a native on his own shore. And the other human shadows flitting there had a stealthy and verminlike quality, a mysterious haunting corruption, suggesting the water's edge, and the meeting of foreign plague with foreign plague. I walked about the shabby little square briskly, drawing hungry lungfuls of the prowling keen March air—a Titan, he, in a titanic city—until in sudden excess of elation and aggression growing suddenly too hot with life, as if to come to grips with an opponent, I took off my long coat; and sinking down on a bench, I clapped my knee and swore the oath of battle and of triumph. The first part of a wide journey was accomplished. At least that part in space. I swore to keep on. Yes, if it took a lifetime, I must get to know the West.

Well, mine was not oath of battle in the militaristic sense. I was congenitally unmilitaristic. Inwoven in my fabric were the agricultural peace of Asia, the long centuries of peaceful living in united households, of seeking not the soul's good, but the blood's good, the blood's good of a happy, decorously branching family tree. In the old days the most excitement permitted to the individual man, if he got free from the struggle with beloved but ruthless and exacting elements, was poetry, the journey to Seoul, wine, and the moons that came with every season. His wife, usually older than himself and chosen by his mother and father, would be sure to know no poetry, but she would not begrudge him a feminine companion in Seoul, or even in some market place nearby—one of those childlike ladies who having bought—or more often inherited—the right to please by the loss of other social prestige, must live on gaiety, dancing, and fair calligraphy. But any wholehearted passion would have shivered too brutally the family tree. And I had done far worse. I had refused to marry my appointed bride. I had repeated that I would not marry, at the ripe age of eighteen. I had said, with more pride than Adam ever got out of sinning in Eden, that I must choose the girl, unhelped by my forefathers or the astrologers or the mountain spirits. And this rebellion against nature and fatality I had learned from the West. Small wonder I had struggled with my father over every ounce of Western learning. I had gone against his will to mission schools, those devilish cults which preach divorce in the blood, and spiritual kinships, which foster the very distortions found, says the golden-hearted Mencius, in the cleverish man. I had studied in Japanese schools and it must be confessed, my studies had brought ever increased rebellion and dismay—to me as well as my father.

The military position of Japan—intrenched in Korea in my own lifetime—forced me into dilemma: Scylla and Charybdis. I was caught between—on the one hand, the heart-broken death of the old traditions irrevocably smashed not by me but by Japan (and yet I seemed to the elders to be conspiring with Japanese)—and on the other hand the zealous summary glibness of Japan, fast-Westernizing, using the Western incantations to realize her ancient fury of spirit, which Korea had always felt encroaching, but had snubbed in a blind disdain. Korea, a small, provincial, old-fashioned Confucian nation, hopelessly trapped by a larger, expanding one, was called to get off the earth. Death summoned. I could have renounced the scholar's dream forever (plainly scholarship had dreamed us away into ruin) and written my vengeance against Japan in martyr's blood, a blood which like that of the Tasmanians is strangely silent though to a man they wrote. Or I could take away my slip cut from the roots, and try to engraft my scholar inherited kingdom upon the world's thought. But what I could not bear was the thought of futility, the futility of the martyr, or the death-stifled scholar back home. It was so that the individualist was born, the individualist, demanding life and more life, fulfilment, some answer to his thronging questions, some recognition of his death-wasted life, some anchor in thin air to bring him to earth though he seems cut off from the very roots of being.

And this it was—this naked individual slip—I had brought to New York.

"Dream, tall dreams," I thought. "Such are proper to man. But they must be solid, well-planned, engineered and founded on rock."

Had I not reached the arena of man's fight with death? I sat there on a park bench, savouring rebellion, dreaming the Faustian dream, without knowing of Faust, seeing myself with the Eastern scholarship in one hand, the Western in the other. And as I sat it grew colder. I had thought a little of spending the night on that bench. It appealed to me to wake up here with the dawn and find myself in New York. It would not be the first night I had slept roofless in a large city. But in the inner lining of my cap, I had four dollars, all I had left, in fact, after my long gestation by boat and by train. I decided to get myself the birthday present of a room.

"Begin tomorrow, trouble. See if I can't have some good dream. An unpleasant dream in this dark lonely park would be bad luck."

Clouds over the denser uptown regions trembled with the city's man-made whiteness, a false and livid dawn light, stolen from nature. I turned my face toward the dawn light as to a pillar of fire. And as I walked, steadily progressing toward the harsh curt lights and the Herculean noise, I wondered if the sight of a rainbow would be lost, the sound of thunder drowned here.

At last I found a hotel to my liking, neither as tall as a skyscraper—to choose such a one would not be modest the first night—and yet not a dingy one either, which would be inauspicious. The hotel had many lights inside, but not too many, not the naked glare which clashed from canyon to canyon along the outer runways of the great hive; these had a luminance more proper to honey cells and inner coffers. The fat six-foot doorman with red face seemed an imposing sentinel. Past him, I saw inside the people walking to and fro... talking mysteriously, perhaps of Michelangelo, but more likely of stocks and bonds. I tried to catch his eye. Always he looked past me, or without looking exactly at me, he would shake his head mournfully, directing his thumb toward a side door. But while he was engaged with one of the fortunate insiders who came outside, I went in. To me the gilded lamps, the marble floorway with its carpet of red, were luxurious and full of splendor. How gentlemanly, engaging, yet frankly businesslike, the sandy-colored hotel clerk, as I asked for a room, in my best high-school English which I had prepared to say before coming in!

And as I wrote my name down—Chungpa[1] Han—in my unmistakably Oriental handwriting, which unconsciously dwelt on a stroke, or finished in a quirk that was not Western—I was elated that I had voted not to spend the night with the waifs and strays, but was enrolled there tangibly as a New Yorker.

I had engaged a small room for two dollars. This was half of all I had. I was satisfied. I thought I had a bargain. I had heard that all the hotels in New York cost ten and twenty dollars a night.

"They are worth that!" I thought, as the elevator boy danced up, a rich tobacco brown, well-formed and neatly mannered like his dress. He seized my big suitcase of brown cloth purchased in Seoul, Korea, a roomy bag which yet carried little besides a few books, some letters of introduction and a toothbrush.

The elevator went zk! and up we shot. A funny cool ziffy feeling ran into my heart. It was my first elevator. Fast climb... I thought... like going to heaven....

---

1 Younghill Kang spells the name of his protagonist inconsistently, alternating between "Chung-pa" and "Chungpa." We chose the spelling that appeared more often, "Chungpa."

2
(Mary Paik Lee, 1900—1995)
白广善

作者简介

白广善（Mary Paik Lee，1900—1995），美国朝鲜裔作家，出生于朝鲜平壤（Pyongyang）。1905 年，日本帝国主义在朝鲜半岛日益猖獗，白广善一家逃到夏威夷（Hawaii）。白广善的父亲没有了原本体面的工作，只得在一家糖料种植园打工。他们生活窘迫、备受鄙夷，于 1906 年搬至加利福尼亚州的河滨市，靠母亲给人做饭来勉强维持生计。

白广善的自传《安静的奥德赛：美国的朝鲜先驱女性》（*Quiet Odyssey: A Pioneer Korean Woman in America*，1990）是为数不多的美国亚裔女性作家回忆录之一，也是唯一一本几乎跨越整个 20 世纪的美国朝鲜裔女性作家回忆录。作为最早一批赴美的朝鲜开拓者，白广善对 20 世纪社会文化的审视具有先导性的启发意义。

选读部分摘自《安静的奥德赛：美国的朝鲜先驱女性》第十三章《歧视》（"Discrimination"）。选文不仅回溯了朝鲜人的悲惨遭遇，还详述了来自中国、日本等地的东方人，以及黑人、墨西哥人等在学业、就业、政治生活与娱乐生活中受到的或显性或隐性的不公正对待。他们好心救人的热情被误解，他们英勇杀敌的战功被忽视，他们的生命财产安全随时面临威胁。白广善终其一生都在与偏见和歧视作斗争，她的语言平和但富有张力，读起来让人心生悲悯之情。

作品选读

Quiet Odyssey: A Pioneer Korean Woman in America

Chapter 13 Discrimination
(excerpt)
By Mary Paik Lee

As we looked around at our friends in Los Angeles, we could see the progress our people had made since 1906. The only work available for men at that time had been farm work, eight to ten hours a day at ten to fifteen cents an hour, depending on the good nature and kindness of the employer. It was several years before women were allowed to do housework in American homes. Although not being able to speak English was a big problem, after long hours of hard labor, no one had the time or energy to study English.

As their children grew up and helped them with their language problems, Orientals were able to try something else. Some families started small grocery stores, tobacco shops, chop suey joints, dry-cleaning and pressing shops, or laundries. Those enterprises were the first step up toward a better way of life. Fruit and vegetable stands became very popular with Americans, which helped in many ways to break down the barriers between people.

Our black friends, who had lived here longer, were in the same situation as Orientals. They spoke English, but that did not help them in their struggle for a better life. My black girl friend cried as she related all the hardships of her people. "Why did God make me black to be hated and ignored by white people?" she asked. She told me I was lucky not to be black. I replied that her color did not seem to be the problem, that we were all in the same situation. The Mexican people were here first, but they were in the same hopeless state. Due to our mutual problems, all minorities felt a sympathetic bond with one another. We patronized one another's stores, to help out. The first generation laid the foundation for the future by teaching their children to be honest—never to steal or do anything that might cause ill feeling towards our people. We felt that was the only way we could prove to Americans that we are also human beings.

Our daily relations with Americans were improving, but once in a while something happened to remind us of the past. When my oldest son Henry was in the fifth grade, he came home one afternoon in high spirits because his class had had a spelling match, the guys against the girls, and he had won. The teacher had told them that the real match would be the next day, and there would be a prize for the winner. I felt like saying something, but decided to wait and see. He returned home the next day, feeling very angry and disgusted with school. He said that though he had won the match, "old lady Stone" had given the prize to the girl. I told him what my father had told me a long time ago, when the same thing had happened to me. "It doesn't matter who got the prize as long as you know the correct answer. The person who won so easily, without knowing the correct answer, has not learned anything. Just be sure that you know it and don't forget it. The knowledge you have in your brain can never be taken away by anyone."

A few days later, a young lady about twenty years old came to our roadside stand on Leffingwell Road. She said she was Henry's teacher. I asked, "Are you 'old lady Stone'?" "That's what the children call me," she replied. "I wanted to explain why I didn't give Henry the prize the other day. The girl's mother is the president of the PTA. I knew she would have me fired if I gave Henry the prize. I am very sorry and want to apologize. I am trying to earn enough money to go to college and get my teacher's certificate. It's very difficult to find a job these days. That's why I was forced to give the prize to the girl." I was so surprised by her unexpected thoughtfulness and courage in speaking to me like that. It reminded me of what my father told us long ago—that there are good people everywhere, but we just had not met them yet. Times were getting better.

Once an American lady friend asked me if I was going to vote that day. I said I was too busy and couldn't get away. She started to give me a lecture about my civic duty. I looked at her in wonder. She considered herself well educated and thought she knew everything. Yet she didn't know that the reason I didn't vote was that Orientals were not allowed to be citizens, so we didn't have the right to vote. She became very angry and said, "That's not so! Everyone in America has equal rights." But she came back a few days later and said a lawyer friend had told her that I was right. We remained good friends, anyway.

In the 1950s, most of the "For Whites Only" signs on public restrooms, swimming pools, and so forth, were removed. But although there were no signs on barber shops, theaters, and churches, Orientals were told at the door that they were not welcome. In northern California, some gas stations and towns had signs on the highway stating: "Japs are not wanted here."

Young Korean students who were just starting their careers with high hopes found themselves caught in the fury of this anti-Oriental sentiment. We had a young friend who had graduated from medical college with honors and was serving his internship at the Stanford University Hospital. One evening a man from a prominent family was badly injured in an automobile accident, lost a lot of blood, and needed an immediate blood transfusion. No one present would volunteer his blood, so our friend offered his to save the man's life. The family refused it, saying they didn't want "dirty Jap blood" put into the man's body. So the man died. The incident broke the spirit and ambition of our friend. He was too young and naive to realize what our world was like. Years later, our black friends laughed when the doctors told them that their blood was acceptable for the blood bank.

As the Japanese families were being taken to concentration camps, their sons of military age volunteered or were drafted for army duty. They proved their courage and loyalty to America by joining the famous Japanese battalion that was sent to Europe. The battalion won more medals than any other unit of its size in the army. Many men were killed. One captain in that battalion later became Senator Daniel Inuoye from Hawaii. He was wounded and had one arm in a sling when he landed in San Francisco after the war. He thought he should get a haircut and make himself presentable before joining his family in Hawaii. He was wearing his captain's uniform as he entered the barber shop. The barber took one look at him and said, "I don't serve Japs in my shop." His uniform didn't mean a thing to the barber.

In Los Angeles in 1950 we found many minority women working in sewing factories making garments of every sort for fifty cents an hour, eight hours a day. After several years, the wage went up to one dollar an hour. The sewing rooms were dirty and very dusty, with lint and dust filling the air like fog. The rooms had no air conditioning and no windows. The dust settling on the heads of the women made their hair look gray by the end of the day. The loud power-driven sewing machines working at full speed all at once made a thundering noise that deafened the ear. It was a frightful thing to listen to for eight hours every weekday. I tried it once for several months; the experience made me admire all those women who endured it for years in order to send their children to colleges and universities. I have seen those children return home as doctors, lawyers, and engineers, thus rewarding their parents for their sacrifices. Those pioneers took the first step toward raising the standard of living for the second and third generations of Orientals here.

There is a good example among Koreans which makes me feel proud of what people can accomplish despite hardship. Mr. and Mrs. Lee (no relation to us) had a son named Sammy. The first time I saw him, he was only eleven months old. I watched his progress all the way through the University of Southern California School of Medicine, where he became a doctor, specializing in ear, nose, and throat ailments. He was always playing in the swimming pools and became interested in high diving. The coach at USC took an interest in him and helped him to develop into an expert high-platform diver. Sammy Lee won the Olympic Gold Medal for high-platform diving in 1948 and successfully defended his title in 1952. In 1953 he became the first non-Caucasian to win the James E. Sullivan Memorial Trophy. His parents helped with all his expenses by working in their chop suey restaurant for many years.

Orientals were not the only ones who suffered from discrimination. A neighbor told me her family had to move to Los Angeles because her son was not accepted in most universities back East because he was Jewish. There was discrimination of every kind in those days, and it has not disappeared completely. As recently as 1982 a Chinese man was killed by two white men. They had been laid off their jobs at an automobile plant because of all the Japanese cars coming into America. Without knowing or even thinking that there are many Orientals who are not Japanese, they vented their rage on the first Oriental man they saw. He was savagely beaten with a baseball bat. The local police were reluctant to do anything about it until the Chinese community rose up in sorrow and anger and complained to the federal government. The two men were convicted, but their sentences were light, considering the crime they had committed.*

*Mrs. Lee is referring to the Vincent Chin case, in which a Chinese American was clubbed to death by two unemployed white autoworkers in Detroit. One of them was acquitted and the other, though convicted and sentenced to twenty-five years in prison, never served time, because his conviction was overturned on a technicality. *Editor.*

3

(Margaret K. Pai, 1914—)
玛格丽特·K. 帕伊

作者简介

玛格丽特·K. 帕伊（Margaret K. Pai, 1914— ），美国韩裔作家。她曾在夏威夷瓦胡岛（Oahu）上凯卢阿（Kailua）、罗斯福（Roosevelt）和法灵顿（Farrington）的高中教授英语，退休后开始撰写有关于夏威夷的短篇传奇故事、诗歌和个人回忆录，并在当地的写作比赛中获过一些奖项。

关于早期韩裔移民在夏威夷的生活鲜有记载，回忆录《两个移民之梦》（*The Dreams of Two Yi-min*, 1989）展示了日帝暗黑期夏威夷韩裔移民社区的社会和文化结构，涉及独立运动协会架构、夏威夷卫理公会教会的政治运作方式等，具有宝贵的历史价值。20世纪初期，日本占领朝鲜半岛并实行殖民统治，侵略者不仅大肆掠夺资源、侵袭土地，还在思想上实行奴化教育，强制人们使用日语教学。频发的战争与严酷的殖民统治造成人口大量外流，"照片新娘"、劳工、流亡人士等纷纷涌出。《两个移民之梦》就处于这一历史背景之下，标题中的"两个移民"指的是父亲权道仁（Kwon Do In）和母亲李熙京（Hee Kyung Lee）：父亲性格古怪、聪明智慧，把室内装潢的生意逐步做得风生水起；母亲坚韧不拔、正直勇敢，身为"照片新娘"的一员嫁到檀香山，1919年回到母国后因参与"三·一"运动示威而被日本人监禁。《两个移民之梦》正如一幅生动、逼真的画像，它通过描述早期普通移民寻找美好生活的故事，折射出宏观意义上生活在夏威夷的韩裔移民群居史。

选读部分摘自《两个移民之梦》第十章《最终的成功发明》（"A Successful Invention at Last"）：父亲勤恳工作、不断创新装潢技巧；母亲任劳任怨、操持一家老小的家务。虽然经济大萧条给一家人带来了挑战与困扰，但他们还是向着美好的移民梦不断挺进。

作品选读

The Dreams of Two Yi-min

Chapter 10 A Successful Invention at Last
(excerpt)
By Margaret K. Pai

  During the Depression, instead of laying off his employees, my father engaged them in testing his newest patent idea. He brightened the large showroom by adding more lightbulbs. The plain walls of the store were covered with displays of his innovative bamboo blinds and draperies. The upholsterers Yin Hong and Jimmie learned to install the bamboo hangings under cornices, which were built and painted by the carpenter and the painter. Only old Ordway hammered and coughed in the background, working on the few reupholstery jobs that trickled in.

  My mother looked with anxiety on these efforts to keep the employees busy. She must have thought they were all crazy spending day after day playing with Father's toys.

  To her amazement, his invention began to sell. One wealthy client after another replaced their worn, faded draperies with new draperies made of bamboo. Furthermore, the new bamboo installed in their homes promoted sales of rattan-trimmed custom furniture. The clients enjoyed the tropical setting created in their homes by combining bamboo draperies and rattan furniture.

  The bamboo material, which came from Japan, was made up of one-sixteenth inch split bamboo strips woven together with heavy threads. The green peel, or bark, of the bamboo pole from which the drapery material was made was extremely durable.

  In Honolulu the best-known importer of Japanese goods was the firm Iida. My father bought dozens of ready-made blinds from Iida, then stripped and discarded the pulleys and cords attached to them; the horizontal strips of bamboo in Iida's roll-up shade then could be turned to work in vertical strips in a drapery. It wasn't long before he realized how foolish he was to squander money and labor purchasing the shades and dismantling them before converting the bamboo material into draw draperies.

As sales of the new draperies increased, a way was found to import the bamboo material in continuous rolls, like cloth yardage. The shipments of woven, peel, split bamboo began arriving in rolls of one hundred running feet. They were warehoused above the store. The rolls looked strange, standing like thick stumps of trees of varying heights lined up for inspection. A few rolls came in three foot heights; most were five, six, and seven feet tall—the heights needed most frequently for windows and doors in Hawaii's homes. Later, rolls of eight, nine, and ten feet were ordered for the arches and windows in commercial buildings.

The new bamboo came raw and unfinished, unlike the polished staves of the blinds from Iida. So the material had to be blow-torched to remove loose, needly fibers. Yin Hong or Jimmie lay a cut-to-measure piece of the material over two horses and swung the blow torch back and forth until the surface was smooth enough for one's hand to run over it without feeling splinters.

My father was the best salesman for the new bamboo draw draperies and the new bamboo folding shade—his two innovations for windows. He could speak for hours extolling their virtues with irresistible enthusiasm. A skillful craftsman and an adept handyman, he promised he could make his inventions fit any window, no matter how different it was from the ordinary. And he promised the bamboo would last the customer's lifetime, although he had no proof. He believed it was important to hem the sharp edges of the cut bamboo with a cotton tape, which my mother sewed on. Our super-power sewing machine ran easily over the woody fibers. Soon Yin Hong and Jimmie became installers of these draperies and blinds in homes all over the city.

I wondered how my father was able to handle draperies with such proficiency. Then I recalled the experience he had while at Bailey Furniture Co., especially one time when he was involved with the "fanciest curtains" he had ever seen. The Princess Theatre on Fort Street, which in Honolulu in the 1920s served as a first-class movie theatre and symphony hall, had called on my father to take charge of the replacement of the proscenium curtains. For several nights he sat next to me at the kitchen table in the Pele Street house while I studied, making crude drawings of swirling drapes on wrapping paper. He arranged and rearranged the pattern of loose, flowing folds: a sheer inner curtain that parted gracefully to the sides and the heavy upper curtains rising to reveal the full stage. He hummed as he worked with numbers—how many yards of soft material? How many folds per swirl? How many swirls in all? I asked at one point what the heavy marks on the side in one drawing represented. He replied, "Those are the ties, the tassels."

There came a time when my father felt so pressured he said he wished he had twelve pairs of hands. Every custom order of furniture and drapery seemed to require his personal attention. Women cried and begged him for special treatment of their jobs. My poor father was sought after from the moment he opened the doors of the store in the morning. The customers clamored, "Mr. Kwon, *will* you do this for me?" "Mr. Kwon, *can* you do that for me?" Then terse, stronger demands followed: "Kwon, you *must* do this for me!"

He made excuses and offered apologies for late deliveries. He had to resort to telling lies. The sheer diversity of orders required a variety of abilities; an employee often felt stymied and needed help before he could proceed with his work.

My father happened to be on the phone one day talking to an irate woman. He said, "I'm sorry, I hurt my hand—got it caught in a machine." The same woman, looking very sympathetic, inquired a week later when she stopped in the store, "How is your hand?" He asked, "What hand?" When the woman reminded him of her call, he hastily replied, "Oh, that—it's all okay now."

When he ran out of excuses, apologies, and lies he decided to hide himself far back in the carpenter shop where no one could find him.

There was one woman, however, who was clever enough to ferret him out of hiding. Not believing that "Mr. Kwon is not here," she brushed aside all the employees who tried to stop her from entering the carpenter shop. Dressed in shorts and zori slippers, wearing huge sunglasses, Doris Duke Cromwell, the tobacco heiress, swept through the shop looking for my father. Obviously tired of peddlers of goods fawning over her, she found my father refreshing and a challenge. But he did not favor her. In fact, he did not particularly care to do business with her. He said she was overly demanding and demeaning. She haggled over the price of every item. Perhaps because she had years of fending off cheaters, she had acquired a style of bartering when buying.

He found her especially unreasonable with *time*. He did not mind if she acted like many other women who expected special attention. But when he was forced to make an appointment at 5:30 P.M. at her home, a most inconvenient hour for a man who started work at 5:30 A.M., and he was made to wait and wait once he got to her home until her swim lesson with Duke Kahanamoku was over, he was angry. Her maid, feeling sorry for him, offered to take him on a tour of the tobacco heiress' home, the famous Shangri-la at Black Point, which was just being completed. But he told her he was too tired.

But my father had great respect for most of his clients, especially the gracious *kamaaina* wives of wealthy businessmen in Hawaii. He referred to them as "ladies." He noted their modulated voices, their expressions of appreciation, their trust in his billing as fair.

My mother, who had to divide her time between the shop and home, found little time to rest. She even had to give up regular church attendance. Our house on Nehoa Street, she said, needed so much of her attention. She alone had planted all the grass around the house, a coconut tree in the front, and an avocado tree in the back. A lawnmower was purchased and we depended on Father to push it occasionally around the property. After six days at the factory, my mother spent most of her Sunday cleaning the house and washing clothes. Every Sunday I helped with the laundry—most of which was boiled in soapy water in a five-gallon square tin, set up outside over a crude arrangement of stones. I didn't understand why we had to go through the arduous task of stirring, boiling, and retrieving the laundry, carrying it dripping to the wash trays in the garage to be rinsed. We hoped for sunny Sundays, for the wash could be dried on the lines outside, then ironed in the afternoon. On Sunday nights we could sleep on crisp, clean, pressed sheets and our clothes for the week would be ready.

We all felt an urgent need to save time somehow. My father had the idea that if he bought a family car, then Mother would not have to take the bus to the shop. She could then spend more time at the store.

The difficult task of teaching her to drive the new Ford Model A touring car fell on him. What stormy driving lessons they must have had, for when they returned from one he would be shouting as they walked in the house: "I told you to step on the brake *and* clutch at the same time. Why do you forget? How many times must I remind you?"

She looked indignant but determined to succeed. We children cheered her, and made faces at her instructor when he wasn't looking. We couldn't wait for her to get her license and take us riding in the open green car with the narrow running board.

One day when we got home we noticed part of the jungle across from our house was being cleared. We were pleased; we could be expecting neighbors soon. As we had hoped, one house started going up, then another. Then we found both houses torn down several weeks later and the ground leveled. What was going on?

Trees and shrubs were being cut down every day until the area looked cleared for about twenty or more houses. The bald ground revealed a gently rising slope from

Nehoa Street. The land rose sharply and met the hill behind; steep ridges and bare clefts showed.

Instead of houses, one large building began to take shape. Its architecture was Mediterranean; its roofing, colorful tile. Before it was completed we learned it was to be the new Roosevelt High School. The new building when finished looked stark—like a fortress or a prison—situated alone on a rise of the land. But later, with plantings around the structure, the lines of the school softened. Roosevelt graduated its first class of seniors at the location in June 1933, and I was one of them.

At the beginning of that summer my mother started packing for a trip to Korea. I had been so excited about graduation and planning for college I hadn't been aware of my mother's plans.

"Omoni, where are you going?" I asked.

"Oh, don't you know, Chung Sook? I'm going to visit my—my—parents." Her eyes misted and she made an effort to control her tears by biting her lips.

"Why? Are they ill?" My grandparents' son, a doctor, would be able to care for them. "Are they very ill?"

"No. I don't think so. But there is something not quite right going on there. I have to go and see..."

"This trip is sudden, isn't it?" I said to her. "How long will you be gone? Just for the summer?"

"I cannot say. I hope I can come back soon."

The words sounded ominous. A lump formed in my throat. I was more concerned, I was ashamed to admit, about myself faring at home without Mother than for her safety. "It's going to be hard for us without you, Omoni. Maybe I should stay out of college this year if you plan to stay a while."

"No. No. You will be able to manage, I'm sure. Your father says you can look for someone to come in and help with the housework and the cooking while I'm gone. Remember this: your father and I insist you register to enter the University of Hawaii this fall. You must get an education. No matter what happens at home."

4

(David Hyun, 1917—2012)
玄大卫

作者简介

玄大卫（David Hyun，1917—2012），美国韩裔随笔作家、建筑师，出生于汉城（Seoul，今首尔）。其父亲玄舜（Soon Hyun）在1919年参加韩国独立运动，之后带一家人逃至上海，并帮助组建了大韩民国临时政府。1924年，一家人搬至夏威夷考艾岛（Kauai）定居，玄舜成为临时政府在美官方代表。

玄大卫生活经历丰富，做过剧院引座员、管家以及电气、土木、结构工程绘图员，也曾在甘蔗种植园与罐头厂工作。1947年，他搬到洛杉矶（Los Angeles），在南加州大学（University of Southern California）学习建筑，成为首位美国韩裔建筑师，并于1953年创办公司。其作品赢得若干国家和地区奖项，最为人所熟知的是1978年为洛杉矶小东京设计的日本村广场（Japanese Village Plaza）和日式高架塔楼（Yagura Tower）。

此外，玄大卫还于20世纪70年代在加州大学洛杉矶分校（UCLA）学习创意写作和小说课程，并成为该校的研究员，曾担任美国韩裔联盟（Korean American Coalition）、美国韩裔国家博物馆（Korean American National Museum）主席以及南加州大学韩国遗产图书馆的创始名誉主席。他通过短篇小说、日记和自传等形式记述家国历史、时事要闻、个人轶事。选读部分摘自《我在甘蔗田干活》（I Work Sugarcane Fields），从孩童的视角再现了甘蔗种植园童工们的日常：孩子们单纯善良、乐观向上，日薪30分的微薄收入丝毫没有影响他们苦中作乐的生活热情。

作品选读

I Work Sugarcane Fields

(excerpt)
By David Hyun

Papa served the Korean people who labored in the sugarcane fields of Kauai by traveling all around the island: Lihue, Hanamaulu, Kapaa, Kealia, Kilauea on the wet side and Puhi, Koloa, Eleele, Makaweli, Kekaha on the dry side. The Korean families were only one, or two, or three in each of these plantation towns, except in Kapaa which had about ten Korean families.

Papa had to travel every Sunday to conduct services or to minister to practical needs in these towns except for the first Sunday of each month when services were held at the Kapaia Church. Then I had to drive to collect families without cars to come to church and to drive them home after church service and after a grand luncheon prepared by Omma. Omma worked a week to buy and prepare the luncheon for 50 to 75 guests, but on Christmas and Easter, service and luncheon were for as many as 150 men, women and children. For these holiday luncheons, Omma did the purchasing and much of the chopping. The ladies came early to finish the chopping and to cook while service went on in the church. One long table was set inside the house and two were set outside in the garden between the church and the house. People sat in turns at benches to partake of the luncheon.

For many children, these holiday luncheons would be the best eating for the year. The luncheon was a Korean feast: sliced beef, short ribs, and chicken marinated in Korean sauce——shoyu, vinegar, sesame oil spiced with ginger and garlic—and a variety of seasoned vegetables that Omma had cooked and stored in the icebox during the week, rice dumplings in seaweed soup, rice, and kimchee. Omma was physically tiny, less than five-feet tall but she had the strength and endurance of ten men. Omma was like forever, a warm good-for-hugging miracle worker.

Papa did not have enough money to serve the Korean people who earned $22 monthly working for the plantation. Papa received $70 monthly for his ministry and additional stipends from the Rice, Wilcox, and Isenberg families of Kauai. Papa's ministry was not only inspirational spiritual messages, Papa had to give practical help to Koreans in distress like sickness, loss of jobs, immigration and police troubles, et cetera, et cetera, et cetera. Papa used most of his income for his ministry and was always short on cash for the family's daily needs. That is why Omma asked Joshua and me to work summers in the cane fields. Joshua was twelve and I was ten when we began working in the cane fields.

Omma woke Joshua and me at 4:30 a.m. Omma had to fight for my pillow, which I hugged tightly. The pillow and I slept together, Omma would say, "please" about three times without separating me from my pillow. It was just a warning for her next step. Omma put her hand under the blanket and rubbed her fingertips on the bottom of my feet. My feet bottoms have 110-volt tickles. I cannot stand the tickling of my feet bottoms. I had to clutch my legs and let go of the pillow.

Then I awoke, ready to do a man's work. I washed my face, brushed my teeth with forefinger and salt, put on my precious long pants to protect my legs from the saw-edged cane leaves, long-sleeve shirt (ugh) to protect my arms, a straw hat with string straps, and then looked over my trusty bare feet. I gulped a cup of hot chocolate and off I went marching side by side with Joshua, each of us carrying a sharp hoe in rifle position and a carry-on lunch can to join our Kapaia gang down by the hanging bridge.

It was five o'clock; the night was still dark. Stars were bright and moonlight helped us see our way up the trail to the main road and then to the Hanamaulu train station almost two miles away. The train left at 5:30 and carried us to the proximity of the day's work. We then marched another ten to fifteen minutes to the location of the cane field.

Some nights we did not go to the train station or truck station in Hanamaulu. Instead we marched directly to cane fields on the road to the Waialua waterfalls. Marching on the Waialua mountain road was more fun than train or truck except where the Waialua Road began at the main road near Kapaia town. Right at this intersection to the right of the Waialua Road, when marching up to work, was an old almost abandoned cemetery. We were all afraid to march past the cemetery. Stories told us that neglected and unhappy dead arose from their graves to snatch small boys. We heard that the unhappy dead shot white fireballs up into the air from their graves. Doug, the small Japanese from across the river, said, "My uncle, he saw real ghosts. They chased after him. My uncle, run like hell. He almost get caught; he was real scared.

Before walking up the Waialua Road, we had begun with talk story, laughing, and arguing in Kapaia town. When we suddenly realized that we were coming to the cemetery, every mouth that was open did not make even one tiny sound. No can talk. The walking group became smaller because the guys on the right tried to get on the left side. Protection was to let the ghost catch the guy nearest to the grave, so jostling began.

Doug was on the right; he started to walk fast so that he could cut in to the left. He failed because we kept up. Doug made an abrupt stop and fell behind and into the left side. Kazu was now nearest to the grave.

Kazu yelled, "I no scare ghost," and began running ahead. Everyone ran. When Kazu was tired, he stopped running. Kazu said, "Why you guys run? I no scare ghosts. I run for feel good."

Doug said, "You bullshit. You make me scared more than ghosts."

Vincent said, "Kazu scared of ghosts. Me, I not scared. I only keep up."

I turned back to look at the cemetery. I yelled, "White fireball. I see white fireball; white ghost coming."

Nobody spoke; everybody ran.

After this ghost experience, we detoured past the cemetery because no can tell when the ghost come out to catch little boys.

5

(Ronyoung Kim, 1926—1987)
金兰英

作者简介

金兰英（Ronyoung Kim, 1926—1987），亦音译作金容雍，本名格罗丽娅·金（Gloria Kim），美国韩裔作家。其父亲是农民，母亲是贵族，二人在日本吞并朝鲜半岛前逃到美国。金兰英在洛杉矶韩国城（Koreatown）出生并长大，19岁时嫁给外科医生理查德·韩（Richard Hahn），并育有四个孩子。中年时期她重返校园，在旧金山州立大学（San Francisco State University）学习远东艺术与文化，获得了文学学士学位。1976年，金兰英被确诊乳腺癌，于是她加紧创作具有自传性质的《泥巴墙》（*Clay Walls*, 1987），小说出版后不久，金兰英遗憾去世。

《泥巴墙》是较早讲述韩国移民家庭在美经历的小说，曾获普利策奖（Pulitzer Prize）提名。目前这部作品的价值并未被充分发掘，具有广阔的研究空间。小说讲述了在20世纪20年代，农民全（Chun）和贵族惠秀（Haesu）逃离日本统治，不远万里来到美国加利福尼亚州，但两人的阶级差异加之美国的种族歧视导致他们的生活步履维艰。惠秀毅然带着三个孩子回到故乡，但不堪忍受日本人的极端统治而返回美国。在此期间全沉迷于赌博，颓废萎靡，最终客死他乡。惠秀最终卖掉了自己在韩国的土地，象征着她失去了与母国最后的情感连接。这部小说既关注第二次世界大战期间美国韩裔的生活状况，比如珍珠港事件后众多韩国人被误认为日本人而遭受打击；也关注社会文化中种族、性别和阶级关系的不对称所带来的冲突与误解。

选读部分摘自《泥巴墙》第一章。惠秀辞掉保洁员的工作，希望另谋一份体面的职业，而丈夫对此并不支持，两人在世界观、人生观、价值观方面的冲突初露端倪。此外，这一阶段的韩国移民多为政治难民，他们在美国身份卑微、处境尴尬，但不乏仁人志士心系母国反日运动，推动实现民族独立。

作品选读

Clay Walls

Chapter One
(excerpt)
By Ronyoung Kim

"You've missed a spot," Mrs. Randolph said, pointing. "Dirty." Haesu had been holding her breath. She let it out with a cough.

Mrs. Randolph shook her finger at the incriminating stain. "Look," she demanded, then made scrubbing motions in the air. "You clean."

Haesu nodded. She took in another breath and held it as she rubbed away the offensive stain.

"Th-at's better." Mrs. Randolph nodded with approval. "Good. Clean. Very good. Do that every week," she said, scrubbing the air again. She smiled at Haesu and left the room.

Haesu spat into the toilet and threw the rag into the bucket. "*Sangnyun!*" she muttered to herself. "*Sangnyun, sangnyun, sangnyun!*" she sputtered aloud. She did not know the English equivalent for 'low woman', but she did know how to say, "I quit" and later said it to Mrs. Randolph. The woman looked at her in disbelief.

"I don't understand. We were getting on so well. I..." Mrs. Randolph pointed to herself "teach you." She pointed at Haesu. "You do good. Why you say, 'I quit'?"

"Toilet make me sick."

"That's part of the job."

"No job. No toilet. Not me. I go home." Haesu held out her hand, palm up to receive her pay.

Mrs. Randolph stiffened as she backed away from Haesu's outstretched hands.

"Oo-oh no. You're supposed to give me adequate notice. I'm not obligated to pay you anything."

They were words not in Haesu's vocabulary. Perhaps she had not made herself clear. Haesu raised her hand higher.

Mrs. Randolph tightened her lips. "So you're going to be difficult. I'm very disappointed in you, Haesu, but I'm going to be fair." She motioned Haesu to stay put and left the room.

Haesu sighed with relief and put down her hand. She knew that Mrs. Randolph's purse was on top of the dresser in the bedroom; the woman had gone to get the money. As she waited, Haesu looked around. It was a beautiful room. She had thought so when she first agreed to take the job. Later, when she ran the vacuum over the carpet, she had admired the peach-like pinks and the varying shades of blues of the flowing Persian pattern. She felt an affinity with the design. Perhaps what some historians say is true, that sometime in the distant past Hittites were in Korea. She ran her fingers over the surface of the table. The mahoghany wood still glowed warmly from her earlier care. She had not minded dusting the furniture. It was cleaning the toilet she could not stand.

Mrs. Randolph returned carrying a coin purse. She gestured for Haesu to hold out her hand, then emptied the contents of the purse into the outstretched palm. The coins barely added up to one dollar. Haesu held up two fingers of her other hand.

Mrs. Randolph gave a laugh. "No. You quit. Two dollars only if you were permanent." She shook her head; it was final.

Carefully, so as not to scratch the surface, Haesu placed the coins on the table. She picked up a dime. "Car fare," she explained.

Mrs. Randolph glared at Haesu. She began to fume. "Why you insolent yellow..."

Haesu knew they were words she would not want translated. She turned on her heels and walked out.

The dime clinked lightly as it fell to the bottom of the coin box. Haesu found a seat by the window. She would put her mind to the scenes that passed before her and forget the woman. She enjoyed her rides on streetcars, becoming familiar with the foreign land without suffering the embarrassment of having to speak its language. In three months, she had learned more about America from the seat of streetcars than from anywhere else.

The ride from Bunker Hill to Temple Street was all too brief for her. Only a few minutes separated the mansions of well-to-do Americans from the plain wood-framed houses of the ghettos. But it might as well be a hundred years, she thought. Her country's history went back thousands of years but no one in America seemed to care. To her dismay, few Americans knew where Korea was. This was 1920. The United States was supposed to be a modern country. Yet to Americans, Koreans were "oriental", the same as Chinese, Japanese, or Filipino.

As shops began to come into view, Haesu leaned forward to see the merchandise in the windows. In front of the Five and Ten-cent Store, children were selling lemonade. A discarded crate and hand-scrawled signs indicated they were in business. Charmed, Haesu smiled and waved at the children. When she recognized the shops near her stop, she pulled the cord to signal the conductor she wanted off.

Clara's house was several blocks away. Although the rambling Victorian was really the meeting house of the National Association of Koreans, Haesu thought of it as Clara's. It was because of Clara that Haesu and her husband, Chun, were given a room, a room usually reserved for visiting Korean dignitaries. It was because of Clara that Mr. Yim, her husband, had agreed to make an exception to the rule.

The front door was open. Rudy Vallee's tremulous voice filtered through the screendoor. Clara was practicing the foxtrot again. Haesu stepped out of her shoes and carried them into the house.

"I quit my job," she announced, loud enough to be heard over the victrola.

Clara stopped dancing and took the needle off the record. "But you've just started," she said.

Haesu set her shoes on the floor and plopped into the sofa. "It was horrible. That *sangnyun* stood over me while I worked. I had to practically wipe my face on her filthy toilet to satisfy her."

"Oh, *Onni,* how terrible," Clara said, looking as if she had swallowed something distasteful.

The expression on Clara's face made Haesu laugh. "*onni*", older sister. The honorific title further softened her anger. "The work wasn't hard. I could have done it," Haesu said confidently. "I have to admit the *sangnyun* has good taste. Beautiful furniture, Carpets this thick." She indicated the thickness with her forefinger and thumb. "Such lovely patterns. Like the twining tendrils on old Korean chests. Do you think we have Persian blood in us?"

Clara laughed. "I wouldn't know. You're the one who always says you're one hundred percent Korean."

"I am. But I'm talking about way back. Long, long ago. It would be fun to know." She absent-mindedly picked up one of the round velvet pillows Clara kept on the sofa and ran her hand over it, smoothing down the nap of the fabric. "What difference does it make now?" she said with a sigh. "What difference does it make who our ancestors were? I don't have a job."

"A lot of difference, *Onni*. Your ancestors were *yangbans*. No one can ever deny that. Everyone knows that children of aristocrats are not supposed to clean toilets," Clara declared.

Haesu tossed the pillow aside with such force that it bounced off the sofa onto the floor. "Then what am I doing here?"

Clara picked up the pillow and brushed it off. "How many times are you going to ask me that? You're here ..."

"Living with you and Mr. Yim because Chun and I can't afford a place of our own," Haesu said.

"Why do you let that bother you? Mr. Yim and I don't mind. We want you here." Clara sat down next to Haesu and slipped her arm into Haesu's. "You're like a sister to me. If you were in my place, you would do the same."

Haesu looked earnestly into Clara's eyes. "I would, that's true. We had such fun in Korea, laughing at everything, worrying about nothing."

"It will be that way again. We haven't been here long enough. I've only been here a year and you've hardly had time to unpack. We'll get used to America." Clara leaped from her seat and pulled at Haesu's arm. "Put on your shoes and let's do the foxtrot. I think I'm getting it."

Laughing as she pulled away, Haesu protested, "No, no. I can't do that kind of dance."

"Yes you can. Just loosen up. You act like an old lady, Haesu. You act like you're eighty not twenty." Clara put Rudy Vallee on again and began dancing around the parlor, gliding effortlessly on the linoleum rug.

Haesu drew her feet onto the sofa out of Clara's way. She reached for the cushion and held it in her lap. Clara's enthusiasm amused her. It also puzzled her. Rudy Vallee stirred nothing in Haesu to make her want to dance.

Haesu stood at the screendoor waiting for Chun. Since Monday she had been thinking about what she would say to her husband. She knew what she would not say to him. At dinner on Monday, when Haesu had explained to Mr. Yim why she had quit her job, Clara had chimed in with, "It's so hard here. Haesu's right. We had such fun in Korea, laughing at everything, worrying about nothing."

Mr. Yim's jaw had dropped, the *kimchee* he held in his chopsticks falling onto his rice, causing a momentary lapse in his usual courtly manners. "Laughing at everything and worrying about nothing?" he had said incredulously. "Then, tell me, what are we doing here?" While Haesu and Clara had searched for an answer, Mr. Yim had sardonically added, "As I recall, no one I knew was laughing at Japanese atrocities. Everyone I knew was worrying about persecution." Haesu had shrunk with embarrassment; Mr. Yim was a Korean patriot who had suffered torture in a Japanese prison, and was now forced to live in exile to escape death. "How thoughtless of me," she had replied. "Please forgive me."

Up until two weeks ago Haesu walked with Chun to Clara's house on Thursdays. Chun had found them work as live-in domestics. But Haesu could not bear being summoned by the persistent ringing of a bell and, after two months, had quit. Chun had insisted upon staying on, choosing the security of room and board and five dollars a month. Haesu now saw him only on his days-off.

As soon as she recognized his slight build and flat-footed gait, she flung open the screendoor and walked out to meet him.

Chun did not stop for her. She had to turn around and walk alongside him, matching her steps to his. "I quit my job," she said.

"Let's talk about it later," he said, speeding up. "I have to go to the bathroom. The damn food makes me sick." He hopped up the front steps and disappeared into the house.

Later that night, when they were alone in their room, Haesu told her husband the details of her quitting.

"You'll get used to the work," he said.

"Never! I'll never get used to cleaning someone else's filth."

"It takes two minutes to clean a toilet. It won't kill you," he said as he climbed into bed.

Haesu felt the heat rise to her cheeks. "I'll never understand how you do it, how you can remain mute while someone orders you to come here, go there, do this, do that... like you were some trained animal. They call you a houseboy. A twenty-five year old man being called 'boy'."

"They can call me what they want. I don't put the words in their mouths. The work is easy. Work for pay. There's no problem as long as they don't lay a hand on me. Just a job, Haesu. Work for pay."

"Cheap pay and demeaning work," she said.

Chun shrugged his shoulders. "No work, no pay. No money, no house, no food, no nothing. It's as simple as that."

"That's not good enough for me and I won't disgrace my family by resorting to menial labor," she whispered hoarsely, keeping her voice down as her anger rose. She was obliged to maintain the peace of her host's home.

"I haven't met a *yangban* yet who thought any work was good enough for him. Me? I'm just a farmer's son. Any work is good enough for me. Isn't that right?" He pulled the covers over him.

"I don't want to talk about that now. I have an idea. Are you listening? Riding home on the streetcar, I saw these little stands where people were selling things. Nothing big and fancy. Little things. Standing in the sun selling... things. It didn't seem like hard work. Why can't we do something like that? Are you listening?" She shook his shoulders.

Chun snorted. "You? Selling things? Out in the sun where all the Koreans can see you?"

Haesu pulled the blanket from his shoulders. "I don't care about that. All I care about is that we be our own boss. Can't you see that? No one will tell us what to do."

Chun pulled the blanket from her. "Let a man get some sleep, will you?" He covered himself then turned his back to her.

Haesu walked over to his side of the bed. She leaned over him and put her lips close to his ears. She spoke softly. "I will never work for anyone. Do you hear me. Chun? I'll never clean someone else's filth. Never! You'll never make enough money as a houseboy to support us. Do you hear me, Chun? As soon as we make enough money, we are going back to Korea. We don't belong here. Just tell me, what are we doing here?" She really had laughed at everything and worried about nothing in Korea; a daughter protected from the world by her parents, groomed in seclusion for marriage.

6

(Richard Eun Kook Kim, 1932—2009)
金恩国

作者简介

　　金恩国（Richard Eun Kook Kim，1932—2009），美国朝鲜裔作家，出生于朝鲜咸镜南道的首府咸兴（Hamhung），其童年正值日本占领朝鲜半岛末期。1950至1954年间，他加入韩国海军陆战队与大韩民国陆军，成为步兵中尉，早年的参战经历为其后期的写作积累了广泛的一手素材。金恩国退役后来到美国求学深造，1955至1959年，他在明德学院（Middlebury College）学习政治学和历史；1960至1963年，他先后获得约翰斯·霍普金斯大学（Johns Hopkins University）写作硕士学位、爱荷华大学作家工作坊（University of Iowa's Writers Workshop）艺术硕士学位（MFA），以及哈佛大学远东语言文学硕士学位。成名之后，金恩国曾在马萨诸塞大学安姆斯特分校（University of Massachusetts Amherst）、雪城大学（Syracuse University）、圣地亚哥州立大学（San Diego State University）、首尔大学（Seoul National University）授课，并在首尔大学担任富布赖特教授。此外，1981至1984年，他还担任《韩国先驱报》（*The Korea Herald*）和《朝鲜日报》（*The Chosun Ilbo*）的专栏作家。金恩国荣誉等身，曾荣获1962—1963年福特基金会的外国区域基金（Ford Foundation Foreign Area Fellowship）、1966年古根海姆奖学金、1974年现代韩国文学翻译奖（Modern Korean Literature Translation Awards）、1978—1979年美国国家艺术基金会奖金（National Endowment for the Arts Fellowship）。

　　金恩国著有小说《牺牲者》（*The Martyred*，1964）、《无辜者》（*The Innocent*，1968），短篇小说集《失去的名字：韩国的童年场景》（*Lost Names: Scenes from a*

Korean Boyhood,1970)、儿童故事《蓝鸟》("A Blue Bird",1983)及文章《寻找逝去的岁月》("In Search of Lost Years",1985)等。

  金恩国的处女作《牺牲者》是最为成功的一部作品,小说聚焦朝鲜半岛战争,被翻译成十种语言,长期跻身《纽约时报》畅销书排行榜,并被提名国家图书奖(National Book Award)和诺贝尔文学奖(Nobel Prize in Literature)。小说围绕战争与宗教的关系,探讨了公众在战争期间遭受的巨大苦难以及信仰、希望、忏悔与真理的意义。选读部分摘自《牺牲者》第十九章。朝鲜半岛战争伊始,十二位基督教牧师离奇死亡,叙述者李上尉(Captain Lee)奉命调查此事。为了误导舆论走向,幸存的申牧师被迫背上背叛的罪名,从而达到诋毁共产党、拉拢基督徒的目的。选文看似节奏缓和,但字里行间透露出权力话语的对抗与角逐,具有扣人心弦的魅力。

作品选读

The Martyred

Chapter 19

(excerpt)

By Richard Eun Kook Kim

  For some time after the ministers had left in an atmosphere of confusion and uneasiness, a heavy silence prevailed among the four of us. Park and I stood by the window; Chaplain Koh sat quietly near the stove; while Colonel Chang leaned back in his swivel chair behind the desk, gazing at the ceiling. It was getting dark outside. The wind blew hard. A streetcar clanged by, spattering pale sparks in its wake.

  Colonel Chang at last broke the silence by sitting up abruptly in his chair. "Captain Lee," he said, "you asked me what it was that I knew and you didn't about the execution of the twelve ministers. Do you remember?"

  Park and the chaplain looked at the colonel, who now sat with his hands clasped on the desk.

  "It's true, I do know something that all of you here do not know. I had hoped that I would never have to tell you what I know, but now I feel I have no other choice. The prisoner was telling you the truth about the ministers, although he exaggerated and understandably so. Among the twelve there were some who betrayed their fellows; they were unable to resist the Reds and allowed themselves to be manipulated into denouncing the others. I needn't say anything about Mr. Shin or about the young minister. You have heard the prisoner's words."

"Colonel, how long have you known all this?" I asked.

"Ever since I was assigned to the case. Of course I didn't know everything in detail. But that there were betrayers I knew for certain prior to the capture of Major Jung. Under the circumstances I had no other choice than to suspect Mr. Shin and Mr. Hann. I now know they are innocent. We have Major Jung's word for the fantastic and complicated but true circumstances regarding the last moments of the execution. It was only when I got his confession that I was able to understand why Mr. Shin at first denied any knowledge of the execution. He decided to tell a small lie rather than a big lie about the martyrdom of the twelve, rather than reveal the truth about the shameful frailty and infidelity of some of them."

Colonel Chang's thin lips curled with disdain.

"Now," he continued after a pause, "Mr. Shin has vanished in the face of angry Christians who accuse him of an alleged betrayal. He wants to resign from the ministry and from his church. What are we to make of this? Consider for a moment that you are in his position, that you are falsely accused of a shameful act which you did not commit; consider also that you are subjected to unspeakable humiliation—such as having your house smashed by those for whose sake you are keeping silent. Captain Lee, I accept what you said—that Mr. Shin is guarding the truth, that the others may not want the truth. But I am afraid of what he might do, of what he may be thinking of doing."

Chaplain Koh said, "Mr. Shin did not say anything about his intention of resigning until this morning. He hasn't explained why he wants to resign, or what he plans to do afterward."

"That is why I am disturbed," Colonel Chang said.

"Are you afraid that he might speak the truth?" I said.

"The truth which you don't want?" said Park bitterly.

Colonel Chang scowled at Park.

"Colonel, are you sure," the chaplain said, "that what you have just told us is beyond question?"

"Yes, I am sorry to say I have all the details—the names of the ministers, what they did and said, what confessions they gave to the Reds. I regret to say that I have the evidence."

"Colonel, may I...?" said Park.

Colonel Chang interrupted him. "I know what you would like to know, Captain Park," he said gravely. "You can be proud, as we all are, that your father was the bravest man of them all. He was magnificent, Captain. Even Major Jung admitted that your father could inspire a certain kind of awe and respect among the Red torturers. Rest assured, Captain, he is a great martyr."

Park, with eyes closed, remained silent.

Colonel Chang said, "Chaplain, where is Mr. Shin?" And when there was no response, "It doesn't matter whether you tell me or not. I shan't disturb him. But tell me, do you have any idea what he is thinking of doing?"

The chaplain shook his head. "No."

"Does he know what happened to his house?"

"He knows what they did."

"How did he take it? Was he angry?"

"Yes!" shouted the chaplain, jumping up from his chair. "Yes, he was angry. What did you expect? I've never seen him so angry. He didn't want to go away. I forced him to go. I admit that it was my way of revenge. I hated those petty Christians who behaved like mice yesterday and today are howling like hungry beasts!" He stopped for breath. "All right, he is at the service headquarters of my brigade in Chinnampo. I thought I could keep him over there for a while, at least until the memorial service is over. But is there going to be a memorial service?" Chaplain Koh glanced furiously about him. "For whom? To commemorate whom?"

Colonel Chang brought his fist down on the desk. "Yes! There is going to be a memorial service. To commemorate whom? The twelve martyrs, of course, the twelve glorious martyrs! What do you think! Never mind what I told you. You've heard it, and now forget what you know. I told you only because I wanted you to help me, to help the Christians."

"To help your propaganda, too?" said the chaplain.

"Yes! To help the Army's propaganda, too. Why not, after all! I am not going to let anyone defile our cause. I am not going to let anyone give the Reds an upper hand. Understand that. I don't care who betrayed whom. All I care is that the betrayers and the betrayed alike were murdered by the Reds. That is what you must remember. That is what we must emphasize. And that is the most important thing to tell the whole nation. Army Intelligence has been compiling the data about the inhuman practices of the Reds; we are especially interested in collecting evidence on how the Reds treat Christians. The murder of the twelve ministers cannot be dismissed lightly just because there were a few weak human beings among them. What counts is they were murdered by the Reds, and don't forget it!"

"Aren't you overlooking something?" cried the chaplain. "We are dealing with martyrs, religious martyrs! If you wanted a hundred heroes out of a hundred Army deserters, very well, you should have them. But, by God, you are not going to manufacture religious martyrs. It would be the most despicable blasphemy. Martyrs serve the will of God, not the ephemeral needs of men!"

"Leave your god out of this, Chaplain," the colonel said. "You know I don't give a damn for your god."

"You are unnecessarily blasphemous, Colonel," the chaplain said indignantly.

"Am I? How do you know that what I am going to do—manufacture martyrs as you say—well, how do you know it is what your god may not want? How do you know that I may not be doing a greater service to your Christianity by presenting twelve martyrs than by exposing all the dirty linen under the holy garments of those miserable ministers?"

For a moment Chaplain Koh was too furious to reply. Then he said, "Something must be said to explain Mr. Shin's act, to explain that he has nothing to be ashamed of. You must tell the truth, Colonel, or I shall!"

"Well, Captain Lee," said the colonel, "you have been quiet. What is your opinion? Do you also insist that I tell the truth?"

There was in the tone of his voice an unmistakable challenge. Feeling upon me the silent gaze of the chaplain and Park, I said, "With your permission, sir, let me say I don't understand why you are all so disturbed. What I would like to remind you is that we are talking about *your* truth, Colonel. We have *your* truth before us and we are arguing what to do with it. But it seems to me you have forgotten about Mr. Shin. What about him? What is he going to do? What is *Mr. Shin*'s truth? That is the heart of the matter."

"I don't understand you," said the colonel.

"Sir, the Christians will be more willing to believe what he tells them than what you tell them," I said.

"Hm, don't be too sure of that. But I am glad you brought Mr. Shin up. Why does he want to resign? I'll tell you why. I am afraid he has become rather emotional about the whole damned affair. I fear he has come to a decision to speak out the truth, all the filthy truth about the betrayers. Otherwise, why resign from his calling? It is not a simple thing for a minister to accuse and expose the crimes and failings of fellow ministers. So he quits to make a clear way for his conscience."

"And if he states the fact," Park said, "that there were betrayers, what do you propose to do about it?"

"He won't say that," Colonel Chang said angrily.

"But suppose he does."

"I will do my best to deny it."

"And claim that he says so because he wants to hide his own guilt?" said Chaplain Koh.

Colonel Chang glared at him. "We must persuade him not to lose his head and do anything rash. That's why I said I need your help. We must do our best to stop him from resigning, first of all, and then persuade him to tell the Christians that no minister was guilty, including himself and Mr. Hann, of course. And I will back him up."

"With enough evidence, I hope, sir," I said.

"I don't want to hear any more nonsense from any of you," he shouted. "And I remind you that you are not to divulge any part of this confidential information, you understand."

"You assume," Park said quietly, "that he will either speak the truth or distort it for your benefit, or even maybe his own. But why not assume that he just might say nothing, as he has not so far? Suppose he continues to keep an absolute silence? What then?"

"Nonsense! Sooner or later, he has to clear himself. Otherwise, everyone will be convinced that he is really guilty of something terrible, as many have already begun to think."

"It is imperative that Mr. Shin's innocence be established," said the chaplain.

"How would you accomplish that, Chaplain?" the colonel asked.

"Tell the truth," the chaplain said in anger. "How else? I am a Christian and a chaplain and I was once a pastor myself, but that does not mean I should compromise the truth, however painful it might be to the cause and interest of Christians. Truth cannot be hidden away. Perhaps, it was God's will that such a painful truth as this should have come to Christians."

"And you, Captain Park? What do you say to that?" said the colonel.

Brooding, Park did not reply.

"And you, Captain Lee?"

"I cannot agree with you, sir," I said. "I cannot twist the truth to suit it to the purpose of our propaganda. Besides, sir, as Chaplain Koh has pointed out, the truth has to do with the religious nature of martyrdom, a matter which must be dealt with by religious authorities."

"You then refuse to understand my position," said the colonel.

"Colonel, my only argument is that truth must be told for the sake of its simply being the truth. I must make it clear that I have no other motives. If Mr. Shin were to be found guilty of betrayal, I would insist that he be brought to account for his crime. That's all, Colonel."

"Why must truth be told?" Exasperated, the colonel sprang up from his chair and began pacing the room. "Truth can be buried and still be the truth. It doesn't have to be told."

"The problem in our case, sir, is that you are obliged to say something about the execution of the ministers," I said. "You have created the situation as it stands now, and I am afraid there is no way out of it for you, no way other than either to tell the truth or, as you insist, to distort it. It is your choice, Colonel."

"And what is your choice, Captain? Suppose you were in my position, what would you do?"

"I would tell the truth," I replied.

"And make the damn Reds happy and bring all the disgrace to us, eh?"

"I would have no other choice."

"Enough!" Colonel Chang cried impatiently. "We must persuade Shin to cooperate with us."

"You mean, cooperate with you," said the chaplain.

"Suppose he refuses to be persuaded or to cooperate with you?" I said.

"Then I won't have any other choice. I will have to force him, no matter how much I may be disinclined to do so."

"Do you really think he is the kind of man you can force to do something against his principles?" the chaplain said.

"Ah, that we shall see."

"How would you force him, may I ask?" retorted the chaplain.

"I would rather not say anything about it at this stage."

A long moment of silence followed. At last the chaplain turned to me. "Captain Lee, do you remember, some time ago I told you of a certain problem which is exclusively my own?"

"Yes, I remember," I said. "Why do you ask?"

"You remember I asked you what you would do if you were in my place?"

I nodded.

"What are you talking about?" said the colonel, darting a vexed look at me and at the chaplain.

"I am merely trying to pose a question," the chaplain said. "You asked Captain Lee what he would do in your position. What would you do, Colonel, if you were in Mr. Shin's place?"

"What would *you* do?" said the colonel, frowning.

"I confess," Chaplain Koh sighed, "I wouldn't know what to do."

"I would tell the truth," I said.

"Enough!" cried Colonel Chang once again. "Enough of this nonsense."

7
(Sook Nyul Choi, 1937—)
崔淑烈

作者简介

崔淑烈（Sook Nyul Choi, 1937—），美国朝鲜裔作家，出生于朝鲜平壤，朝鲜半岛战争期间前往韩国避难，之后移民到美国深造。1962年在曼哈顿维尔学院（Manhattanville College）获得学士学位之后，崔淑烈曾在商界短暂工作，并在纽约（New York）和马萨诸塞州（Massachusetts）的公立和教会学校教书二十年。朝鲜半岛战争对崔淑烈影响颇深，磨炼了她面对残酷不公的勇气与意志。其作品多以自身经历为基础，探讨战争、自由、国际政治等主题，在一定程度上反映了亚洲国家的社会地缘政治与历史，是许多中学社会研究课程以及大学政治学课程的推荐书目，并被《当代作家》（*Contemporary Authors*）、《儿童文学评论》（*Children's Literature Reviews*）等多部文学选集与评论收录。

崔淑烈著有《无法告别的一年》（*Year of Impossible Goodbyes*, 1991）、《白长颈鹿的回声》（*Echoes of the White Giraffe*, 1993）、《哥哥与野餐》（*Halmoni and the Picnic*, 1993）、《采珍珠》（*Gathering of the Pearls*, 1994）、《最好的姐姐》（*The Best Older Sister*, 1997）、《云米与哥哥的旅行》（*Yunmi and Halmoni's Trip*, 1997）。其中，处女作《无法告别的一年》荣获朱迪·洛佩兹图书奖（Judy Lopez Book Award）、美国图书馆协会优良图书奖（ALA Notable Book），并被青少年图书馆服务协会评为"青年最佳图书"（Best Books for Young Adults），被纽约公共图书馆评选为"青少年最佳图书"（Best Books for the Teen Age）等。

《无法告别的一年》是崔淑烈最为著名的一部作品，已被翻译成朝鲜语、法语、意大利语和日语。该小说聚焦十岁朝鲜女孩在日帝暗黑期以及第二次世界大战后的生活，展现了家庭成员间不离不弃的爱以及他们不惜一切代价获得自由的决心。小说的第五章是小说最精彩的一章，讲述了主人公苏根（Sookan）首次去日本学校上学的所见所闻：教职人员采取一系列非人道措施同化本地学生，孩子们所遭受的不公正待遇背后是一个国家动荡不安的民族悲剧。

作品选读

Year of Impossible Goodbyes

Chapter 5

(excerpt)

By Sook Nyul Choi

Like porcelain dolls, all the girls sat in their seats with their hands folded. They stared straight ahead at the blank chalkboard. There were no extra seats, so I quickly went to a corner and sat quietly on the floor hoping to stay out of trouble for the rest of the day. I had thought there might be a minute or two to chat and meet the other girls, but I was mistaken. Narita Sensei sat at her wooden desk and fussed about arranging her belongings. Then she took out her black book and surveyed the class. She motioned for me to come to her. "*Aoki Shizue*," she said. I didn't say anything. That was not my name. I knew my brothers had Japanese names that they used at school, but at home we called them by their Korean names or Christian baptismal names. To me they were just "*oppa*," which meant "older brother." I knew our last name was "Aoki" in Japanese, but I was not used to "*Shizue*." I stood before her, feeling confused and afraid.

Narita Sensei banged her ruler on her desk, which sent a pencil flying. It hit me in the eye and I started to cry. I wished she would let me go and sit down. Instead, she shouted, "You refuse to talk to your Sensei?" Unhi rushed up and said something to Sensei. This made Sensei even angrier. She pounded on her desk, and motioned for Unhi to sit down. I learned that the worst thing one could do was to speak up for your friend. We were to mind our own business at all times. Narita Sensei resumed the class. Everyone's name was called. Mine was called again and I answered as all the other children had by saying, "*Hai, Sensei*" and raising my right hand. I knew I had no choice. My baptismal name and my Korean name would be used only at home from now on. Here I would have to answer to this strange Japanese name; I was someone I did not want to be and I had to pretend.

We then had to sing the "*Kimigayo*" all over again and pledge our undying devotion to the Emperor. I was relieved that I had learned the pledge, for Narita Sensei was watching me carefully. I did not want to get my family in trouble. I knew that if I did not behave, they might cut our rice ration or do something worse. Captain Narita knew exactly how best to punish us. I thought of how pale my mother looked that morning, and how skinny Inchun looked. They couldn't take much more.

Finally, it was time to sit down and open our notebooks. I went back to my place on the floor. I wanted only to stay out of Narita Sensei's sight. Sensei put up two poster-boards. One was a picture of two Japanese pilots standing in front of a shiny airplane with Japanese flags painted on the wings. The other was a picture of two tall American soldiers in green fatigues, their faces painted black. Their planes were dirty and dilapidated. Narita Sensei pointed to the Japanese soldiers and had us repeat after her, "*Hikoki, hikoki, gawai hikoki*," which meant, "Airplane, airplane, pretty airplane." Then, pointing to the other picture, she said, "The White Devils are losing the war. See how funny they look." She laughed and the children imitated her. She moved her pointer back and forth from one picture to the other, and I watched the children reciting these chants over and over as if they were familiar old songs. Narita Sensei smiled. "Well done, children," she said.

One by one she called on every child to come up to the front of the classroom and lead the recitation. Unhi went first. She did exactly as she was told and the class repeated after her, and then the next girl went up. I looked at them in astonishment. How could they repeat these ridiculous slogans so easily? I felt sorry for them, and I wondered if these little girls really believed what they were saying. I was glad that I knew something about America.

There was no break from these tedious recitations. I wanted to go to the bathroom, but did not dare attract attention. As I was out of her line of vision, Narita Sensei seemed to have forgotten me. I was grateful to be left alone; I didn't care that I didn't have a desk or chair. As I listened to Narita Sensei's shrill voice, I looked around. I saw one girl wiggling in her chair. Pretty soon, a little puddle formed beneath her. I looked around the room and counted four other little puddles. I looked up at their faces and saw them continuing to recite their lessons as if nothing were wrong. I couldn't wait much longer myself and I sat squeezing my legs together hoping that I could manage to wait until she let us out.

Narita Sensei called on yet another girl to come up to the front of the room and lead the recitation. The girl had wet her pants. She was ashamed, and just sat in her chair, looking nervous and frightened. Narita Sensei whacked her ruler against the side of her desk and shouted at the girl to come up to the board. The girl stood up. The back of her skirt was dripping wet. Narita Sensei looked at her in disgust and asked the whole class to take out their cleaning bags. Each girl had a little bag with some rags and some polishing wax. The children started to push all the chairs and tables back to one side of the classroom, and got on their hands and knees to wax the whole floor. It all seemed very routine to them. No one spoke. Those who had wet their pants seemed relieved to clean up the little puddles they had made.

I stood and watched. She made us all feel worthless and ashamed of ourselves. Unhi saw me and quickly tossed me a rag and part of her stick of wax. We crawled about the floor polishing it as best we could. When we finished, the girls arranged all the desks and chairs, and put their rags and sticks of wax neatly in their desks. They sat quietly and waited for Narita Sensei to continue with the lessons. I was amazed at their efficiency. I knew that this would soon become routine for me, too.

I took my place on the floor. After a long while, Narita Sensei looked up at the class and said with a big smile, "You Koreans are so good at following orders. You are lucky that the Japanese soldiers are here to protect you from the White Devils, aren't you?" "*Hai, Sensei!*" the children shouted in unison. "Remember your happiness depends on the victory of the Imperial soldiers," she said as the bell rang. Our hands were dirty and caked with wax, but we sat and ate our lunches in silence. I tried to take out the splinter in my finger. Then like the others, I started eating my lunch.

Narita Sensei left the room and an older girl came in to watch us. I looked over at the little girl who had put me at the head of the line. She had been one of the girls who had wet her pants. I felt sorry for her. I noticed she had no lunch box. All she had to eat were two little rice balls sprinkled with salt. I pushed my lunch box over toward her. There were still some beans left, and a bit of egg. It smelled so good because Mother had cooked with a little bit of sesame oil, and I knew the little girl would like some. The big girl saw me sharing my lunch, and immediately took it away. She walked out with it, and that was the last time I saw the beautiful lunch box that Grandfather had made. Later Unhi grabbed me and said, "Mind your own business. Never help any of the other girls in the class. It's a bad thing to do. Just take care of yourself."

After lunch, the whole school gathered in the yard. The June sun was hot, but I was glad to be out of that classroom. We were given big burlap bags and told to fill them with sand and pile them against the wall. After about an hour of this, a voice over the loudspeaker said, "That's enough. Now get those stones and pile them up near the sand bags. When the White Devils come, we need those stones to throw at them." I looked at the boys on the other side of the yard, and saw that they were doing something with the bamboo poles. "Line those bamboo spears neatly against the wall," said the voice over the loudspeaker "Remember when the White Devils come each must grab one and stab them."

That was my first day of school. When I went home, Mother did not ask me any questions. She looked at my dirty hands and my sunburnt face. I knew she saw that I didn't have my lunch box. I told her about my new Japanese name and I asked her to call me by my Korean name at home as often as she could. I started to sob. "Sookan, Sookan," she murmured as she held me tightly in her arms and rocked me gently. Her body felt very hot against mine, and I knew she was sick. "The war will be over soon and the Japanese will leave, right Mother?"

"Yes, yes, soon," she replied. "Soon it'll all be better" Exhausted from the afternoon, I rested my head on Mother's lap as I listened to her reassuring words. How glad I was to be at home for the evening.

I wished morning would never come, but it did, all too soon. I felt like announcing, "I am not going to that horrible place again this morning." But I knew if I didn't go to school, my family would be in trouble with Captain Narita and the police. She handed me two little balls of rice and millet wrapped in a damp white handkerchief to keep them moist. She forced a smile. Quietly, I took my lunch and left for school. I thought of all the other girls in my class who had to endure this with me. They had been there much longer than I had. Maybe it won't be so bad today, I kept thinking as I walked along the streets Aunt Tiger had shown me.

8

(Chan E. Park, 1951—)
朴灿应

作者简介

朴灿应（Chan E. Park，1951— ），美国韩裔作家。1995年获得夏威夷大学（University of Hawaii）东亚语言与文学方向博士学位，目前是俄亥俄州立大学（The Ohio State University）的教授，研究方向为韩语、文学与传统口头叙事、亚洲与西方戏剧。

朴灿应在朝鲜族说唱音乐盘索里（p'ansori）、口头叙事传统及其对现代韩语戏剧的影响领域造诣颇深，已开展多场讲座、研讨会、工作坊和表演来推广盘索里研究。她的专著《草席上的声音：关于韩语故事吟唱的民族志》（*Voices from the Straw Mat: Toward an Ethnography of Korean Story Singing*，2003）深入探讨了口头叙事与人文艺术的跨学科关联。

《1903年朴洪波去了夏威夷》（*In 1903, Pak Hŭngbo Went to Hawai'i*，2003）是朴灿应为"韩裔移民抵美百年纪念活动"创作的故事吟唱剧（story-singing play）。该剧的演出伴随着传统民间劳作曲调，展现了第一批韩裔移民流离失所、定居奋斗、劳作收获的悲与喜，将他们在百年前跨越太平洋驶入檀香山港的经历娓娓道来。选读部分摘自这个盘索里式的叙事剧，讲述了一位富有的绅士去世后，将家产全部赠与品行恶劣的大儿子，被驱逐的小儿子朴洪波（Pak Hŭngbo）不得不乘船远赴他乡，开启新的生活。

作品选读

In 1903, Pak Hŭngbo Went to Hawai'i

(excerpt)
By Chan E. Park

Sung:　"*Aigo,* Older Brother!
　　　　You tell your younger brother to get out.
　　　　Where am I to go?
　　　　In this viciously cold winter,
　　　　Where and how may I survive?
　　　　Shall I enter Chiri Mountain,
　　　　Or starve to death on the way?"

　　　　"Stupid! Do I have to tell you where to go?
　　　　Save your breath and go!"

(Slide: Snowing on Paektusan Mountain)

Spoken: Hŭngbo wanders through eight provinces,
　　　　Looking for a place to settle.
　　　　At this time, Japan was intensifying its colonial grip on Korea.
　　　　Many farmlands were being taken,
　　　　Many Koreans were being displaced,
　　　　Many crossed the borders to the Manchurian wasteland.

Sung:

　　　　Chorus: *Arirang, arirang arariyo.*
　　　　　　　　I go over the Arirang Hill.

　　　　1. With a bundle on my back. I go over the Arirang Hill.

2. Father, Mother, hurry, they say the soil in North Kando is good.
   3. Grabbing my aching heart. I go over Paektusan Hill.

Chorus: *Ariari sŭrisŭri arariyo.*
   I ġo over the Ariranġ Hill.

   1. Who took my jade soil, and left me a beggar's gourd?
   2. Enemy, enemy, my enemy, he with the gun is my enemy.
   3. He who argues well went to court, and he who works well went to grave.

Spoken: At a schoolyard in Inch'ŏn,
   Hŭngbo chances upon an announcement that reads:

   (In the Korean traditional style of book recitation)
   "Looking for healthy, well mannered people." That's me!

   "Salary is fifteen dollars a month.
   Work ten hours per day, Sunday off." Hm!
   "Housing and medical will be taken care of by the plantation
   owner. Education is free, and the children can learn English."

   "English? Not Confucian classics?
   Well, beggars can't be too choosy, sign me on."

   Pak Hŭngbo and one hundred one fellow Koreans boarded a ship called
   Genkai Maru.
   The ship sails out to the Pacific.

Sung: (*Chinyanġ*)

   To the middle of the water, the ship sails.
   Endless blue sea, majestic waves.

   Chorus: *Ŏgiya, ŏgiya, ŏhŏ——giya, ŏgiya.*

White duckweeds bloom on the shore,
Seagulls fly up the red reed hill.

Chorus: *Ŏgiya, ŏgiya, ŏhŏ—giya, ŏgiya.*

Out from the estuary of Han River,
Geese circle the harbor in bidding farewell.

(*Chungmori*)

Chorus: *Ŏgiya-ch'a, Ŏgiya-ch'a!*

Set the sail to the gentle wind, weigh the anchor!
Seagulls, high up, frolic through the clouds.

Chorus: *Ŏgiya-ch'a, Ŏgya-ch'a!*

Boundless water, endless sea,
Where are we headed?

(*Chajinmori*)

Chorus: *Ŏgiya-dwiyŏ-ch'a, ŏgiya-dwiyŏ-ch'a!*
　　　　Ehehehe ŏgiya-dwiyŏ—ŏhŏ,
　　　　Ŏŏŏŏ-ŏya, ŏ-hŏgiya...

(Overlaps with a Hawaiian chant.)

(Slide: Black-and-white photo of the old Honolulu Harbor)

All: *Ya! Hawai-da!* (Wow! This is Hawai'i!)

(Local children greet the newcomers with leis.)

All: *Ige muŏyŏ? P'ulmokkŏri-ya? Naemsae ch'aam chotta!*

(What's this? Grass necklace? Smells good!)

(Slide: Photo of the first Korean settlement in Kahuku)

Spoken: In Kahuku a Korean settlement was formed.
        Plantation was a different life altogether.
        But in leisure and in labor,
        The Koreans lived in relative peace and harmony.
        Together they plant, transplant, and weed to the Farmers' Song,
        The Korean-Hawaiian Farmers' Song.

Sung: *(Chungmori)*

      Chorus:
      Turidu-nġ-du-nġ-du-nġ, kkaeġaenġmaek kkaenġmaek kkaenġmaek
      Ŏrŏ-ŏl-lŏl-lŏ-ŏl sanġsadwiyŏ
      Ŏyŏ-ŏhŏ yŏhŏru sanġsadwiyŏ.

      우뚝우뚝 날칼진 코올라우 산상우로
      Over the majestic Ko'olau towering like sharp blades,

      비바람 건듯 불어와, 젖은 등을 말리고.
      Rain blows to cool our sweaty backs.

      Chorus: *Ŏyŏ-ŏhŏ yŏhŏru sangsadwiyŏ.*

      만경창파 물결이 해변에 와그르르르.
      Waves break the shore, *waġŭrŭrŭrŭ*....

      사탕밭 수숫대는 살푸리춤으로 흐느적거린다.
      The willowy sugarcane dance *salp'uri.*

      Chorus: *Ŏyŏ-ŏhŏ yŏhŏru sangsadwiyŏ.*

저녁놀 붉게 피고, 청천하늘에 잔별돋으니
Evening glow spreads, stars come out.

담배붙여 입에울고 북녘바다 쳐다보네.
Lighting tobacco, I gaze at the North Sea.

Chorus: *Ŏyŏ-ŏhŏ yŏhŏru sangsadwiyŏ.*

보고지고 보고지고, 부모처자 형제자매.
I miss my family

가고지고 가고지고, 멀고먼 고향산천.
I miss my home far far away.

Chorus: *Ŏyŏ-ŏhŏ yŏhŏru sangsadwiyŏ.*

Spoken: Different culture, different masters to serve,
Different soils, seasons, calendars, crops,
But they celebrate the first harvest,
Of taros, mangos, papayas, and da sugar!

(Slide: Sugarcane harvest)

Sung: (*Chunġmori*)

Chorus: *Ŏyuhwa pangayo, ŏyuhwa pangayo.*
Ttŏlgŭdŏngttŏng chal tchingnŭnda,
Ŏyuhwa pangayo.

Slippery is millet milling,
After a harsh winter, barley milling,
Good pounding, rice milling,
Deep pounding, water milling,
Sabak sabak, Job's tears milling,

Chigŭl chigŭl, mung bean milling,
Brown grains, white grains,
All through the autumn night,
Ŏyuhwa pangayo.

(*Chajinmori*)

Ŏyuhwa pangayo, Ŏyuhwa pangayo, Ŏyuhwa pangayo.

Entering a valley deep,
Cutting a pine long and straight,
Crafted this mill, yeah?
Ŏyuhwa pangayo.

See how it looks,
A shape of a human!
With legs spread wide,
Ŏyuhwa pangayo.

One leg lifted, one leg lowered,
Up and down,
Strange, intriguing,
Ŏyuhwa pangayo.

Tŏlgŭdŏk ttŏngttŏng, good pounding,
Ŏyuhwa pangayo.

Yummy is sesame.
Sticky is sticky rice,
Ŏyuhwa pangayo.

Sweetest is sugarcane,
Ŏyuhwa pangayo.

Ŏyuhwa panġayo.
Ŏyuhwa panġayo.

Tŏlġŭdŏk ttŏnġttŏng, pound faster,
Ŏyuhwa panġayo.

9

(Theresa Hak Kyung Cha, 1951—1982)
车学庆

作者简介

车学庆（Theresa Hak Kyung Cha, 1951—1982），出生于韩国釜山（Busan），美国韩裔小说家、制片人、导演和艺术家。她于1962年随家人移民美国夏威夷，1964年搬至旧金山湾区（San Francisco Bay Area），在圣心修道院女子学院（Convent of the Sacred Heart High School）学习法语与古希腊罗马经典。车学庆曾在旧金山大学（University of San Francisco）修读一学期，之后转学至加州大学伯克利分校（UC Berkeley）并获得比较文学与艺术双学士学位。1974年至1977年间，她在太平洋电影档案馆（Pacific Film Archive）工作，先后获得文学与艺术双硕士学位。1980年，车学庆搬到纽约，在塔纳姆出版社（Tanam Press）担任编辑和作家。此前她曾三次返回韩国，但没有受到优待。1981年，她在伊丽莎白塞顿学院（Elizabeth Seton College）教授视频艺术，并在大都会艺术博物馆设计部门工作。1982年，在《言说》（*Dictee*, 1982）大获成功后仅一周，她不幸被一名保安杀害。

在创作方面，车学庆受斯特凡·马拉美（Stéphane Mallarmé）句法多变的自由诗和塞缪尔·贝克特（Samuel Beckett）高度简化的戏剧风格影响较大；在艺术方面，她受到艺术家特里·福克斯（Terry Fox）的熏陶，采用一种缓慢柔美、灵活多变的节奏。其作品为后世留下了宝贵的财富，曾在美国、法国、英国等多场展览中展出。学界对于车学庆的研究不断加深，金惠经（Elaine Kim）和诺玛·阿拉尔孔（Norma Alarcón）收集了关于《言说》的评论文章，并编辑出版了《书写自我、书写族群》（*Writing Self, Writing Nation*, 1994）；埃尔文·扎班扬（Elvan

Zabunyan）在2013年出版了关于车学庆的第一部专著。

车学庆的成名作《言说》围绕希腊九位缪斯女神展开九个部分，实现了印刷媒介和视觉媒体的并置交互，显示出开阔的跨文化视野，是现代文学课程的指导书目。选读部分利用多元文本、图像、书法来探索记忆错位和记忆碎片，讲述了车学庆及母亲等女性对苦难的超越。这位前卫艺术家打破了传统的排版设计，对语言进行拆解与实验，善用多语种、重复破碎的短语和频繁的代码转换，赋予作品复杂性和持久美。

作品选读

Dictee

(excerpt)

By Theresa Hak Kyung Cha

CALLIOPE　EPIC POETRY

　　Mother, you are eighteen years old. You were born in Yong Jung, Manchuria and this is where you now live. You are not Chinese. You are Korean. But your family moved here to escape the Japanese occupation. China is large. Larger than large. You tell me that the hearts of the people are measured by the size of the land. As large and as silent. You live in a village where the other Koreans live. Same as you. Refugees. Immigrants. Exiles. Farther away from the land that is not your own. Not your own any longer.

　　You did not want to see. You cannot see anymore. What they do. To the land and to the people. As long as the land is not your own. Until it will be again. Your father left and your mother left as the others. You suffer the knowledge of having to leave. Of having left. But your MAH-UHM, spirit has not left. Never shall have and never shall will. Not now. Not even now. It is burned into your ever-present memory. Memory less. Because it is not in the past. It cannot be. Not in the least of all pasts. It burns. Fire alight enflame.

Mother, you are a child still. At eighteen. More of a child since you are always ill. They have sheltered you from life. Still, you speak the tongue the mandatory language like the others. It is not your own. Even if it is not you know you must. You are Bi-lingual. You are Tri-lingual. The tongue that is forbidden is your own mother tongue. You speak in the dark. In the secret. The one that is yours. Your own. You speak very softly, you speak in a whisper. In the dark, in secret. Mother tongue is your refuge. It is being home. Being who you are. Truly. To speak makes you sad. Yearning. To utter each word is a privilege you risk by death. Not only for you but for all. All of you who are one, who by law tongue tied forbidden of tongue. You carry at center the mark of the red above and the mark of blue below, heaven and earth, tai-geuk; t'ai-chi. It is the mark. The mark of belonging. Mark of cause. Mark of retrieval. By birth. By death. By blood. You carry the mark in your chest, in your MAH-UHM, in your MAH- UHM, in your spirit-heart.

You sing.

Standing in a shadow, Bong Sun flower
Your form is destitute
Long and long inside the summer day
When beautifully flowers bloom
The lovely young virgins will
Have played in your honor.

In truth this would be the anthem. The national song forbidden to be sung. Birth less. And orphan. They take from you your tongue. They take from you the choral hymn. But you say not for long not for always. Not forever. You wait. You know how. You know how to wait. Inside MAH-UHM fire alight enflame.

From the Misere to Gloria to Magnificat and Sanctus. To the Antiphonal song. Because surely. Soon. The answer would come. The response. Like echo. After the oblations. The offering. The sacrifice, the votive, the devotions, the novenas, the matins, the lauds, the vespers, the vigils, the evensong, the nightsong, the atten-dance, the adoration, the veneration, the honor, the invocations, the supplications, the petitions, the recitations, the vows, the immolations. Surely, all these and more. Ceaseless. Again. Over and over.

You know to wait. Wait in the Misere. Wait in the Gloria. Wait in the Magnificant. Wait in the Sanctus. For the Antiphonal song. Antiphonal hymn. The choral answer. In the ebb and tide of echo.

They have not forbidden sight to your eyes. You see. You are made to see. You see and you know. For yourself. The eyes have not been condemned. You see inspite of. Your sight. Let that be a lesson to you. You see farther. Farther and farther. Beyond what you are made to see and made to see only. You pass the mark, even though you say nothing. Everyone who has seen, sees farther. Even farther than allowed. And you wait. You keep silent. You bide time. Time. Single stone laid indicating the day from sunrise to sundown. Filling up times belly. Stone by stone. Three hundred sixty-five days multiplied thirty six years. Some have been born into it. And some would die into it.

The days before the reclamation. Your father. Your mother. Dying while uttering the words. Their only regret. Not having seen with their very eyes, the overthrow. The repelling. The expulsion of the people who have taken you by force. Not to have witnessed the purging by sulphur and fire. Of the house. Of the nation.

You write. You write you speak voices hidden masked you plant words to the moon you send word through the wind. Through the passing of seasons. By sky and by water the words are given birth given discretion. From one mouth to another, from one reading to the next the words are realized in their full meaning. The wind. The dawn or dusk the clay earth and traveling birds south bound birds are mouth pieces wear the ghost veil for the seed of message. Correspondence. To scatter the words.

Mother you are eighteen. It is 1940. You have just graduated from a teacher's college. You are going to your first teaching post in a small village in the country. Your are required by the government of Manchuria to teach for three years in an assigned post, to repay the loan they provided for you to attend the teacher's school. You are hardly an adult. You have never left your mother's, father's home. You who are born the youngest of four children. Always ailing. You have been sheltered from the harshness of daily life. Always the youngest of the family, the child.

You traveled to this village on the train with your father. You are dressed in western clothes. At the station the villagers innocently stare at you and some follow you, especially the children. It is Sunday.

You are the first woman teacher to come to this village in six years. A male teacher greets you, he addresses you in Japanese. Japan had already occupied Korea and is attempting the occupation of China. Even in the small village the signs of their presence is felt by the Japanese language that is being spoken. The Japanese flag is hanging at the entry of the office. And below it, the educational message of the Meiji emperor framed in purple cloth. It is read at special functions by the principal of the school to all the students.

The teachers speak in Japanese to each other. You are Korean. All the teachers are Korean. You are assigned to teach the first grade. Fifty children to your class. They must speak their name in Korean as well as how they should be called in Japanese. You speak to them in Korean since they are too young yet to speak Japanese.

It is February. In Manchuria. In this village you are alone and your hardships are immense. You are timid and unaccustomed to the daily existence of these village people. Outside the room and board that you pay, you send the rest of your pay home. You cannot ask for more than millet and barley to eat. You take what is given to you. Always do. Always have. You. Your people.

You take the train home. Mother... you call her already, from the gate. Mother, you cannot wait. She leaves everything to greet you, she comes and takes you indoors and brings you food to eat. You are home now your mother your home. Mother inseparable from which is her identity, her presence. Longing to breathe the same air her hand no more a hand than instrument broken weathered no death takes them. No death will take them, Mother, I dream you just to be able to see you. Heaven falls nearer in sleep. Mother, my first sound. The first utter. The first concept.

It is Sunday afternoon. You must return to the school. Your students are at the station waiting for you. They see you home and bring you food. It is May, it is still cold in Manchuria. You work Monday, Tuesday, Wednesday, and Thursday passes. On Friday morning you do not feel well. Fever and chill possess the body at the same time. You are standing in the sunlight against the tepid wall to warm yourself. You are giving in. To the fall to the lure behind you before you all around you beneath your skin the sharp air begins to blow the winds of the body, dark fires rising to battle for victory, the summoning the coaxing the irresistable draw replacing sleep dense with images condensing them without space in between. No drought to the extentions of spells, words, noise. Music equally out of proportion. You are yielding to them. They are too quick to arrive. You do not know them, never have seen them but they seek you, inhabit you whole, suspend you airless, spaceless. They force their speech upon you and direct your speech only to them.

You are going somewhere. You are somewhere. This stillness. You cannot imagine how. Still. So still all around. Such stillness. It is endless. Spacious without the need for verification of space. Nothing moves. So still. There is no struggle. Its own all its own. No where other. No time other conceivable. Total duration without need for verification of time.

She could be seen sitting in the first few rows. She would be sitting in the first few rows. Closer the better. The more. Better to eliminate presences of others surrounding better view away from that which is left behind far away back behind more for closer view more and more face to face until nothing else sees only this view singular. All dim, gently, slowly until in the dark, the absolute darkness the shadows fade.

She is stretched out as far as the seat allows until her neck rests on the back of the seat. She pulls her coat just below her chin enveloped in one mass before the moving shades, flickering light through the empty window, length of the gardens the trees in perfect a symmetry.

The correct time beyond the windows the correct season the correct forecast. Beyond the empty the correct setting, immobile. Placid, Extreme stillness. Misplaces nothing. Nothing equivalent. Irreplaceable. Not before. Not after.

The submission is complete. Relinquishes even the vision to immobility. Abandons all protests to that which will appear to the sight. About to appear. Forecast. Break. Break, by all means. The illusion that the act of viewing is to make alteration of the visible. The expulsion is immediate. Not one second is lost to the replication of the totality. Total severance of the seen. Incision.

April 19
Seoul, Korea

Dear Mother,

4. 19. Four Nineteen, April 19th, eighteen years later. Nothing has changed, we are at a standstill. I speak in another tongue now, a second tongue a foreign tongue. All this time we have been away. But nothing has changed. A stand still.

It is not 6. 25. Six twenty-five. June 25th 1950. Not today. Not this day. There are no bombs as you had described them. They do not fall, their shiny brown metallic backs like insects one by one after another.

The population standing before North standing before South for every bird that migrates North for Spring and South for Winter becomes a metaphor for the longing of return. Destination. Homeland.

No woman with child lifting sand bags barriers, all during the night for the battles to come.

There is no desination other than towards yet another refuge from yet another war. Many generations pass and many deceptions in the sequence in the chronology towards the destination.

You knew it would not be in vain. The thirty-six years of exile. Thirty-six years multiplied by three hundred and sixty-five days. That one day your country would be your own. This day did finally come. The Japanese were defeated in the world war and were making their descent back to their country. As soon as you heard, you followed South. You carried not a single piece, not a photograph, nothing to evoke your memory, abandoned all to see your nation freed.

From another epic another history. From the missing narrative. From the multitude of narratives. Missing. From chronicles. For another telling for other recitations.

Our destination is fixed on the perpetual motion of search. Fixed in its perpetual exile. Here at my return in eighteen years, the war is not ended. We fight the same war. We are inside the same struggle seeking the same destination. We are severed in Two by an abstract enemy an invisible enemy under the title of liberators who have conveniently named the severance, Civil War. Cold War. Stalemate.

I am in the same crowd, the same coup, the same revolt, nothing has changed. I am inside the demonstration I am locked inside the crowd and carried in its movement. The voices ring shout one voice then many voices they are waves they echo I am moving in the direction the only one direction with the voices the only direction. The other movement towards us it increases steadily their direction their only direction our mutual destination towards the other against the other. Move.

I feel the tightening of the crowd body to body now the voices rising thicker I hear the break the single motion tearing the break left of me right of me the silence of the other direction advance before... They are breaking now, their sounds, not new, you have heard them, so familiar to you now could you ever forget them not in your dreams, the consequences of the sound the breaking. The air is made visible with smoke it grows spreads without control we are hidden inside the whiteness the greyness reduced to parts, reduced to separation. Inside an arm lifts above the head in deliberate gesture and disappears into the thick white from which slowly the legs of another bent at the knee hit the ground the entire body on its left side. The stinging, it slices the air it enters thus I lose direction the sky is a haze running the streets emptied I fell no one saw me I walk. Anywhere. In tears the air stagnant continues to sting I am crying the sky remnant the gas smoke absorbed the sky I am crying. The streets covered with chipped bricks and debris. Because. I see the frequent pairs of shoes thrown sometimes a single pair among the rocks they had carried. Because. I cry wail torn shirt lying I step among them. No trace of them. Except for the blood. Because. Step among them the blood that will not erase with the rain on the pavement that was walked upon like the stones where they fell had fallen. Because. Remain dark the stains not wash away. Because. I follow the crying crowd their voices among them their singing their voices unceasing the empty street.

There is no surrendering you are chosen to fail to be martyred to shed blood to be set an example one who has defied one who has chosen to defy and was to be set an example to be martyred an animal useless betrayer to the cause to the welfare to peace to harmony to progress.

It is 1962 eighteen years ago same month same day all over again. I am eleven years old. Running to the front door, Mother, you are holding my older brother pleading with him not to go out to the demonstration. You are threatening him, you are begging to him. He has on his school uniform, as all the other students representing their schools in the demonstration. You are pulling at him you stand before the door. He argues with you he pushes you away. You use all your force, all that you have. He is prepared to join the student demonstration outside. You can hear the gun shots. They are directed at anyone.

Coming home from school there are cries in all the streets. The mounting of shouts from every direction from the crowds arm in arm. The students. I saw them, older than us, men and women held to each other. They walk into the *others* who wait in *their* uniforms. Their shouts reach a crescendo as they approach nearer to the *other side*. Cries resisting cries to move forward. Orders, permission to use force against the students, have been dispatched. To be caught and beaten with sticks, and for others, shot, and carted off. They fall they bleed they die. They are thrown into gas into the crowd to be squelched. The police the soldiers anonymous they duplicate themselves, multiply in number invincible they execute their role. Further than their home further than their mother father their brother sister further than their children is the execution of their role their given identity further than their own line of blood.

You do not want to lose him, my brother, to be killed as the many others by now, already, you say you understand, you plead all the same they are killing any every one. You withstand his strength you call me to run to Uncle's house and call the tutor. Run. Run hard. Out the gate. Turn the corner. All down hill to reach Uncle's house. I know the two German shepherd dogs would be guarding one at each side, chained to their house they drag behind them barking. I must brave them, close my eyes and run between them. I call the tutor from the yard, above the sounds of the dogs barking. Several students look out of the windows. They are in hiding from the street, from their homes where they are being searched for. We run back to the house the tutor is ahead of me, when I enter the house the tutor is standing in front of him. You cannot go out he says you cannot join the D-e-m-o, *De. Mo.* A word, two sounds. Are you insane the tutor tells him they are killing any student in uniform. Anybody. What will you defend yourself with he asks. You, my brother, you protest your cause, you say you are willing to die. Dying is part of it. If it must be. He hits you. The tutor slaps you and your face turns red you stand silently against the door your head falls. My brother. You are all the rest all the others are you. You fell you died you gave your life. That day. It rained. It rained for several days. It rained more and more times. After it was all over. You were heard. Your victory mixed with rain falling from the sky for many days afterwards. I heard that the rain does not erase the blood fallen on the ground. I heard from the adults, the blood stains still. Year after year it rained. The stone pavement stained where you fell still remains dark.

Eighteen years pass, I am here for the first time in eighteen years, Mother. We left here in this memory still fresh, still new. I speak another tongue, a second tongue. This is how distant I am. From then. From that time. They take me back they have taken me back so precisely now exact to the hour to the day to the season in the smoke mist in the drizzle I turn the corner and there is no one. No one facing me. The street is rubble. I put my palm on my eyes to rub them, then I let them cry freely. Two school children with their book bags appear from nowhere with their arms around each other. Their white kerchief, their white shirt uniform, into a white residue of gas, crying.

I pass a second curve on the road. You soldiers appear in green. Always the green uniforms the patches of camouflage. Trees camouflage your green trucks you blend with nature the trees hide you you cannot be seen behind the guns no one sees you they have hidden you. You sit you recline on the earth next to the buses you wait hours days making visible your presence. Waiting for the false move that will conduct you to mobility to action. There is but one move, the only one and it will be false. It will be absolute. Their mistake. Your boredom waiting would not have been in vain. They will move they will have to move and you will move on them. Among them. You stand on your tanks your legs spread apart how many degrees exactly your hand on your rifle. Rifle to ground the same angle as your right leg. You wear a beret in the 90 degree sun there is no shade at the main gate you are fixed you cannot move you dare not move. You are your post you are your vow in nomine patris you work your post you are your nation defending your country from subversive infiltration from your own countrymen. Your skin scorched as dark as your uniform as you stand you don't hear. You hear nothing. You hear no one. You are hidden you see only the prey they do not see you they cannot. You who are hidden you who move in the crowds as you would in the trees you who move inside them you close your eyes to the piercing the breaking the flooding pools bath their shadow memory as they fade from you your own blood your own flesh as tides ebb, through you through and through.

You are this
close to this much
close to it.
Extend arms apart just so, that much. Open the thumb and the index finger just so.
the thumb and the index finger just so.
That much
you want to kill the time that is oppression itself. Time that delivers not. Not you, not from its expanse, without dimension, defined not by its limits. Airless, thin, not a thought rising even that there are tilings to be forgotten. Effortless. It should be effortless. Effortless ly the closer it is the closer to it. Away and against time ing. A step forward from back. Backing out. Backing off. Off periphery extended. From imaginary to bordering on division. At least somewhere in numerals in relation to the equator, at least all the maps have them at least walls are built between them at least the militia uniforms and guns are in abeyance of them. Imaginary borders. Un imaginable boundaries.

Suffice more than that, SHE opposes Her.
SHE against her.
More than that. Refuses to become discard decomposed oblivion.
From its memory dust escapes the particles still material still respiration move. Dead air stagnant water still exhales mist. Pure hazard igniting flaming itself with the slightest of friction like firefly. The loss that should burn. Not burn, illuminate. Illuminate by

losing. Lighten by loss.

Yet it loses not.

 Her name. First the whole name. Then syllable by syllable counting each inside the mouth. Make them rise they rise repeatedly without ever making visible lips never open to utter them.

Mere names only names without the image not *hers*

hers alone not the whole of *her* and even the image

would not be the entire

her fraction *her* invalid that inhabits that rise

voluntarily like flint

pure hazard dead substance to fire.

 Others anonymous *her* detachments take her place. Anonymous against *her.* Suffice that should be nation against nation suffice that should have been divided into two which once was whole. Suffice that should diminish human breaths only too quickly. Suffice Melpomene. Nation against nation multiplied nations against nations against themselves. Own. Repels her rejects her expels her from *her* own. Her own is, in, of, through, all others, *hers*. Her own who is offspring and mother, Demeter and Sibyl.

 Violation of *her* by giving name to the betrayal, all possible names, interchangeable names, to remedy, to justify the violation. Of *her.* Own. Unbegotten. Name. Name only. Name without substance. The everlasting, Forever. Without end.

 Deceptions all the while. No devils here. Nor gods. Labyrinth of deceptions. No enduring time. Self-devouring. Devouring itself. Perishing all the while. Insect that eats its own mate.

 Suffice Melpomene, arrest the screen entrance flickering hue from behind cast shadow silhouette from back not visible. Like ice. Metal. Glass. Mirror. Receives none admits none.

 Arrest the machine that purports to employ democracy but rather causes the successive refraction of *her* none other than her own. Suffice Melpomene, to exorcize from this mouth the name the words the memory of severance through this act by this very act to utter one, *Her* once, Her to utter at once, *She* without the separate act of uttering.

10
(Gary Pak, 1952—)
加里·朴

作者简介

加里·朴（Gary Pak, 1952— ），美国韩裔作家、编辑。其祖父母在第二次世界大战期间逃离朝鲜半岛来到美国，祖母在夏威夷的甘蔗种植园工作。加里·朴在夏威夷出生并长大，获得波士顿大学学士学位，之后又于夏威夷大学攻读硕士、博士学位。目前，他是夏威夷大学的英语教授和韩国研究中心成员，同时还是《亚美学刊》（*Amerasia Journal*）的编委会成员。

加里·朴是一位多产的作家，文学成就卓著，代表作品有短篇小说集《崴普那的看守》（*The Watcher of Waipuna and Other Stories*, 1992）、《壁虎的语言》（*Language of the Geckos and Other Stories*, 2005）；长篇小说《米纸飞机》（*A Ricepaper Airplane*, 1998）、《火山的孩子们》（*Children of a Fireland*, 2004）、《同一片天空下的兄弟》（*Brothers Under a Same Sky*, 2013）；电视剧《种植园的孩子：夏威夷的第二代韩国人》（*Plantation Children: 2nd-generation Koreans in Hawai'i*）等；曾获得富布赖特奖金（Fulbright Fellowship）、美国亚裔研究协会2004年散文/诗歌类图书奖（Book Award in the Prose/Poetry）优秀奖等。

《米纸飞机》的场景设置在甘蔗种植园，再现了20世纪20年代夏威夷边缘亚裔的艰苦生活。主人公金成华（Kim Sung Wha）是一位劳动者、爱国者、革命者。他设想用宣纸、竹子和破旧自行车建造一架飞机，然后飞回韩国家人的身边。这是一个关于爱和涅槃的英雄叙事，大气磅礴、感人至深；主人公年事已高却老骥伏枥，坚韧不拔投身革命，对母国热忱丝毫不减。选读部分即摘自《米纸飞机》。

作品选读

A Ricepaper Airplane

(excerpt)
By Gary Pak

But now, how everything is different, everything is changed, now that he and his friends are old and feeble in mind and brittle in body. Now, where is the death that should talk to them in alluring tones and embrace them with promises of release from the omnipresent discomforts and miseries of this life, this penalty of old age? Why do people ready for death live forever? Why hasn't death come to those who are ready for it—to those who wait with pain—and burn them to unthinking dust? Why must we wait so long when there is nothing more to live for? And why does it come down like a merciless vulture attacking, only the flesh is not carrion but young and so vigorous and alive and furious with the warmest, brightest blood?

For three hours, Sung Wha sleeps a dreamless sleep. He is awakened by a soft knocking on the hollow door. The door squeaks as it inches open, finally exposing the naked light bulb of the hallway, which blinds him for a moment.

"Uncle! Uncle! You sleeping?" It's Yong Gil's voice, whispering.

Sung Wha turns from the light and sighs. Farts.

"Uncle... sorry I wake you up. I brought you some food."

Dropping his legs over the side of the bed, Sung Wha sits up and acknowledges his nephew with a yawning nod. He scratches his head and chest. "Come inside," he says, languidly waving in Yong Gil.

Yong Gil takes a tentative step into the room. "You want me shut the door?"

Sung Wha shakes his head. He watches Yong Gil's dark, bent figure with his offering of food.

"This time, I went down to the park, but the boys, yo' friends, they say they never see you the whole day. I thought..."

What you *thought? Dat I wen* maké-*die-dead? No be scared, Yon*ġ *Gil, Say it. Say you thought I* wen maké. *Why you scared say dat? Bettah if I was* maké *already. Bettah for me. Bettah for you.*

"Here. I brought you some *kaukau*. Mary made plenty *kaukau* so I gave some to your friends."

Sung Wha motions his nephew to set tile food on the bureau. He yawns again.

Yong Gil sits on a stool at the foot of the bed. Silence. Then a door opens down the hall: a flip-flopping to the bathroom. The bathroom door closes, is latched.

Then: "Uncle, I know you no like hear what I have to say."

"Den no say it."

Uneasily, Yong Gil draws. In a breath, releases. "I know I brought this up how many times already, but I gotta bring it up again. Mary and me... we want you come live with us. I know I brought this up time and time again, but we're worried about your welfare, your health. We like you move in with us. Think about it, Uncle. You not getting any younger."

"You know my answer already," he says. He clears his throat.

"I know. I know." Yong Gil rattles off.

"Den das dat."

The plumbing in the wall whines. The bathroom door unlatches, and the user returns to his room. It's John-John: Sung Wha can tell by his dragging left foot.

"But I like you think about it," Yong Gil says. "And there's something else."

"What?"

"Uncle Sung Wha ... I don't think you should get so involved with all this business, all this radical stuff, making all this trouble with the landlord."

The words stab Sung Wha. A sharp look at his nephew. "Trouble? What you calling 'trouble'?"

"I know not my business, but all this is making you more sick. Uncle, you one old man already. You cannot keep going on like this. It's bad for your heart. And the landlord, this is his place, he can do what he wants with it. The way you guys act, just like he owes you something. He doesn't owe you nothing."

"Who 'you guys'?"

Yong Gil sighs.

"Every time you come here, you tell me same-same story. You tell me what to do. You no mo' respect fo' yo' elders or what? If you going come here every time and tell me dis same-same thing, no come. I get my own life live. I not asking fo' special-kine treatment. I not asking fo' handouts. Das why I no like live wit' you folks. If live wit' you folks, I not going live da way I like live."

A twisted look on Yong Gil's face. Like a scolded child's.

"No get me wrong. Yong Gil. I love you and Mary. I 'preciate what you folks trying do, thinking 'bout me, bringing me food. But you gotta understand me. No can teach dis old dog new tricks."

"Uncle, we just thinking about you." Yong Gil offers.

"I know, I know. But..."

"Uncle, go eat the food before it comes cold." Yong Gil gets up to bring Sung Wha the food, but the old man holds him back. "Uncle, I just want you to think about it... okay? If you ever need one place to stay, you always have a room with us."

What kine fool you, Sung Wha? Anybody in dis damn hotel would grab da chance right away. You crazy, lōlō. Yo' own nephew, yo' own flesh and blood, asking you come live wit' him. You going get one nice bed sleep, good food eat, one TV watch, somebody always going be around you anytime you like somebody around. And yo' clothes going get wash to' you. Sung Wha, you going live like one king! So den... how come you no like go? No tell me' cause your 'independence!' Das bullshit. You know dat. I know dat. Everybody know dat. Tell dem da reason is you no like take advantage. But dis da real reason?

Eh, Sung Wha, everybody know you old man, so no lie. You like take advantage, no? Everything in you all dried up. You no young guy wit' one hard body and one mind can think straight anymo'. Why you like maké by yo' self, wit' nobody care fo' you? You know you no like maké *by yo'self but here you go, torturing yo'self. Dis mo'worse dan you* maké *with no mo' face.*

"Come." Sung Wha says. "Yong Gil, come. We go take one walk."

Slowly and carefully, Sung Wha puts the parts of himself together: his wallet, his belt, his... they leave the room and step into a back alley of the cooling late afternoon, a gritty but pleasant breeze bringing them the smell of an oily ocean. They walk along a quiet waterfront and sit at the end of an old wharf where mingling smells of diesel fuel and dried aku blood are pungent but resurrecting. They can see only a couple of stars in this stagnant night, probably bright planets, the edge of sky a dying indigo, a fleeing hint of a going day.

"You know, Yong Gil, in da old days, dis time of da day da best. Da plantation workers jus' coming home. Was hard work, dose days. Everybody really work fo' dey money. Now at least I can kick back and relax and watch da sunset. But I no regret all dose hard working days, Yong Gil. I no regret dem days. Da stuff I experience, you can fill one book wit' 'em. Da only thing I regret... my wife not here wit' me." He gazes across the harbor at the city's lights—there's no reflection off the water—then out to the hiding horizon. "And I nevah really see and bring up my children. Das my main regret, Yong Gil. Das da main regret in my life. Maybe by now... maybe by now, I one grandfather already."

They listen to the wind and the water lapping on the pillars of the ailing wharf.

"How is the sunset in Korea?" asks Yong Gil.

"Beautiful. Mo' beautiful dan Hawai'i. You like see one beautiful sunset, you go Korea. You nevah go Korea, eh, Yong Gil? You evah go?"

"No. When I was small kid I went, but I don't remember."

"Den you gotta go. Every Korean gotta go back Korea and see one sunset. You know, dey say Korea is da Land of da Morning, yeah?"

"Land of the Morning Calm."

11

(Cathy Song, 1955—)
宋凯西

作者简介

宋凯西（Cathy Song，1955— ），美国韩裔诗人，出生于美国夏威夷首府檀香山；1971年于威利斯勒大学（Wellesley College）获学士学位，1981年获波士顿大学创意写作硕士学位。

宋凯西的作品包括诗歌集《照片新娘》（"Picture Bride"，1983）、《无框的窗，成块的光》（*Frameless Windows, Squares of Light*，1988）、《学校人物》（*School Figures*，1994）、《福地》（*The Land of Bliss*，2001）、《云推手》（*Cloud Moving Hand*，2007），以及短篇小说集《世上所有的爱》（*All the Love in the World*，2020）。她曾荣获1982年耶鲁大学年轻诗人系列奖（Yale Series of Younger Poets Award），被提名美国国家图书评论奖（National Book Critics Circle Award），1994年获美国诗社颁发的雪莱纪念奖（Shelley Memorial Award）。

第一篇选读诗歌《照片新娘》（"Picture Bride"）选自诗集《照片新娘》，讲述了宋凯西祖母被包办的婚姻。由于移居至美国的韩国人不被允许与当地人通婚，他们只能从母国或其他亚洲国家寻找结婚对象，通常是将女性的照片寄给远方的男性，由他们挑选出自己的妻子并将其接至美国成婚，"照片新娘"由此得名。宋凯西的祖母在二十出头的花样年华离开韩国，远赴夏威夷，嫁给了一位三十六岁的种植园劳工移民。本诗集的大部分内容都涉及此类复杂的家庭关系。

第二篇选读摘自小说集《世上所有的爱》中的同名短篇小说《世上所有的爱》（"All the Love in the World"），讲的是一位病重老人在医院的所思所感。家庭关系的联结是永远无法割舍的爱的纽带，家人的陪伴给了老人无尽的精神力量。他殷切嘱托晚辈，并祈祷每位家庭成员都能永远被爱包围。

作品选读（一）

Picture Bride

By Cathy Song

She was a year younger
than I,
twenty-three when she left Korea.
Did she simply close
the door of her father's house
and walk away. And
was it a long way
through the tailor shops of Pusan
to the wharf where the boat
waited to take her to an island
whose name she had
only recently learned,
on whose shore
a man waited,
turning her photograph
to the light when the lanterns
in the camp outside
Waialua Sugar Mill were lit
and the inside of his room
grew luminous
from the wings of moths
migrating out of the cane stalks?
What things did my grandmother
take with her? And when

she arrived to look
into the face of the stranger
who was her husband,
thirteen years older than she,
did she politely untie
the silk bow of her jacket,
her tent-shaped dress
filling with the dry wind
that blew from the surrounding fields
where the men were burning the cane?

作品选读（二）

All the Love in the World

(excerpt)

By Cathy Song

"Alex? Kitty?"

"Go to sleep, Dad. We're here, " Alex said, rising from the chair she had been curled up in. She pressed her face against his. "Don't worry, we're here."

"Where? Where's Kitty?"

Alex moved aside to point to Catherine asleep on the two chairs she had joined to form a makeshift cot.

He relaxed, falling back into an open air marketplace where he was being swept against his will by a crowd pushing and yelling, going in the opposite direction. Sellers hawking wares, jugglers hurling balls, butchers running with knives, mimes gesturing toward the sky—everyone but him seemed to be in costume, carrying the implements of trade. Among the trinkets, wristwatches, cheap handbags, he saw the suitcase he was looking for, but he couldn't reach the stall. The strong current of the crowd turned into a river carrying him toward a narrow passage where he could feel the softness of moss against his head, where he could see every leaf sparkling in a tunnel of branches. He drifted, alone, into a great dispersion of silence. When he woke up, he told his sleeping daughters that their mother had come to bathe him.

He was exhausted, barely hanging on. The line of visitors kept coming to say goodbye. He wanted to be cheerful for each one of them. They deserved to be greeted with cheerfulness.

He didn't need any promptings from Catherine, who stood by ready to interpret in the event of confusion. He didn't need any more notes to tell him where he was, where he was going, who was who. He remembered every person who came to his bedside, some tearfully, some shyly, some collapsing in fits of grief. He clasped their hands and told them what he felt they needed to hear. He thanked them for stopping by, which they knew was his way of thanking them for everything. To his two grandsons, he told James the eldest to look after the others, and Luke the youngest to be a warrior. He told Kristin, Amelia, Frances, Anuhea, and Hoku, his five granddaughters, to be sweet and kind like their mothers.

He saw everything clearly—that his son Aidan had already become the patriarch of his wife Malia's family; that Catherine and David, having patched whatever had been broken between them, would find the fruits of forgiveness in becoming grandparents together; that Alexandria and Ben would settle companionably into the best kind of old age, an uneventful one. He had brought his family as far as he could in the twelve years since Eleanor had died, carrying them alone through the rough times of raising their own children. He had no more to give. He saw everything clearly, and it was done.

He was forgotten momentarily as the room emptied at the news that the pizzas had arrived in the lounge. Aidan stayed behind, and once he was alone, he embraced his father, and wept.

"When's the bus leaving, son?" Sung Mahn asked, beginning to drift back into the silence that was waiting for him, that peacefulness of drifting on a great body of water.

"Soon, Dad. Soon."

Before the family would let him go, they returned. He could smell garlic and pepperoni on their breaths as they continued one by one to cover his face with kisses.

"Let's get this show on the road," he said, which prompted a rearrangement of chairs.

"C'mon," he added, afraid he would miss it. "Time to board the bus. Which bus should we take?"

There was laughter. He wasn't trying to be funny. He heard laughter but mostly he heard crying.

The women started to dance hula to a song he didn't recognize. The music was coming out of someone's phone. He watched his daughters and granddaughters bump into one another, their circular arm motions scrambled, depicting waves or swaying palm trees or rain rushing down the mountains, he couldn't tell. It was his turn to laugh, because he knew they weren't trying to be funny.

When the hula ended, to his relief, his granddaughter Frances asked the family to gather themselves into a circle. His hands were held in that circle. Once he felt his hands being grasped, he didn't wait for the coughing and the shifting of feet to stop. He launched into the prayer he had said every night, thousands of recitations of that long list including so many who had entered into that dispersion beyond. Saying their names all these years had given him courage to face this very moment, the strength of his voice lifting him closer to the moment when all would be silent, a great body of silence drowning out the noise, the pain of striving, the ache of continuing. He ended with the only psalm he knew, "The Lord is my shepherd ..." Those who knew the words joined in, their voices lifted by his. And when it was over, he looked around the circle of those he had carried for as long as he was able, and said, "I wish all of you all the love in the world." It was finished. It was done. And it was good.

12

(Walter K. Lew, 1955—)
沃尔特·卢

作者简介

沃尔特·卢（Walter K. Lew, 1955— ），美国韩裔诗人。他曾在布朗大学（Brown University）、康奈尔大学（Cornell University）、米尔斯学院（Mills College）、迈阿密大学（University of Miami）和加州大学洛杉矶分校教授创意写作、东亚文学和美国亚裔文学，现居住在纽约布鲁克林（Brooklyn）和宾夕法尼亚州伯利恒（Bethlehem）。

沃尔特·卢是美国较早关注无声电影叙事的艺术家，与刘易斯·克拉尔（Lewis Klahr）等多位视觉艺术家有过合作。他对韩国文学及美国亚裔文学的翻译和研究作品已被广泛收录，其纪录片已在哥伦比亚广播公司新闻（CBS News）、公共广播电视网（PBS）、英国独立电视台（British ITV）和日本广播协会（NHK-Japan）播出。

沃尔特·卢的代表作包括《美国韩裔小说灯塔选集》（*Kori: The Beacon Anthology of Korean American Fiction*, 2001）、《乘风：诗歌和多媒介文本》（*Treadwinds: Poems and Intermedia Texts*, 2002）、《文化的要务》（*Imperatives of Culture*, 2013）、《闭着眼》（*With Eyes Closed*, 2014）等。此外，他还参与了《疯狂的瓜和中国的苹果：弗朗西斯·钟的诗歌》（*Crazy Melon and Chinese Apple: The Poems of Frances Chung*, 2000）、北美亚裔诗歌选集《预感》（*Premonitions*, 1995）的编辑与撰写，先后获得美国国家艺术基金会奖金、美国笔会文学奖（PEN Center USA Literary Award）、美国亚裔文学奖（Asian American Literary Award）。

《从修道院下来》（"Down from the Monastery"）出自《乘风：诗歌和多媒介

文本》，灵感源于诗人在檀香山和韩国学习时认识的一位牧师。《在马诺阿奔跑》（"Mānoa Run"）最早于1998年刊登在《竹岭》（*Bamboo Ridge*）期刊，探讨了韩国移民文化的延续性与传承性，具有现代主义色彩，体现了诗歌重塑语言、再现场景的魅力。

作品选读（一）

Down from the Monastery

By Walter K. Lew

Priest Baba jabs
quickly through a spill of photographs
and finds a tiny sepia tint

of five Korean schoolgirls in hanbok
Curved together on a wild hill,
sky-drunk as they gaze off

Over the camera,
Part of the Japanese empire.
Some hold onto stalks
Of pampas grass, the wind is that strong
And certain clouds are about to
Slide away forever.
Baba slaps his feet and sighs:
"That mood will never return.
Too bad you didn't live *then*
You could have fallen in love with a country girl
When you were 14 or 15 and
Written a beautiful sad story."
He points at the most dewy-faced girl:

"Maybe she was never that pretty again!" I tell him,
That's my mother! I knew that, he laughs, then shuts up
to not
Parch their gazes.
For a moment I imagine
He is about to sing another bar song,
But he doesn't. He makes me promise
I'll read the sutras
Then goes down the hall to get me cold water
Because "guys" my age always eat so fast
They forget to drink with their food.

Baba, why did you laugh so hard?
You can't even remember your mother.
When you were a boy chanting
Kwanseŭm posal, Kwanseŭm posal
All dawn in the mountain temple,
You kept saying *inside*
Omŏni ŏdi, Omŏni Ŏdi—Where's
my mommy Where's my mommy
When you beat all the orphan taunters
With your dragon drawings
And returned with the valley school's prize,
A bad monk tore them up and said, "Can you make
Rice with this? Will it
Bring your mommy back?"
                      Bless, you said
The old ill priest who rose from his cell,
Pieced the paper back together.
Blew dirt off the gleaming dragon eyes,
And kept winking as he praised them.
Unwrapping candy, he made you promise to continue
Even if he leaves soon.

Baba, let's wander together—

It's true we still have pictures

But have lost our souls. Let us lose
Our loss together
And feed at last
The children cold inside us.

Kwanseŭm posal, Kwanseŭm posal

All dawn in the mountain temple

作品选读（二）

Mānoa Run

By Walter K. Lew

If I stretch it out, turn and go

Up the hill, the circling road
Behind the widow's house

I will see an ocean sunset, flotillas

Of cirrus blazing in their chassis.
I will follow the curve, the lush bend up into the better

Neighborhood: silk dogs, children tumbling like deaf-mutes,

The crying iridescent flora
Shrubbed and rinsed and shaken clean.

A cold flame of wind will grab fallen, lung-sized

Kamani leaves and gust them into
A walking companion

Rushing and treading beside me, at shoulder-height:

Its head's milled peat, belly, shins
Unceasingly thrashed and shat into each other,

As if this were no mere exercise

But a face of the hidden urge, whispered
Mind of things to pace and speak with us.

By this I will be made helpless, and jog on

Knowing like a scar, that I cannot remember, cannot
Say the spell exactly, or dare to embrace

The falling figure, weep and pray

For the burning prisoner kneeling into his
Dissolving shins. *Grandfather!* I may whisper. *Father!*

My father says all his life here. The flame withdraws,

The head keels, flops open like a gourd
Into a hopping gyre of mute leaves

On the black road, if I stop and turn around.

13

(Myung Mi Kim, 1957—)
金晏密

作者简介

金晏密（Myung Mi Kim，1957— ），美国韩裔诗人。她出生于韩国汉城（今首尔），九岁时随家人移居美国，在中西部地区长大。金晏密在欧柏林学院（Oberlin College）获得学士学位，并分别在约翰斯·霍普金斯大学与爱荷华大学（The University of Iowa）取得文学硕士学位和艺术硕士学位。毕业之后，她曾在旧金山州立大学教授创意写作，担任过加州圣玛丽学院（St. Mary's College）的杰出访问诗人，目前是纽约州立大学布法罗分校（SUNY Buffalo）的英语教授与诗学研究项目的核心教员。

金晏密的诗集《在旗帜下》（*Under Flag*，1991）大胆进行语言实验，探索碎片化与错位实践，荣获当年多元文化出版商交流优秀奖（The Multicultural Publisher's Exchange Award of Merit）。她还著有诗集《奖金》（*The Bounty*，1996）、《平民》（*Commons*，2002）、《贫穷》（*Penury*，2009）等，获得杰拉西艺术村项目（Djerassi Resident Artists Program）奖学金、纽约州立大学校长奖（State University of New York Chancellor's Award）等一系列荣誉。

作为一名后现代主义先锋派诗人，金晏密不拘泥于传统的排版布局与行文规范，善于使用支离破碎的语言与大篇幅的页面留白，在作品中探讨殖民、移民、文化融合、母语丧失以及历史余波等问题，精准认知并捕捉全球资本主义以及不断演变的暴力、灾难、恐怖形势，极大地影响了21世纪美国亚裔诗歌的发展方向。诗歌《在旗帜下》（"Under Flag"）选自同名诗集《在旗帜下》，再现了朝鲜半岛战争期间惨烈的战争场景，以一种坚定的声音直击痛苦主题的核心，把对战争的批判与抵制展现得淋漓尽致。

作品选读

Under Flag

By Myung Mi Kim

Is distance. If she knows it
Casting and again casting into the pond to hook the same turtle
Beset by borders conquered, disfigured

One house can be seen
Then another thatched roof
On this side of the sea the rancor of their arrival
Where invasion occurs according to schedule
Evacuees, a singular wave set against stubbled bluffs
Rigor of those who carry households on their backs

Above: victims.
Below: Chonui, a typical Korean town. In the distance,
a 155-mm shell has exploded.
Of elders who would have been sitting in the warmest part
of the house with comforters draped around their shoulders
peeling tangerines
Of an uncle with shrapnel burrowing into shinbone
for thirty years
A wave of much white cloth
Handful of millet, a pair of never worn shoes, one chicken
grabbed by the neck, ill-prepared for carrying,
carrying through

Not to have seen it yet inheriting it
Drilled at the core for mineral yield and this, once depleted,
never to be replaced
At dawn the next morning, firing his machine gun, Corporal Leonard H.
was shot and instantly killed while stopping the Reds' last attempts
to overrun and take the hilltop
The demoralized ROK troops disappeared but the handful of Americans,
completely surrounded, held out for seven hours against continuous
attack, until all ammunition was exhausted
General D.'s skillful direction of the flight was fully as memorable
as his heroic personal participation with pistol and bazooka

Grumman F9F
Bell H-130s
Shooting Stars
Flying Cheetahs
They could handle them if they would only use the weapons we have
given them properly, said Colonel Wright
Lockheed F-04 Starfire
Lockheed F-803
Bell H-13 Sioux
Bell H-13Ds
More kept coming. More fell

Is distance. If she could know it
Citizens to the streets marching
Their demands lettered in blood
The leader counters them
With gas meant to thwart any crowd's ambition
And they must scatter, white cloths over their faces

Every month on the 15th, there is an air raid drill sometime during
the day, lasting approximately 15 minutes. When the siren goes off,
everyone must get off the streets. An all clear siren marks the
end of the drill.

And how long practice how long drill to subvert what borders are
What must we call each other if we meet there
Brother sister neighbor lover go unsaid what we are
Tens of thousands of names
Go unsaid the family name

Sun, an affliction hitting white
Retinue of figures dwindling to size
The eye won't be appeased
His name stitched on his school uniform, flame
Flame around what will fall as ash
Kerosene soaked skin housing what will burn
Fierce tenement of protest

Faces spread in a field
On the breeze what might be azaleas in full bloom

Composed of many lengths of bone

14

(Don Lee, 1959—)

多恩·李

作者简介

多恩·李（Don Lee, 1959— ），美国韩裔小说家、文学期刊编辑。他是第三代美国韩裔，其父亲是一名国务院官员。多恩·李的童年在日本东京（Tokyo）和韩国首尔度过，之后于加州大学洛杉矶分校获得文学学士学位，于艾默生学院（Emerson College）获得艺术硕士学位。他曾在爱默生学院担任四年的兼职讲师，并在文学杂志《犁头》（*Ploughshares*）担任主编长达十七年。2007年，多恩·李获得匹兹堡大学（University of Pittsburgh）创意写作项目针对新生代作家发起的弗雷德·布朗文学奖（Fred R. Brown Literary Award）。2007年至2008年，他先后在玛卡莱斯特学院（Macalester College）与西密歇根大学（Western Michigan University）教授创意写作，目前在坦普尔大学（Temple University）任教，并创办了线上文学期刊 *TINGE Magazine*。此外，他还是《乔治亚评论》（*The Georgia Review*）、《新英格兰评论》（*The New England Review*）、《阿格尼》（*Agni*）等文学期刊的独立咨询顾问。

多恩·李获奖众多，其处女作短篇小说集《黄色》（*Yellow*, 2001）荣获苏·考夫曼奖（Sue Kaufman Prize for First Fiction）以及美国亚裔作家研讨会颁发的成员选择奖（Members Choice Award）；长篇小说《起源之国》（*Country of Origin*, 2005）荣获埃德加奖（Edgar Award for Best First Novel）、美国图书奖（American Book Award）等；《破坏和毁灭》（*Wrack and Ruin*, 2008）入围瑟伯奖（Thurber Prize），《集体》（*The Collective*, 2012）荣获亚裔/太平洋美国文学奖（Asian/Pacific American Award for Literature）；短篇小说《可能的丈夫》（"The Possible Husband"）获得欧·亨

利奖（O. Henry Award），《中国鸡蛋的价格》（"The Price of Eggs in China"）获得手推车奖（Pushcart Prize）。

《黄色》讲述了罗萨里塔海湾虚构小镇上几位美国亚裔青年的故事，其中第一篇《中国鸡蛋的价格》是一部关于艺术与爱的短篇小说：韩裔马塞拉·安（Marcella Ahn）与华裔卡洛琳（Caroline）是诗坛上的竞争对手，高级家具设计师迪恩（Dean）为了给精神濒临错乱的女友卡洛琳扫清障碍，不惜冒险犯罪，却迎来了意料之外的反转结局。

作品选读

The Price of Eggs in China

(excerpt)

By Don Lee

"There haven't been any phone calls all week," Caroline said inside his truck.

"I know. Maybe she's decided to stop."

"No," Caroline said, "she'd never stop. Something's going to happen. I can feel it. I'm scared, Dean."

He dropped her off at Da Bones, then drove up Skyview Ridge Road and nestled in the woods outside Marcella's house. On schedule, she left for the Y.M.C.A. at six P.M. After a few minutes, he strolled to the door as casually as possible. She didn't have a neighbor within a quarter mile, but he worried about the unforeseen—the gynecologist lover, a UPS delivery, Becklund deciding belatedly to serve a restraining order. Wearing latex surgical gloves, Dean inserted a lock pick and tension bar into the keyhole on the front door. The deadbolt opened within twenty seconds. Thankfully she had not installed an alarm system yet. He took off his shoes and walked through the kitchen into the garage. This was the biggest variable in his plan. If he didn't find what he needed there, none of it would work. But to his relief, Marcella Ahn had several cans of motor oil on the shelf, as well as some barbecue lighter fluid—it wasn't gasoline, but it would do. In the recycle bin, there were four empty bottles of pinot grigio. In the kitchen, a funnel and a dishrag. He poured one part motor oil and one part lighter fluid into a bottle, a Molotov cocktail recipe provided by the Internet. In her bedroom, he pulled several strands of hair from her brush, pocketed one of her bracelets, and grabbed a pair of platform-heeled boots from her closet. Then he was out, and he sped to his house in Vasquez Canyon. All he had to do was press in some boot-prints in the dirt in front of the lumber shed, but he was running out of time. He drove back to Marcella's, hurriedly washed the soles of the boots in the kitchen sink, careful to leave a little mud, replaced the boots in the closet, checked through the house, and locked up. Then he went to Santa Cruz and tossed the lock pick set and voice changer into a dumpster.

He did nothing more until three A.M. By then, Caroline was unconscious from the sleeping pills. Dean drove to Marcella Ahn's again. He had to make sure she was home, and alone. He walked around her house, peeking into the windows. She was in her study, sitting at her desk in front of her laptop computer. She had her head in her hands, and she seemed to be quietly weeping. Dean was overcome with misgivings for a moment. He had to remind himself that she was at fault here, that she deserved what was coming to her.

He returned to his own property. Barefoot and wearing only the latex gloves and his underwear, he snagged the strands of Marcella's hair along the doorframe of the lumber shed. He threw the bracelet toward the driveway. He twisted the dishrag into the mouth of the wine bottle, then tilted it from side to side to mix the fluids and soak the rag. He started to flick his lighter, but then hesitated, once more stalled by doubt. Were those mystery novels he read really that accurate? Would the Hair & Fiber and Latent Prints teams be deceived at all? Was he being a fool—a complete amateur who would be ferreted out with ease? He didn't know. All he knew was that he loved Caroline, and he had to take this risk for her. If something wasn't done, he was certain he would lose her. He lit the rag and smashed the bottle against the first stack of zelkova inside the shed. The fire exploded up the boards. He shut the door and ran back into the house and climbed into bed beside Caroline. In a matter of seconds, the smoke detectors went off. The shed was wired to the house, and the alarm in the hallway rang loud enough to wake Caroline. "What's going on?" she asked.

Dean peered out the window. "I think there's a fire," he said. He pulled on his pants and shoes and ran to the shed. When he kicked open the door, the heat blew him back. Flames had already engulfed three boules of wood, the smoke was thick and black, the fire was spreading. Something had gone wrong. The sprinkler system—his expensive, state-of-the-art, dry-pipe sprinkler system—had not activated. He had not planned to sacrifice this much wood, one or two stacks at most, and now he was in danger of losing the entire shed.

There was no investigation, per se. Two deputies took photographs and checked for fingerprints, but that was about all. Dean asked Becklund, "Aren't you going to call the crime lab unit?" and Becklund said, "This is it."

It was simple enough for the fire department to determine that it was arson, but not who set it. The insurance claims adjuster was equally lackadaisical. Within a few days, he signed off for Dean to receive a $75,000 check. Dean and Caroline had kept the blaze contained with extinguishers and garden hoses for the twenty-two minutes it took for the fire trucks to arrive, but nearly half of Dean's wood supply had been consumed, the rest damaged by smoke and water.

No charges were filed against Marcella Ahn. After talking to Becklund and a San Vicente County assistant district attorney, though, she agreed—on the advice of counsel—to move out of Rosarita Bay, which was hardly a great inconvenience for her, since she owned five other houses and condos. Caroline never heard from her again, and, as far as they knew, she never published another book—a one-hit wonder.

Caroline, on the other hand, finally submitted her second book to a publisher. Dean was relentless about making her do so. The book was accepted right away, and when it came out, it caused a brief sensation. Great reviews. Awards and fellowships. Dozens of requests for readings and appearances. Caroline couldn't be bothered. By then, she and Dean had had their first baby, a girl, Anna, and Caroline wanted more children, a baker's dozen if possible. She was transformed. No more nightmares, and she could nap standing up (housekeeping remained elusive). In relation to motherhood, to the larger joys and tragedies that befell people, the poetry world suddenly seemed silly, insignificant. She would continue to write, but only, she said, when she had the time and will. Of course, she ended up producing more than ever.

Marcella Ahn's chair was the last Dean made from the pristine zelkova. He would dry and clean up the boards that were salvageable, and when he exhausted that supply, he would switch to English walnut, a nice wood—pretty, durable, available.

He delivered the chair to Marcella just before she left town, on May 11, as scheduled. She was surprised to see him and the chair, but a promise was a promise. He had never failed to deliver an order, and she had prepaid for half of it.

He set the chair down in the living room—crowded with boxes and crates—and she sat in it. "My God," she said, "I didn't know it would be this comfortable. I could sit here all day."

"I'd like to ask you for a favor," Dean said as she wrote out a check for him. He held an envelope in his hand.

"A favor?"

"Yes. I'd like you to read Caroline's new poems and tell me if they're good."

"You must be joking. After everything she's done?"

"I don't know poetry. You're the only one who can tell me. I need to know."

"Do you realize I could have been sent to state prison for two years? For a crime I didn't commit?"

"It would've never gone to trial. You would've gotten a plea bargain—a suspended sentence and probation."

"How do you know?" Marcella asked. "Your girlfriend is seriously deranged. I only wanted to be her friend, and she devised this insidious plot to frame me and run me out of town. She's diabolical."

"You stalked her."

"I did no such thing. Don't you get it? She faked it. She set me up. She was the stalker. Hasn't that occurred to you? Hasn't that gotten through that thick, dim-witted skull of yours? She burned your wood."

"You're lying. You're very clever, but I don't believe you," Dean said. And he didn't, although she made him think for a second. He pulled out the book manuscript from the envelope. "Are you going to read the poems or not?"

"No."

"Aren't you curious what she's been doing for the past six years?" Dean asked. "Isn't this what you came here to find out?"

Marcella slowly hooked her hair behind her ears and took her time to respond. "Give it to me," she finally said.

For the next half hour, she sat in his chair in the living room, flipping through the seventy-one pages, and Dean watched her. Her expression was unyielding and contemptuous at first, then it went utterly slack, then taut again. She breathed quickly through her nose, her jaw clamped, her eyes blinked.

"Are they good?" Dean asked when she finished.

She handed the manuscript back to him. "They're pedestrian. They're clunky. There's no music to the language."

"They're good," Dean told her.

"I didn't say that."

"You don't have to. I saw it in your face." He walked to the door and let himself out.

"I didn't say they were good!" Marcella Ahn screamed after him. "Do you hear me?

I didn't say that. I didn't say they were good!"

Dean never told Caroline about his last visit with Marcella Ahn, nor did he ever ask her about the stalking, although he was tempted at times. One spring afternoon, they were outside on his deck, Caroline leaning back in the rocker he'd made for her, her eyes closed to the sun, Anna asleep in her lap. It had rained heavily that winter, and the eucalyptus and pine surrounding the house were now in full leaf. They sat silently and listened to the wind bending through the trees. He had rarely seen her so relaxed.

Anna, still asleep, lolled her head, her lips pecking the air in steady rhythm—an infant soliloquy.

"Caroline," he said.

"Hm?"

"What do you think she's dreaming about?"

Caroline looked down at Anna. "Your guess is as good as mine," she said. "Maybe she has a secret. Can babies have secrets?" She ran her hand through her hair, which she had kept short, and she smiled at Dean.

Was it possible that Caroline had fabricated everything about Marcella Ahn? He did not want to know. She would, in turn, never question him about the fire. The truth wouldn't have mattered. They had each done what was necessary to be with the other. Such was the price of love among artists, such was the price of devotion.

15

(Don Mee Choi, 1962—)
崔东美

作者简介

  崔东美（Don Mee Choi，1962— ），美国韩裔诗人兼翻译家，出生于韩国汉城（今首尔），目前在西雅图（Seattle）从事成人基础教育研究。她著有《晨间新闻激动人心》(*The Morning News Is Exciting*, 2010)、《几乎无战争》(*Hardly War*, 2016) 以及其他一些诗歌和散文集，曾获怀丁奖（Whiting Award）、莱南文学奖（Lannan Literary Fellowship Award）、卢西恩·斯特雷克亚洲翻译奖（Lucien Stryk Asian Translation Prize）、古根海姆奖学金等。此前，崔东美还为韩国著名诗人金惠顺（Kim Hyesoon，1955— ）翻译了诗集《死亡自传》(*Autobiography of Death*, 2018)。这部传记着眼于女性身份，对于死亡这一严肃主题进行了深入挖掘与思考，荣获2019年加拿大格里芬国际诗歌奖（Griffin Poetry Prize）。

  诗集《DMZ 殖民地》(*DMZ Colony*, 2020) 是崔东美的代表作，荣获2020年美国国家图书奖。此作品在艺术风格上交织了诗歌、散文、照片、图画以及幸存者叙述，极具震撼力，仿佛在用这种七零八落的艺术形式诉说殖民地人民支离破碎的生活。选文摘自《DMZ 殖民地》，分别回顾了主人公的童年及其在一所废弃学校参观时的所见所思；残酷的战争给普通民众带来翻天覆地的变化，导致无数孤儿流离失所、食不果腹；反观商品经济时代冲击下，部分人放松警惕，历史感逐渐消弭。崔东美试图借助文字重新唤起大众对于暴力、恐怖、战争、不公的社会记忆，促使人们在当下以史为鉴、居安思危。

作品选读

DMZ Colony

(excerpt)
By Don Mee Choi

What I remember about my childhood are the children, no older than I, who used to come around late afternoons begging for leftovers, even food that had gone sour. The drills at school in preparation for attacks by North Korea kept me anxious at night. I feared separation from my family due to the ever-pending war. I feared what my mother feared—my brother being swept up in protests and getting arrested and tortured. Our radio was turned off at night in case we were suspected of being North Korean sympathizers. At school, former North Korean spies came to give talks on the evil/leader of North Korea. I stood at bus stops to see if I could spot any North Korean spies, but all I could spot were American GIs. My friends and I waved to them and called them Hellos. In our little courtyard, I skipped rope and played house with my paper dolls among big, glazed jars of fermented veggies and spicy, pungent pastes. I feared the shadows they cast along the path to the outhouse. Stories of abandoned infant girls always piqued my interest, so I imagined that the abandoned babies might be inside the jars. Whenever I obeyed the shadows, I saw tiny, floating arms covered in mold. And whenever it snowed, I made tiny snowmen on the lids of the jars. Like rats, children can be happy in darkness. But the biggest darkness of all was the midnight curfew. I didn't know the curfew was a curfew till my family escaped from it in 1972 and landed in Hong Kong. That's how big the darkness was. ...

I went on a tour of Ilya Kabakov's *School No.6*. It's an imaginary school, abandoned in the desert just like an orphan. One famous critic said that the school house and children represent the future, a utopia! No, this is not speech. I may be the only one who thinks this but representation can be magical. Cruelty and beauty—how do they coexist? I wish the eight orphans could have attended this school. They could have shown the Russian children how to make green noodles from camellia leaves. And the Russian children could have read to them their favorite fairy tale, "Snow White." The guide told us that a big snake lives alone in the school courtyard among overgrown grass and dead trees no birds will perch on. What a void! But the music room was enchanting. There were many stories written by schoolchildren. They wrote about their class events, how they repaired their school, how they behaved on a trip to the museum, and so on. Their notebooks strewn on the dusty wooden floors were not that different from mine—"discarded notebooks that no one needs," according to the artist. I wish the orphan girls could have written their school stories too. I was thinking that the floors could use a good rubbing with sesame oil, the way children polished the floors at my old school, when I noticed a faded butterfly postcard on the floor. Another card next to it had pink roses. How perfect! The artist had thought of everything, as a child does. The roses looked like camellia blossoms, so I made a quick sketch for my mother. My mother always looked for camellia blossoms in our flight. I wish the orphan girls could have sketched the roses for their mothers too. I didn't know Snow White also flew with snow geese. But that's what the artist painted, pretending to be one of the schoolchildren: Illustration for the fairy tale by Ostrovsky, "Snow White." In fact, he pretends to be all the children at the imaginary school while I pretend to be deaf. I may be the only one who thinks this, but his translation of "The Snow Maiden" as "Snow White" is sublime. As I said, representation can be magical. Anyway, Snow White is displayed in the glass case of the school announcement board. I wish paintings of orphan girls could be on display, too, behind the glass. Then they could live forever inside a utopia! I wish and wish! It looks as if Snow White can touch the Milky Way! I wish and wish!

16

(Marie Myung-Ok Lee, 1964—)
玛丽·李

作者简介

玛丽·李（Marie Myung-Ok Lee，或 Marie G. Lee，1964— ），美国韩裔作家。她在美国偏远的矿业小镇希宾（Hibbing）长大，1986 年毕业于布朗大学，获得文学学士学位。玛丽·李曾在耶鲁大学（Yale University）教授小说创作，是母校布朗大学美国研究客座讲师，并在哥伦比亚大学（Columbia University）教授创意写作。此外，她还是美国亚裔作家工作坊（Asian American Writers' Workshop，AAWW）的前理事长和创始人之一，该组织成立于 1991 年，旨在支持纽约有色人种作家的创作。

玛丽·李在文坛成就斐然，曾获欧·亨利奖荣誉奖（O. Henry honorable mention）、罗德岛州艺术委员会（Rhode Island State Council on the Arts）奖金，担任国家图书奖、国际笔会/E.O.威尔逊文学科学写作奖（PEN/E.O. Wilson Literary Science Writing Award）的评委。其代表作有小说《寻找我的声音》（*Finding My Voice*, 1992）、《如果不是因为尹珠》（*If It Hadn't Been for Yoon Jun*, 1993）、《道别》（*Saying Goodbye*, 1994）、《F 代表 Fabuloso》（*F Is for Fabuloso*, 1999）、《某人的女儿》（*Somebody's Daughter*, 2005）、《晚间英雄》（*The Evening Hero*, 2021）等，并在《卫报》（*The Guardian*）、《纽约时报》等报纸上发表多篇文章。

《寻找我的声音》被看作第一部由主流出版商发行、美国亚裔作家创作并以当代美国亚裔为主人公的青少年小说，1993 年获得美国作家之友（Friends of American Writers）颁发的青年文学奖（Young People's Literature Award），1994 年被国际阅读协会列入"青少年选择"（Young Adults' Choices）名单，1997 年被美国图书馆协会列入"青少年流行平装书"（Popular Paperbacks for Young Adults）名单。第一段选文摘自《寻找我的声音》第十章。主人公艾伦·宋（Ellen Sung）是学校唯一一名美国韩裔学生，老师和同学们的偏见让她倍感孤立，家人的过高期待与严格要求又加重了她的心理负担。如何找到自我、表达自我诉求成为困扰艾伦·宋的一大难题。

《晚间英雄》是玛丽·李的最新小说，探讨了移民离开家乡前往新的国度时，失去了什么，又获得了什么。随着主人公容曼（Yungman）的秘密逐渐浮出水面，他小心呵护的美国梦濒临破碎。在这部小说中，美国医疗体系的漏洞、当地人的种族主义偏见、战争带给大众的身心创伤均有所指涉。第二段选文摘自《晚间英雄》第一章。妇产科医生容曼被无端解聘之后，不甘心碌碌无为的生活状态，在儿子爱因斯坦（Einstein）的建议下，容曼准备前往一家医疗保健公司应聘。

作品选读（一）

Finding My Voice

Chapter 10

(excerpt)

By Marie Myung-Ok Lee

"Clear off your desks," Mr. Carlson says gleefully as he begins to pass out our next calc test. "No rubbernecking—and Beth, no necking."

Every time we have a test, Mr. Carlson says his famous necking line to either me or Beth. We both hate being the only girls in the class.

When the dittoed test plops on my desk, all my inner alarm bells go off. I can hear Michelle, Mom, and Father chorusing: "If you want to get into Harvard, first you need good grades." I grip my pencil tighter.

"Okay, students, go to it."

Twenty-three pencils hit the papers with a resounding *thok-scribble-scrabble*.

I scan the first problems, but nothing clicks. Already, Beth's head is determinedly close to her desk, and she is writing furiously, an arm curled protectively around her paper.

When I move down to the story problems—*Say we are on another planet, where the laws of physics follow the principles of integral calculus*—they are a complete mystery whose secret is locked away somewhere.

With my stomach tightening, I move back to the short-answer problems, which are worth only two points each. But as I stare, the figures sprawl crazily before me, exponents rising and swimming away like protozoans.

I try to remember how to integrate. Finally, I recognize one of the problems as being similar to one we had for practice. I disassemble it, and the answer slowly forces itself into place.

After solving the first one, I crack the next ones like nuts, lining up the solutions neatly in their boxes and leaving the debris of my thought processes in the margins.

I check my watch and see how the precious minutes have slipped by. I jump to the story problems, but they still seem as mysterious as the Dead Sea Scrolls: *If two trains are approaching each other at* x *miles an hour* ... I don't even have a clear idea of how to draw a little diagram of the trains approaching each other.

I move back to the short-answer problems to check them, and some of my new answers don't match. Is it the checking, or was I wrong the first time? My pulse speeds up.

I frantically do the two-point problems over again—and again—until I arrive at a consensus with the answers.

I hear a chair scrape. Beth rises and walks up to Mr. Carlson's desk and places her test on it. Mr. Carlson smiles at her, his eyes crinkling into little raisins.

I hear another chair scraping, and my hand freezes on my pencil. There are fifteen minutes of class to go. If people are already getting up, I'll never be able to concentrate, feeling like such a slowpoke.

My left hand, I notice, is curled into a fist on my lap. I open it and see the tracks of red crescent-shaped nail marks running down my palm.

I stare hard at one of the stubborn story problems, waiting for a mathematical epiphany. I wish I could just shake the answer out, like a marble, from my brain. Doggedly, I try to at least set up each problem.

"Five minutes, class," says Mr. Carlson. Everyone is getting up now.

I flail and flail, drowning in figures and words that have suddenly become unfamiliar.

"Time to hand 'em in," Mr. Carlson says.

I surrender my test. My nose is warty with droplets of sweat, and I sigh. The good thing about tests is that they have to end eventually; the bad thing about grades is that they stay with you forever.

I DROP MY calc book, as though it were leprous, into my bag before heading to gymnastics.

Even on the mat I can't get calc worries out of my mind, and I am fervently praying that I'll get partial credit for the story problems I set up but didn't solve.

"Hey, ching ding-a-ling—watch it!" Marsha Randall's voice reverberates through the gym. I am standing, with my thoughts, in the middle of the mat, in her way.

I step off the mat with leaden feet. Everyone else is looking away, like that day on the bus. I hear the hollow *thunk-thunk* of someone working on the bars. Satisfied, Marsha zooms down the diagonal to do a tumbling pass.

I gather my sweats and walk out of the gym, anger and sadness mixed inside me like oil and vinegar. I hear laughter spilling from the gym, and it all sounds so foreign.

I park myself, sweats and all, in Barbara's office. It's time to let her know that things have gone too far.

Amidst all the sports trophies, I sit on the hard wooden chair by her desk. There is a picture on the wall in front of me of Marsha Randall, smiling on the beam. I turn the chair so I won't have to look at it.

Beth is the first to pass the office on her way to the locker room. She gives me a smile of encouragement but doesn't stop. Marsha Randall and Diane Johnson flutter by, laughing and chattering as loudly as a bevy of quail. Neither glances at me when they pass.

Finally, Barbara comes in, lugging the heavy vault springboard. She stands it against the wall and then looks at me. "Can I help you?" she says.

"Yes." I get up and shut the door. "I'd like to quit."

"What?" she says, looking at me as if I've gone dotty.

"I want to quit," I say. "I've had enough."

"What are you talking about?" she says.

Where has she been when Marsha Randall has been saying these things? On Mars? From her office, you can hear everything that goes on in the locker room.

"I've had enough of people calling me names," I say patiently.

Barbara looks at me. "Names?"

"Like ching ding-a-ling is not my name!" I have a sudden morbid urge to laugh.

"Ellen," Barbara says, putting her arm around me like a sympathetic older sister, "I don't know what you're talking about—and you don't have to name names—but I'm sure they don't mean it."

"I think it's getting worse," I say, stiffening.

Barbara paces around the office, her huge body seeming to fill the small room. "Oh, you know how kids can be mean to each other," she says, rifling through some old score sheets. "Don't take it personally."

I feel my blood pressure rise. *Don't take it personally*—easy for her to say! I feel like yelling this to her face, but I let the stony silence of politeness take over.

"Listen, Ellen," she says, still rustling the score sheets. "You're doing really well this year, and I was thinking of putting you on as an alternate for floor exercise if we go to state."

An alternate for floor exercise? My ears unexpectedly perk up. That would mean a letter for sure.

"I don't want you to quit," she continues. "So how about it?"

My mind is swimming. Too much for one day.

"Well?" Barbara asks.

I remember how much I love gymnastics. I remember how proud I was the day I did a Valdez on the beam. I remember all the times I've envisioned myself in an emerald-green letter jacket. I can't quit, I decide, just because Marsha Randall wants me to. If I quit, that would be one more triumph for her.

"All right," I tell Barbara. "I'll stay."

THAT NIGHT I am slogging through more calc problems, trying to see where I went off the road during the test. Jessie is probably at home listening to music or watching TV. Isn't that what the teen years are for—to hang out and be mellow? I never knew there was going to be this much stress or this much homework.

"Ellen, phone for you." Mom's voice is muffled against my closed door.

I flop onto my parents' bed and grab their phone. When I pick it up, I hear the click of Mom hanging up downstairs.

"Hi, Jessie," I say. "You're calling early tonight."

"This ain't Jessie," says a deep voice in my ear. "This here is Tomper."

I grip the receiver a little tighter and sit up.

"Hi, Tomper," I say. "What's up?"

"Not much," he says. "I just wanted to know if you've done the vocab assignment for English."

"No," I say. "I'm scheduled to give my book report tomorrow."

"Oh yeah," he says. "What'd you read?"

"*The Bell Jar.* What'd you read?"

"Nothing yet. I go next week."

I can't decide if I should be thrilled about his calling me or not. Lately, I've tried to give up on him, since I see him a lot at Marsha Randall's locker—which means that they're probably going steady.

"Well," he says. "At least you don't have to worry about the vocab assignment."

"Yes," I say.

"Well, I guess I'll see you around," he says.

"Yes, see you."

"Okay, bye."

"Bye."

"See you later, Gator."

"Would you hang up already?" In spite of my uncertain mood, I feel lightened.

"Right, Gator," he says.

"Good night, Tomper," I say.

WHEN MR. CARLSON hands back our tests, I can't look at mine. I keep it facedown and eye it warily; it's like a bomb that might explode.

I crane my neck until I can see Beth's score. An *A* sits like a happy tepee at the top of her paper. Maybe, by some act of God, the real answer to the story problems is that they are all unsolvable.

I lift the corner of my paper. A D-plus? How can that be? With all my troubles, I've never even gotten a C in here.

"How'd you do?" Beth asks me cheerfully.

"Awfully," I say, whipping the test back over. I listen closely to determine if I can hear the doors to the colleges slamming in the distance.

FROM CALC, I have to move right to English, where everyone is bustling more than usual because it's the first day of our oral presentation of book reports.

"I heard Mike Anderson tell Marsha Randall that he just copied his out of Cliff Notes," Beth says to me, her nostrils flaring with self-righteous fury.

"I believe it," I say, although it seems silly of him because Mrs. Klatsen gave us the option of reciting a memorized passage from the book or just writing a summary and reading that; it can't get much easier.

Marsha Randall goes first. She dramatically flips her hair back before reading her summary of *National Velvet*.

"Teenage Velvet was like any other girl who's horse crazy," she reads, bending her platinum head close to the sheet. "But who else would dare chop off her hair, don jockey's clothes, and enter the world's most grueling steeplechase?"

Beth looks at me and rolls her eyes. "That's from the summary on the back of the book," she whispers to me. "I know because I read it."

"Mike, you're next," Mrs. Klatsen says.

Mike walks up to the podium, sets his paper down, and then squints at it as if it's a script and begins.

"*The Lilies of the Field* deals with the interesting juxta... juxtapositioning of Homer Smith, an ex-GI on the open road, and Mother Maria Marthe, a nun topped off with the disposition of a drill sergeant."

I look over at Mrs. K., who is sitting impassively with a slight smile on her lips. I wonder if she is concerned about people like Mike and Marsha who try to sidle through high school without bumping into anything that might work their brains or teach them something.

"Ellen, you're up," is all Mrs. K. says when Mike is done. I leave all my things on my desk and walk up to the front of the room. Twenty-four pairs of eyeballs roll to stare at me. I clear my throat.

"This piece is from Sylvia Plath's *The Bell Jar,*" I say, surprised at how clear and resonant my voice can be. "I picked this passage because it captures the mood of the narrator slowly becoming depressed." I fold my hands in front of me, forget everyone, and speak. Before I know it, I am done.

There is a loud noise as people break into applause; I'm back on earth. Mrs. K. is beaming. Feeling my cheeks begin to flame, I return to my seat.

"That was beautiful, Ellen," Mrs. K. says. "Class, you should all take this as an example of a good reader and a good writer interacting. Ellen has managed to pick out a particularly sensitive piece of prose, and her delivery was excellent."

"You're a bomber," Mike Anderson says admiringly to me. Mike Anderson, admiring me?

After class, I start walking to my locker, and Tomper follows.

"Your report was really good, Ellen," he says.

"Thanks," I say. "It was just memorization."

"No, you're really smart," he insists. "And you care about what you do."

I look at him. He's just read me like a book—and I like what he's seen.

"Thank you," I say. "And you're very smart, too."

"In what way, I'll have to find out—because it sure isn't grade-wise," he says, his eyes studying my face.

There is a cord of tension between us that is being stretched tighter and tighter. Who knows what will happen when it breaks?

"HOW DID YOU do on your calculus test?" Father asks at dinner.

My fork accidentally drops. I bend down to the floor to pick it up.

"All right," I say, carefully wiping it off.

"Did you get an A?"

"No."

"What did you get?" Father's voice rises.

"A B-plus," I say, crossing my fingers. "It was a hard test."

"Bs aren't good enough," he says. "I think you'd better stay in and study until your grade gets back to an A—that means no gymnastics, either."

"No gymnastics?" I echo.

"No gymnastics." The tone of his voice makes me stop in my tracks.

"Yes, Father." What would he have done if I told him I'd gotten a D-plus? I must be the only kid in school whose parents are like this. Now how am I going to earn my letter, or get to go out with Jessie, or do any of that?

作品选读（二）

The Evening Hero

Book I

(excerpt)

By Marie Myung-Ok Lee

Yungman liked his loafers. They slipped on and off easily. They had a gold ornament in the front, looking a little like the bit of a horse's bridle. The substantial heel gave him a nice lift. Overall, the shoe had a nice design, its tongue curved at the top like a gladiator's helmet. He'd been so proud buying these dressy shoes in Korea. White collar, white coat, white shoes. As close to being a white American as he could possibly get, he'd thought at the time.

However, come to think of it, he hadn't seen anyone else wear this kind of shoe here in the actual America.

Einstein handed him the oxblood brogues, redolent of pungent cedar shoe trees. He stood there while Yungman tried them on. Even though Einstein's feet were a half size bigger, the tapered style pinched. But now, his feet trussed by the skinny laces, he was committed. His son smiled approvingly as Yungman walked gingerly, unfamiliarly downstairs, where a delightful scent of batter was wafting up.

Marni was dressed in tight yoga clothes that gave off a kind of iridescent sheen. Their waffle maker was the kind they had at hotel buffets, an antigravity clamshell that dropped the finished product into the waiting plate, with no handling of hot objects needed. When Einstein was little, Yungman used to try to make waffles on Sunday mornings, establish a family tradition. Einstein would stand up on his chair and, in defiance of Yungman's warning to keep away, naughtily reach toward the waffle iron's outer surface. "Hot? Hot?" It became almost a game, one that Yungman didn't have the time or inclination to play. He had enough to worry about—getting the waffles done, the frozen sausages made, the Aunt Jemima on the table and everything done in time to hustle them off to church while wondering which one of his patients would be in labor by the end of the sermon. One day, when Einstein teasingly probed his chubby finger a little too close to the steaming lip of the iron Yungman helped it along the rest of the way. The tiny finger had blistered immediately. Einstein screamed. "I said it's hot! This is what happens when you don't listen to your father!" Yungman had screamed back. His son wouldn't have lasted a day trekking on foot to Seoul during the war. And yet, Yungman felt the rebuke now, in the mere selection of their house appliances. Undoubtedly Einstein had told all this to Marni, probably characterizing it as a lasting "childhood trauma," language he'd learned from the therapist he'd been seeing since college.

"We'd better get going," Einstein said. The waffles weren't for Yungman anyway. He wondered about his breakfast, but wouldn't trouble them to ask.

Einstein's Military Utility Recreational Vehicle spanned almost a full highway lane. He seemed to enjoy the reactions—surprise, resentment, curiosity—from drivers and pedestrians alike at this ten-foot-tall armored vehicle with a rotating gun on top.

Despite the vehicle's size, its giant oblong gas reservoirs crowded the inside. Yungman felt something prodding his back. He fished out a bag of blackening pepperoni.

"Oh, that's Reggie's." Einstein threw it merrily out the window. "He likes to eat his 'roni in the car."

THE MALL OF AMERICA
The Biggest Mall in the Nation!
Next Exit

It didn't look as imposing as Yungman remembered. What drew his attention now was the quartz-crystal-shaped spire seemingly growing out of the ground next to it. In gold letters across its base was written

~The HoSPAtal ~A Passion for Excellence ~

The road looked like it was going to run right through the quartz, but then a door opened. It shut after they'd driven through.
"Like the Bat Cave!" Einstein said with boyish glee.

~MDiety PARKING~

"Isn't that cute?" said Einstein. "Here, physicians are 'MDieties'—get it?"
A young dark-eyed man took his keys. "Good morning, Dr. Kwak."
"Hey, thanks, José," Einstein said.
"It's Benedicto, " the man said. "José left two weeks ago."
"Sorry."
They were in the basement. Einstein took Yungman to an elevator that said "To SUB Basement."
One door said:

~Mall-Based Medical Retail Outlet Human Capital Department

The other:

~Caution: *Ionizing Radiation in Use!*

"Ready to be a doctor of the future?" Einstein asked, thankfully taking him to the door that did not have the universal sign for radiation on it. It opened to a waiting room with a few dozen people seated on hard chairs. Facing them were an additional two doors: PRIMARY CARE PHYSICIANS and SPECIALISTS. A man poked his head out of PRIMARY CARE PHYSICIANS. "Nygaard? Dr. Soren Nygaard here?"

"Just answer to your name when you're called, " Einstein said. "I called ahead and put you in the queue."

The SPECIALISTS door listed:

Nephrology
Radiology
Psychiatry
Ophthalmology
ENT
Oncology
Neurology
Urology
OB-GYN

Yungman was pleased-OB-GYN at Horse's Breath General was considered primary, not specialty, care, which he always thought was erroneous, as surgery went beyond primary care. He was every bit the surgeon Mitzner was.

"I have to get going; I'll call you later." Einstein's body was already facing away. He paused. "Oh, wait—you don't have a cell phone." For a moment a look of uncertainty, of dawning panic, crossed his face. "I won't know where you are."

Yungman and his son were separating in the same building, not on different sides of the ocean. "Hmm, " Einstein said, that same troubled look from his Sears baby portrait. "Hmm." If his son blanched at the thought of being out of touch with his father for an hour, Yungman thought, could Einstein even begin to fathom what it was like to be one of the Korean "separated and scattered families" who were once each other's dearest hearts and now were on different sides of a military border, not even knowing who was alive and who was dead?

17

(Chang-rae Lee, 1965—)
李昌来

作者简介

李昌来（Chang-rae Lee，1965— ），美国韩裔小说家，出生于韩国汉城（今首尔），三岁时移居美国，于菲利普艾斯特中学（Phillips Exeter Academy）就读，1987年获得耶鲁大学英语学士学位，并于1993年获得俄勒冈大学（University of Oregon）艺术硕士学位。李昌来先后在俄勒冈大学、纽约城市大学（The City University of New York）、普林斯顿大学（Princeton University）教授创意写作，任韩国延世大学（Yonsei University）客座教授，目前在斯坦福大学（Stanford University）任教。

李昌来是当代韩裔作家的重要代表，其小说多次斩获大奖。《说母语者》（*Native Speaker*，1995）获得海明威笔会奖（Hemingway Foundation/PEN Award）、美国图书奖、俄勒冈州图书奖（Oregon Book Award）、巴诺书店发现作家奖（Barnes & Noble Discover Great New Writers Award）等；《手势人生》（*A Gesture Life*，1999）获得阿尼斯菲尔德·沃尔夫文学奖（Anisfield-Wolf Literary Award）、美国亚裔文学奖等；《在高处》（*Aloft*，2004）获得亚裔/太平洋美国文学奖；《投降者》（*The Surrendered*，2010）获得代顿文学和平奖（Dayton Literary Peace Prize），并入围普利策小说奖提名；《在浩瀚大海上》（*On Such a Full Sea*，2014）被提名美国国家图书评论奖。

《说母语者》是李昌来的处女作，小说以一名美国韩裔工业间谍的抉择为切入点，展现了移民在融入美国生活时的艰难曲折，探讨了人际关系的疏远和背叛等主题。第一段选文摘自《说母语者》，李昌来对1992年洛杉矶种族骚乱事件进行改写，射杀非裔青年的韩国店主被法院无罪释放之后，纽约非裔社群开展了大规模抗议运动，主流媒体借此向公众传输虚假意识，试图维系移民的模范少数族裔形象。

《手势人生》讲述了老年医疗用品推销员富兰克林·秦（Franklin Hata）试图通过音乐摆脱早年的创伤记忆，融入美国主流社会所作出的努力。第二段选文摘自《手势人生》第二章，讲述了父女对于练习钢琴的不同态度。这背后反映出的是他们在身份认同、人生价值、生活方式等方面的潜在冲突。

作品选读（一）

Native Speaker

(excerpt)

By Chang-rae Lee

He poured me more *soju*. "I just wanted to meet you. Janice gave me a copy of your résumé. You must be smart to have gone to such a good school. I hope the same for my sons. You were born where?"

"Here."

"Yes. As you've seen, there aren't many Koreans working for me aside from the students from CUNY. No *adults*, as it were, except for you."

"I guess I should be an investment banker or lawyer."

Kwang laughed. "I'm happy you're not! Ah, I know that is what all the young Korean Americans are doing. Some in medicine, engineering. Good for them. We need them all to succeed. My wife's niece, Sara, is already a vice president in mergers and acquisitions. She's only twenty-eight. Whenever I see her she asks if I'm thinking of selling my business. 'Is there a buyer?' I asked her last time. 'Give me eighteen hours,' she said so seriously. I had to tear away her cellular phone. All she'd have to do is talk half a minute with my accountant to know there's nothing to interest her. She thinks I'm much bigger than I am. Much bigger. She says if I run for mayor she wants to be comptroller, of all things."

"Is she electable?"

"Eminently," he answered, smiling. "She's dynamite."

I took the obvious opening. "The real question," I said to him, "is whether you're going to run."

He replied without looking up from his dish. "The papers seem to think so."

This was true. I had read numerous editorials in the last few months that had questioned De Roos' interest in genuinely improving the city, suggesting that he had grown comfortable and cynical and out of touch with his job, being now in his second term. Assuming a third. But the feeling was that the city was beginning to buckle under its burdens. Businesses were relocating to New Jersey because of high taxes and crime. There was a string of deadly subway accidents. Some schools were spending more on metal detectors than on lab equipment. There were no neighborhoods—even on the Upper East and West sides of Manhattan—that were safe. De Roos, suddenly, was looking as if he had been asleep at the wheel. The editorialists suggested John Kwang, among others, as someone who could bring a fresh face to confront the city's ills, a politician who could better understand the needs of the rapidly changing populace.

Mostly, it was the season's language. Kwang, it was easy to see, was already running into his first real troubles. The press was having a field day. They had multiple boycotts to cover. Vandalism. Street-filling crowds of chanting blacks. Heavily armed Koreans. Fires in the night. The pictures were the easiest 11 P.M. drama. Nothing John Kwang could say or do would win him praise. His sympathy for either side was a bias for one. He couldn't even speak out against the obvious violence and destruction, after black groups had insisted they were "demonstrations" against the callousness of Korean merchants and the unjust acquittal of the Korean storeowner who'd shot and killed Saranda Harlans. The papers and television stations were starting to go back and forth with "information" and "statements". Reporters talked to anyone on the street. What I was noticing most was the liberty they took with the Koreans. A reporter cornered some grocer in an apron, or a woman in the door of her shop, both of them looking drawn and weary. The lighting was too harsh. The Koreans stood there, uneasy, trying to explain difficult notions in a broken English. Spliced into the news stories, sound-bited, they always came off as brutal, heartless. Like human walls.

"Sometimes I have serious thoughts about running," he said, pausing now from the eating. He leaned forward on the table with his forearms. "But I'm suspicious. It's usually after some round of clamor. That's not a good sign, obviously. I find myself getting caught up. When others construct and model you favorably, it's easy to let them keep at it, even if they start going off in ways that aren't immediately comfortable or right. This is the challenge for us Asians in America. How do you say no to what seems like a compliment? From the very start we don't wish to be rude or inconsiderate. So we stay silent in our guises. We misapply what our parents taught us. I'm as guilty as anyone. For instance, this talk that I'm the one to revitalize the Democratic party in New York."

"That's the mayor's secret mission," I replied. De Roos had been pushing this angle since the last campaign. He had an idea to remake the image of the local party machinery. He himself had mentioned John Kwang as a part of that vanguard, though his implication was then cast only in terms of *succession*. "But people think that the shoe fits better on you."

"In theory," John said, "all in theory." By the tone of his voice I thought he was going to drop the subject, but he downed his *soju* and filled both our cups again. His voice cracked with the fume of the liquor. "But the fact is, Henry, that it's a one-party system. We only need one party."

"What party is that?"

"It's the party of jobs and safe streets and education. These are the issues. Are you for them or against them? Please nod. Good. Of course you are. Every politician in this city wants the same things. And the people know very well any one politician can only do so much. So what's left is that we set out to capture their imagination. We let them think that change will come to their lives. How many politicians have walked through the Carver housing projects in the last twenty-five years? How many rallies and speeches have been made there? How many words of hope have been spoken? And what does it still look like? Would you live there for any price? Generations have been lost in those buildings. Thousands of people. A black mayor couldn't change that. What can a Korean do for them?"

"Still, black groups should be supporting you," I said. "I can't think of any other prominent officials who are minorities."

"Some of the organizations do," he answered. "The church community seems open to talking. That's why I'm going to meet *them* next week, and not with more political groups. The NAACP has invited me to certain forums but I feel token there. Everybody is hesitant, cautious. They study me carefully. I can see they're not sure if I'll promote an agenda that suits them. I can support social programs, school lunches, homeless housing, free clinics, but if I mention the first thing about special enterprise zones or more openness toward immigrants I'm suddenly off limits. Or worse, I'm whitey's boy.

It's a grave reaction. I don't think I'll ever get used to it."

"It's still a black-and-white world."

"It seems so, Henry, doesn't it? Thirty years ago it certainly was. I remember walking these very streets as a young man, watching the crowds and demonstrations. I felt welcomed by the parades of young black men and women. A man pulled me right out from the sidewalk and said I should join them. I did. I went along. I tried to feel what they were feeling. How could I know? I had visited Louisiana and Texas and I sat where I wished on buses, I drank from whatever fountain was nearest. No one ever said anything. One day I was coming out of a public bathroom in Fort Worth and a pretty white woman stopped me and pointed and said that the Colored in the sign meant black and Mexican. She smiled very kindly and told me I was very light-skinned. 'Orientals' were okay in those parts, except maybe the kind from the Philippines. I remember saying thank you and bowing. She gave me a mint from her purse and welcomed me to the United States. What did I know? I didn't speak English very well, and like anyone who doesn't I mostly listened. But back here, the black power on the streets! Their songs and chants! I thought *this* is America! They were so young and awesome, so truly powerful, if only in themselves, no matter what anybody said."

I told him how I was too young to understand any of it. How my father never bothered with what was happening. He got passionate only once, when he got angry that a young teacher let us out early the day they arrested Bobby Seale. My father was like Mr. Beah. So focused on his own life. He couldn't understand anything about rights. "What a big noise," he'd mutter at the television. *Egoh joem ba, tihgee sekinohm mehnnal nahwandah. Look at this, every day these black sons of ... show up.* He'd shake his head slowly, as if to say, *Useless.* The sole right he wanted was to be left alone, unmolested by the IRS and corrupt city inspectors and street criminals, so he could just run his stores.

Kwang nodded, beckoning me to eat and drink. I noticed that his gestures were becoming tighter than before, that somehow he appeared more calm and ordered, which seemed to me unusual, given how we were drinking.

"Who can blame him?" he said loudly. "Your father's world was you and your mother. He didn't have time for the troubles of white and black people. It was their problem. None of it was his doing. He was new to the situation. The rights people could say to him, 'We're helping you, too, raising you up with us,' but how did he ever see that in practice?"

"He wouldn't have looked if they had," I said.

"Don't be so hard on your father," he quickly answered. He cleared his throat. "Likely, I know, you are right. But I understand his feeling more than I ever have. Everyone can see the landscape is changing. Soon there will be more brown and yellow than black and white. And yet the politics, especially minority politics, remain cast in terms that barely acknowledge us. It's an old syntax. People still vote for what they think they want; they're calling on a bright memory of a time that has gone, rather than voting for and demanding what they need for their children. They're still living in the glow of civil rights furor. There's valuable light there, but little heat. And if I don't receive the blessing of African Americans, am I still a *minority* politician? Who is the heavy now? I'm afraid that the world isn't governed by fiends and saints but by ten thousand dim souls in between. I am one of them. Lately I've been feeling like the great enemy of the oppressed. You look knowledgeable for your years, Henry. You have a kind face. You should know, how there must be a way to speak truthfully and not be demonized or made a traitor."

"Very softly," I said to him, offering the steady answer of my life. "And to yourself."

Steadily the other dishes were brought in, a half dozen or so of them, one varied and progressive course. Koreans like to taste everything at once, have it all out on the table, flagrantly mixing the flavors. Sashimi, spicy soup, the grilled meat, fried fish. More *soju*. He poured as I grilled. He obviously wasn't a drinker, I mean a drinker in the way I'd seen real drinkers, which is to say the liquor was beginning to affect him in a manner I couldn't predict or call. Old Stew might rant, he might take you by the collar, become belligerent, even stumble on the stairs when going to sleep, but none of it was a surprise. A man like that was eminently navigable. From the first glass you could see the whole dark trip of his evenings, every black jetty, every cove.

But John Kwang was affecting me. A good rule of thumb when you drink with a subject is that you keep yourself twice as sober as he is. Jack calls it the Taxi Rule. This means that you can get drunk, for the sake of building ambience and camaraderie (and for your own taut nerves), but still keep in mind that you haven't done right if you don't eventually bear him home. Call a taxi and tuck him in. Tonight I was working unscrupulously. I usually abstained completely on the job, much less matched a subject shot for shot. But soon I found myself pouring the drinks, too, joking with him for no other reason but to share a simple pleasure.

作品选读（二）

A Gesture Life

Chapter 2
(excerpt)
By Chang-rae Lee

  I remember first walking Sunny into the foyer, with all that dark wood paneling that was still up on the walls and ceiling, smelling from the inside of rot and dust, the lights fading now and then, and she actually began to titter and cry. I didn't know what to do for her, as she seemed not to want me to touch her, and for some moments I stood apart from her while she wept, this shivering little girl of seven. She had learned some English at the orphanage, so I asked her not to worry or be afraid, that I would do my best to make a pleasant home, and that she should be happy to be in the United States and have a father now and maybe a mother someday soon. She kept crying but she looked at me and I saw her for the first time, the helpless black of her eyes, and I could do little else but bend down and hold her until she stopped.

  And so after her arrival, it seemed that my every spare moment away from the store was devoted to fixing the house, at first attempting the renovations myself, and then calling in tradesmen, and finally, after disappointments with slow, shoddy work and the high expense, again taking on the projects solo. And there were many projects, too numerous to remember, but one that stands out is the smallest of them, the time I had to change the mirror and vanity in her bathroom upstairs.

  I was cleaning the house as always that Sunday morning, vacuuming and dusting and disinfecting the kitchen and bathrooms. Sunny was nearly ten years old, and though she was more than capable of helping, I didn't think it was right to have her do such things. The house was still a terrible mess, and because I felt there was so much improving to do, it was clear I shouldn't include my daughter in the mundane drudgeries. My wish, as I had always explained to her, was that she study hard and practice her piano and read as many books as she could bear, and of course, when there was free time, play with her friends from school. A child's days are too short, and my sense then was that I should let her focus on activities that would most directly benefit her.

And so, besides the major ongoing renovations, I took up general maintenance of the house with the usual care and thoroughness, but as it happened every week something seemed to stall my efforts. Everything would go smoothly until a cabinet door wouldn't catch, or a hinge began to squeak, or a drain was too slow, and then a vise-like tightness came over me. That time in Sunny's bathroom, trying to rub out a persistent cloudy stain in the vanity, I somehow cracked the mirror, and my fingers began bleeding from the edges of the spidery glass. I must have kept rubbing and blotting, for it was only some moments later that I realized Sunny was watching from the doorway, her splintered reflection looking up at me.

Her round face, pretty and dark in complexion, was serene and quiet.

"Have you already finished practicing your Chopin?" I asked her.

"Yes."

"I couldn't hear you. What were you playing?"

"Nocturnes," she said, staring at my hand. "The ones you like. From Opus Nine and Thirty-two."

"I must have been vacuuming," I said, wrapping a rag about my fingers. "Would you play some of them again?"

"Okay. But can I help you now?"

"No, dear," I said to her, trying to stay the throbbing in my hand, my arm. "Why don't you play some more? Your teacher wishes that you practice more than you do. You must push yourself. It may be difficult for you to see, but even great talent is easily wasted."

"Yes."

"Sunny?"

"Yes," she said, folding the lacy hem of her green dress for Sunday school, where I would take her in the afternoon.

"Please leave the living room doors open, so the music can travel. And, Sunny?"

"Yes."

"You should do what we talked about last week. About addressing me."

"Yes, *Poppa*," she said, saying the word softly but clearly.

She went downstairs, and I stood before the broken mirror, waiting for the first notes to rise up the stairs. She began playing Opus 32, 1, a piece she was preparing for an upcoming recital, and one I especially liked. The composition calmed me. Aside from the lyrical, impassioned musings, there are unlikely pauses in the piece, near-silences that make it seem as if the performer has suddenly decided to cease, cannot go on, even has disappeared. These silences are really quite magical and haunting. And just at the moment it seems the pianist has stopped, the lovely notes resume.

As I listened, Sunny played beautifully, with a style and presentation much beyond her years. She was as technically advanced as other gifted children, but she also seemed to have a deep understanding of a given piece of music, her playing rich with an arresting, mature feeling. And yet in the end, she never attained the virtuosity the best young performers must have in order to be promoted to the next ranks. In competitions Sunny was mostly magnificent, but it seemed that there were always a few difficult and even strangely blundering moments in her performances, perplexing passages marring what was otherwise wholesale surety and brilliance. It was perfection—or even near-perfection—that somehow eluded her, and as she grew up, the notion of attempting it seemed to fall farther and farther from her desire. Early in high school she ceased practicing seriously, and eventually she dropped playing altogether.

We had many arguments and bad feelings over her quitting, and for a long time during that period the two of us hardly acknowledged each other in the house. She was old enough then to move about as she pleased, and her friends with cars would often pick her up in the mornings before school, and not drop her off until late in the evening, ten or eleven at night. I'd hear the car roll up the cobblestone drive, the sweep of its lights in my window, the slam of the passenger door, her restless keys, the lock, the quick shuffle that trailed straight to her room. And then the quiet again. This went on, I'm afraid, for many months. In the mornings she seemed to wait until I had begun my swim to come downstairs, when she would leave the house and walk down the block to await her rides.

Perhaps I grew too accustomed to our distance. Initially I had tried to leave indications that I was unhappy with our relationship, putting out a bowl and spoon and a box of cereal for her, a glass of juice, a soft-boiled egg, but each morning when I came in from my swim the setting was just as I had left it, unmoved, untouched. I knew she'd seen it. I had watched her once from the pool, my goggled eyes skimming along the surface of the water; she stood staring at the place at the table, as if it were some kind of museum display, not to be disturbed, and then she turned away. But I continued each morning, and eventually I began sitting down to eat the breakfast myself, with more a taste of sorrow than spite. It wasn't long before I mostly forgot about Sunny refusing my offerings, and it became simply habit, part of my waking ritual that I still do now, without fail.

But then everything eventually shifts, accommodates. We began communicating again at some point, for no obvious reasons. This would prove a short time before she left the house for good. There was little warmth, I know, but at least she was hearing me, meeting my eyes. And there was talking, when it suited us. One day I went out to skim leaves and twigs from the pool, where she was sunbathing, and she asked if I was going to sell the piano.

"The piano?" I repeated, surprised by the notion. "Is there a reason why I should? I don't understand. Besides, you might want to begin playing again someday."

She didn't answer, turning over onto her back. She had on wraparound sunglasses, and was lying in the recliner in the full sun. She had just turned seventeen that June, and in the fall would start her final year at Bedley Run High School. I thought she was spending too much time going to the seniors' post-graduation parties, staying out most of the night and then sleeping late, only coming out of her room to lie in the sun. I had often asked her if she would take better care with her skin, having seen certain patients come into the store suffering from melanoma, but in those days it was desirable to be tanned as dark as one could get, and Sunny was one who never had trouble in that regard.

"It's stupid to have the piano, when no one's ever going to play it."

"I hope that's not true," I replied.

"It is true," she said tersely, slinging her forearm over her face. "I don't like having to see it every day. It sits there for no reason."

"It doesn't bother me. I like it."

She didn't reply immediately to this. I kept working, gathering the flotsam with the long net. After a moment, she spoke up again. "I think you like what it says."

"I don't quite understand," I said.

"Of course you don't," she answered. "I'm saying, you like having it around for what it says. About me. How I've failed."

"That's not in the least true."

"Sure it is," she answered, almost affably. But there was real defeat in her voice also, a child's broad welling of it.

I told her, "If anything, Sunny, I should see it as a symbol of my own failure, in inspiring the best in you."

"That's right. I've failed doubly. First myself, and then my good poppa, who's loved and respected by all."

"You can always twist my words," I told her. "But you shouldn't take everything I do so seriously. I'm not doing anything wrong by keeping the piano. I would like you to play again, yes, this is true, but not because of me. Not anymore. I think it would improve you, like reading a book would improve you. Or even something as simple as swimming, which I've taken to heart. I don't believe I've ever compelled you to do anything. I've made suggestions, advised about certain things, like taking up the piano, but I try to follow your interests. Though you don't seem to like many things any longer, which I think I can fairly say."

"You *only* fairly say."

"Please, Sunny, I don't always enjoy your word games."

"Sorry, Doc."

"I wish you wouldn't call me that."

"I won't, then," she said, with some finality. Then she rose from the chaise. She wrapped the towel around her waist and headed for the house, and I didn't see or hear her for the rest of the day. I thought perhaps that this would be the start of another strained period for us, but the next day she left a note saying she was going to Jones Beach with her friends, and would be staying in the city over the weekend, at someone's apartment. She signed her name and added a "Don't worry!" on the end. I was worried, of course, and was annoyed that she hadn't mentioned her plans for the weekend earlier, but part of me was also greatly appreciative of the fact of the note, pleased by the simple thing of it, which she would have never thought to leave me some months before.

18

(Nora Okja Keller, 1965—)
诺拉·奥卡佳·凯勒

作者简介

诺拉·奥卡佳·凯勒（Nora Okja Keller，1965—），美国韩裔作家，出生于韩国汉城（今首尔）。其父亲为德国人，母亲为韩国人，凯勒三岁起就跟随母亲在美国夏威夷生活，故将自己划归美国韩裔。凯勒就读于夏威夷最著名的私立学校——普纳荷学校（Punahou School），在夏威夷大学获得心理学和英语双专业学士学位，并在《檀香山明星报》（Honolulu Star-Bulletin）等担任自由撰稿人，之后她在加州大学圣塔克鲁斯分校（UC Santa Cruz）获得文学硕士和博士学位，目前在普纳荷学校任英语教师。

凯勒曾参与编辑《相交的圈：诗歌和散文中哈帕女性的声音》（Intersecting Circles: The Voices of Hapa Women in Poetry and Prose，1999）、《美国韩裔在夏威夷的写作》（Yobo: Korean American Writing in Hawai'i，2003），并创作小说《慰安妇》（Comfort Women，1997）和《狐女》（Fox Girl，2002），荣获美国图书奖、艾略特·凯兹奖（Elliot Cades Award for Literature）、手推车奖等重要奖项。两部小说均取材于第二次世界大战以及朝鲜半岛战争期间女性沦为慰安妇的创伤经历，开创性地将这一严肃的历史记忆展现在大众视野，把此前一直被遗忘、被忽视的无名女性呈现至台前，将她们提至平等的视阈与高度。越来越多的读者开始关注这个被禁言、被失声的群体，了解她们所遭受的非人待遇与心理重建的痛苦与挣扎。

第十七章是《狐女》最为精彩的章节。湖水（Sookie）是韩国妓女和美国黑人大兵的孩子，她在走投无路之下被迫成为妓女，生下无名/玛雅（Myu Myu/Maya）并将之遗弃。在贤真（Hyun Jin）的帮助下，混血二代玛雅得以来到美国开始新的生活。玛雅的形象蕴含着韩裔移民意欲开启新篇章的积极尝试与美好愿景。

作品选读

Fox Girl

Chapter 17

(excerpt)

By Nora Okja Keller

The driver set my box down underneath the address sign, then helped me out. "You got everything?" he asked as I handed him two twenties. "Sure you can manage?"

I nodded, already bending to settle Myu Myu into the box. She whimpered, and I jiggled the box. She rolled onto her back. I shifted my arms, adjusting to her moving weight, and left the lid of the box open so she could see my face. "It's going to be all right," I told her. "We're going to hide out here for a while."

Listening to the song of the crickets, which filled my ears in tandem with the beating rhythm of my heart, I followed the fence until I found the gate. Balancing the box against one knee, I lifted the latch and started up the gravel road. There was just enough morning light to make out the long, looming shadows of black-screened hothouses on either side of the path. I edged close enough to one of them to peer through the mesh into a jungle world. Plants in baskets hung from the ceiling, their twisting, groping tendrils long enough to sweep the floor. Palms grew up from the ground, leafy fingers scratching at the sides and tops of the hothouse. And on the rows of tables that filled the enclosure, hundreds of potted plants in various stages of infancy stretched their heads, limbs straining, toward the shadowed sky.

"Halloo!" The greeting was almost immediately drowned out by the baying of dogs. Three large mongrels bounded forward, barking as they circled me. A smaller dog with long, matted fur ran toward my ankles, teeth bared and nipping.

I wrapped my arms around the box, keeping my body between it and the dogs as much as I could. Myu Myu whimpered at their noise and burrowed under my clothes. I kept my eyes on the dogs, afraid to turn my back to them.

"Shoo, shoo! Comet, Cupid, go on, you mangy mutts." A flannel-sleeved arm swung at the dogs. They dodged the blows but slunk away. "Can I help you?"

I looked up into a craggy face, weathered by the sun despite the large straw hat perched above it. "Yes, I... uh." I frowned into the person's face, unsure if this was a man or a woman, unsure of how I should address him or her.

The person smiled, revealing bright blue front teeth, and stuck out a gloved hand. "I'm Geraldine, the big boss. You can call me Gerry." The fingers of the glove were also stained blue. "Oh, excuse me." Geraldine, the-big-boss-Gerry, stuck the glove into her mouth and tugged it off. Grinning around her glove, she offered her bared hand.

"My name Hyun Jin," I told her, touching her palm. "I looking for my uncle. Synang Man Lee. He here?" I glanced around the nursery, almost expecting him to appear, summoned by the commotion.

Gerry frowned. "Singhand, Sigmund, whatever, Lee? No one here by that name."

"I don't understand," I stammered, my knees buckling. The box tilted as inside Myu Myu slid from one corner to the other. "I got, my father got a letter from him. Synang Man Lee. This address."

"Lee. Lee. Lee." Woman slapped her glove across the thighs of her baggy jeans. "Korean guy?" When I nodded, she shouted, "Oh! Down the street a ways, at 789, there's one Lee, a FOB from Korea. Ziggy Lee."

I laughed, embarrassed at remembering the address wrong and dizzy with relief. I turned to walk back down the path, already constructing what I would tell him: how my mother always talked about him, her favorite cousin; how she sobbed when I left her, making me promise to look him up; how she knew that he would look after me and my child.

Then Gerry called out, "But he's not there anymore. Good riddance, I say. Handsome buggah, but turned into one *pakalolo* head, him and his friends."

"Not there?" I repeated. The woman's face swayed in front of me, back and forth like one of the palms in her hothouses.

"Went to California about five, maybe six, years ago. San Francisco, I think," she said. Her words, like the crickets' chirping, sounded both far away and right in my head at the same time. "Strange guy. Whoever heard of a Oriental trying for find hisself?

Thought that was for those *haole* hippies."

The box slipped out of my hands, crashed to the ground with a thump. Myu Myu tumbled out, skidding across gravel, screaming—the high-pitched keening of a wounded animal. The dogs charged forward, frenzied and howling, that little hairy one chasing its own tail and yip-yip-yipping; Gerry shouted, an ongoing siren: "Oh my God! Comet, Cupid, get away! Oh my God! Back, Blitzen! It's a baby! No, Vixen! Oh my God! A baby!" And then it was as if those long-limbed vines in the hothouses burst through the seams, whipped around my head, and yanked. Eyes rolling up into my head, I dropped to all fours, ear pressed to earth, and heard the world singing like the crickets, with that in-and-out beat of the tides, of the blood in our veins, of the panting of the fox. Then everything stopped, went dead, and I knew that it was all over. I had nowhere else to go. I was run to the ground.

We play a game, Myu Myu and I. I wrap a scarf around her eyes—"No peeking!" I scold as she giggles—and place a map of the United States under her fingers. She wiggles her fingers and laughs as if she is tickling herself.

"Myu Myu, point!" I tell her.

From under the cloth, she bites her lip, then pouts. "My name is not Myu Myu."

I scramble, trying to remember her name of the week. "Macy?"

The girl who is not Myu Myu today shakes her head.

"Malia?"

She shakes her head again, then sighs. "I am Maya," she says reproachfully, as if she is deeply hurt by my careless memory but forgives me anyway. Then she sends her hands skittering over the map. The whirlwind settles on a bile-colored square. She peeks under the blindfold.

"What'd you land on this time?" Gerry calls out from the sink where she is peeling and mashing fresh stems of aloe into a poultice for my hands. The skin between my fingers has started to flake off again, exposing the vulnerable pink of fresh meat.

"You gotta wear gloves," Gerry is forever scolding me when it comes time to tend the dieffenbachia. But the rubber gloves make my hands feel like paws, the fingers too thick and clumsy to pluck the wilted leaves from the healthy plant.

Maya taps the map. "Read it! Read it!" she demands. "Where are we going?"

"New Jersey," I sound out and shrug. Saturday we will visit the Waimanalo Book Mobile, poring over its current selection of travel guides and encyclopedias, requesting the books—if any—that feature this state. Gerry will read aloud to us, and we will learn about the state's population, its capital city, its flower, and its bird. By week's end, we will have toured the "hot spots," the museums and the zoos, the arboretums and the occasional Mystery Mansion or dead author's home. By week's end, Myu Myu will have gotten to know that piece of America, will have made it her own, and will have moved on to a new name.

"Hmmmmm," says Gerry. "Never been to Jersey before." After five years of this weekly game, Myu Myu has yet to land on a place where Gerry has visited.

The girl sticks her tongue between her lips and blows what she calls a "cherry." "Have you ever been *anywhere*, Tutu Gerry?" Because she giggles as she says this, and because Gerry is elbow-deep in cactus sap, Maya gets away with her impertinence.

"Las Vegas," Gerry snaps back. "I could tell you stories about that place." She side-eyes Myu, then presses her lips together primly. "When you're older."

"Myu Myu," I growl, warning her. Though Gerry says she's made us family, *hanai*-ing Myu as her granddaughter, I still worry that she might turn on us, throwing us out of this apartment she constructed at the back of hothouse number three. True to herself, Myu ignores me, humming as she studies the map.

Each time we sit at the kitchen table to play this game, I prepare myself for the possibility that the place of the week will be Maryland, where Myu Myu's grandfather lives. Or Los Angeles, where her father dreams of one day seeing her with stars at their feet and flocks of elephants flying overhead. I tell myself that when she points to these places, it will be my signal to begin to tell her about the place she was born in and the people she was born to. But I am afraid to bring those secrets to life. Right now, we are still hidden, underground and safe.

Slipping the scarf down around her neck, Myu Myu suddenly looks serious. She stares at my face, her forehead wrinkled in concentration. I try to turn away, thinking she will see me as the rest of the world does: ugly.

Myu Myu cups my chin in her hands to keep me still. "Your face is a map, Mama," she announces, breathless, solemn. "Your head is the world!" Then, blinking, she explodes with laughter, spraying me with spittle. "I pick to go... there." She waggles her fingers and points to a black pit on my temple.

Relieved, I tickle her. "Well, then your face is a map, too," I say. And I am struck by the obvious truth of my words. Her face *is* a map—an inheritance marked by all who were once most important in my life. I have caught familiar but fractured reflections of Lobetto and Sookie, Duk Hee and even my father. They have traversed time and distance, blood and habit, to reside within the landscape of this child's body.

"No, silly," she answers, smoothing her hands over her cheeks. "I'm clean."

"You think so?" I tease, grabbing her arms. "Then what's this?" I lean over the table and lick at a patch of imaginary dirt on her cheek. "And this?" I say, as, slurping drool, I move to her chin.

"Gross!" she squeals, wrestling away from me. She leaps to her feet, her breath coming in staccato gasps, as she tries to decide whether to run away or attack.

And for a quick moment, it's Sookie I see—sloe-eyed and wild-haired—her presence evoked by the power of my memories. "Sookie?" I whisper, feeling shaky, needing to hear her name. I close my eyes, and when I open them, I see my baby again, hovering over me, her face crinkled with worry. Like the fox spirit—the hunter and guardian of knowledge—this child possesses the gift of transformation.

When I smile up at her, she clucks her tongue. "I told you," she says, "my name is Maya."

"Maya, Mary, Mushu, whoever you are today, here." Gerry plops a bowl of her homemade gel onto the table. "Put that on your mama."

When I hold my hands out, Myu puckers her lips and dips a delicate finger into the aloe. Dabbing at my shredded palms, she rubs a rough patch, and a thin ribbon of translucent skin peels away from my hand. "Ewww," she grimaces. But she raises my fingers to her lips. "Does it hurt?" she asks, and kisses each one.

I suck in my breath, from the pain of it, from the joy of it. Inhaling, breathing her in, I know with absolute clarity that the best of Sookie, of Duk Hee, of Lobetto, of me—everything we could have hoped for and wished to be—is here and has always been here under the skin, in the bone and in the blood, in this jewel of a girl who holds the world in her hand and sees it, loves it, as her own.

19

(Nancy S. Kim, 1966—)
南希·金

作者简介

南希·金（Nancy S. Kim, 1966—），美国韩裔作家，出生于韩国汉城（今首尔），后移居南加利福尼亚州（Southern California）。她在加州大学伯克利分校获得本科学位，并在洛杉矶分校获得法学硕士学位。南希·金是旧金山（San Francisco）一家公司的律师、圣地亚哥（San Diego）的法学教授和专家，曾在世界多所大学任教。

南希·金的处女作《奶奶的秘密》（*Chinhominey's Secret*, 2001）使其一举成名，作品聚焦洛杉矶西部的一个美国韩裔家庭，探讨了移民父母和他们被同化、美国化的子女之间的代际冲突。

《如疾风冲向岩石》（*Like Wind Against Rock*, 2021）是南希·金的最新作品，小说借用日记这种极具个性化的文本形式向读者展示了爱丽丝（Alice）父亲生前隐秘又矛盾的真实想法，将两个家庭的历史娓娓道来，相似的命运与交织的情愫不断推进情节的发展。选读部分摘自《如疾风冲向岩石》的第二十至第二十一章，分别是爱丽丝视角的叙述与爱丽丝父亲的日记。这样的设计使读者得以走入多个人物的内心世界，获得多维阅读的体验。随着父亲日记中的秘密逐渐浮出水面，爱丽丝理解了母亲之前的反常行为并重新反思爱情、婚姻和家庭责任的关系。

作品选读

Like Wind Against Rock

(excerpt)
By Nancy S. Kim
CHAPTER TWENTY

"Ay! Ay! Ay!" Ahma scolds, roughly pulling the last box out of my arms even though she is already carrying a large shopping bag around one wrist.

"It isn't that heavy," I say, but she hisses angrily as she trips up the flagstone walkway in her heels. I unlock the door and let her into the house. Ever since I've started to show, Ahma has treated me as though I were made of glass. Even though I am only in my fifth month, my regular clothes no longer fit, except the occasional drawstring skirt or oversize sweatshirt. Against my wishes, Ahma went out and bought maternity clothes that are more stylish than anything I am used to wearing.

"Supermodel design," she says, handing me the oversize shopping bag. I must admit that she has good taste. Inside the bag are two Empire-waist jersey knit dresses, two pairs of black stretch pants, a denim skirt, four funky-patterned long-sleeve shirts, and two strappy tanks with extra support.

"No reason to look ugly when pregnant anymore," she says, without looking at me.

"Thank you," I tell her, resisting the urge to give her a hug that might make her regret her kind gesture.

She is dressed as though ready to go to a nightclub. She met someone who looks promising. A financier, originally from Hong Kong, who is recently widowed. She thinks that they understand each other better because the cultural differences aren't so great. She told me this as she wriggled into her skintight designer denim and fastened her chandelier earrings to her earlobes. Her cheeks were flushed and her eyes sparkled, and I realized that as energetic as she has always been, she's never looked so alive.

"Not bad," she says as she sets the box down in a corner of the living room. "Kind of dark."

"It's just the time of day," I say defensively. "You should see it in the mornings. The light comes streaming in those windows." I point across the doorway to the kitchen windows.

Ahma wanders around the living room. She sees the picture of Mr. Park and his wife on the shelf above the fireplace.

"He married American lady?" she asks.

"Yes."

"He look like your father. Handsome," she says. "But lady look cheap."

I don't tell her that her husband had an affair with the cheap-looking lady.

"It was just the style back then. Everyone used to dress like that."

"Not me," she says. "I was back then, too."

I am struck by the truth of her words, a truth that she doesn't realize. She *was* back then. My parents were married at the time the picture was taken. Had the affair already started? Was Mr. Park's wife going to meet my father later, in that same tube top and miniskirt? It is odd to contemplate. I am grateful now to Mr. Park for leaving the words in my father's notebook untranslated, for just telling me enough to understand him better. It is easier for me to remember what I want about my father without knowing everything. Unlike my mother, who now knows too much.

She must have found his notebook and read it after he died. That would explain why she decided to throw all his things away, why she stopped grieving so abruptly, why she was so determined to *move on* with her life. She may have had her doubts and suspicions about their marriage, but she couldn't have known for certain. Not knowing made it possible for her to continue living their lie.

But after reading his notebook, she could no longer deny the truth. She could throw it away in the garbage with all his other belongings, but she could not unread his words. He had betrayed her. But even worse, for all those years, she had deceived herself. Perhaps that was what hurt the most.

She does not know that I know, and I will not tell her. What would be gained? I want to spare her more shame and hurt, both of which would be compounded by my knowledge. She has changed so much this year. Would she have been able to do that if, every time she looked at me, she was reminded of my father's betrayal? The past would have lurked like a troll under a bridge, blocking the path to her future.

I offer her some tea, but she refuses.

"I have to meet Wayne," she says. Wayne is the financier from Hong Kong, the reason for her sparkling eyes and flushed cheeks. "He take me to dinner. Nice restaurant."

"Not La Chemise," I groan.

"Not French restaurant. Japanese. Best sushi. Very fresh. Famous chef." She looks at me, and a shadow of concern darkens her face. "You want to come?"

I shake my head. "No. What would Wayne think?"

"He don't care. He Chinese!" she says, meaning that he understands that family is part of the deal.

"No. I'm just going to relax and watch some TV and unpack."

"Take lots of rest. Don't let feet get too fat."

"I will. I won't. Have fun."

She gives me a peck on the cheek. I wave to her as she pulls her car out of the driveway.

I make myself a cup of green tea. I will have to replenish Mr. Park's stash before he gets back. His tea comes curled in balls that slowly unfurl as they steep. It doesn't have the bitter edge of the cheap green tea that I buy.

I drink my tea and watch the daylight fade over the hills until there is nothing but a hazy orange across the skies. I get up and start to unpack the last boxes. I want to be ready when the baby comes, and there is still so much I need. Janine promised me a baby shower, despite my protestations. She knows me well enough to realize that even though a shower will embarrass me and make me feel uncomfortable, I will love every minute of it.

My feet hurt so I sit in the leather chair and turn the television channel to a news program about climate change. Melting glaciers, hurricanes, wildfires. I watch patterns of red and green on an illustrated map, and the red rapidly spreading across the screen. I see pictures of a tourist village in Switzerland twenty years ago, a winter wonderland for vacationing Europeans. Pictures of the same village today show dusty brown shops and empty streets. In only a hundred years. Fifty years. Twenty years. This is what it means to live, to build a life, to populate a planet. This is what it means to be part of the universe, to be interconnected. The cumulative effects of billions of people over time.

After I found out I was pregnant, I applied to the master of accountancy program at the university. If I'm going to support a family, I'm going to need a better-paying job. It was a decision that I made alone, and one that I finally shared last week with Ahma and Janine. My mother seemed pleased but didn't say anything.

"But aren't you too... old?" Janine asked. "By the time you graduate, you'll be..."

"The same age I would be if I didn't do it."

There was no point in waiting for the perfect time, the perfect person, the perfect opportunity. I understand better now that there is no choice to opt out of a life. It is about more than simply seizing the day. It is about the accumulation of days, the way each moment, each decision, connects to the next, how just the sheer number of decisions, no matter how small or seemingly inconsequential, can shape your life, can *be* your life. The incrementalism of existence, the winds that eventually create canyons. The years pass, so stealthily, whether you choose to pay attention or not, whether you are ready or not. You have more need of time than it has of you.

It seems so important now to be ever vigilant, ever mindful, of how I spend my days. I stand and stretch, arching my back. I instinctively rub my stomach, even though I have not yet felt any movement. My doctor promises me that I will, any day now.

I empty one more box, the one that Ahma carried in for me. Inside are papers—my passport, old bills, bank statements. Hidden carefully underneath everything is the large yellow envelope. I open it. Inside is Appa's notebook. I look at the characters, my father's handwriting. I wonder whether my father regretted his life, and if so, what parts of it. Did he regret his affair? Marrying Ahma? Having me? It is the last question that troubles me the most. I know that it would have been easier for him to leave my mother if it hadn't been for me.

But I am not to blame for his unhappiness. It was his love for Crystal River that, like a weed, wound its way through our family and stifled the passion that my father must have felt at one time for my mother, strangling the bond that could have grown between them and that was necessary for our family to flourish. It was his love for the woman he could not have that made him unable to love the woman he married.

This thought fills me with sadness. My sympathies had been only with my mother, who loved a man who refused to love her back. But now I understand that my father, too, deserved sympathy, because he was the one who could not be with his true love, and so he was the one who suffered the most.

CHAPTER TWENTY-ONE

April 5, 2010

Last night, I had the most beautiful dream. Shirley appeared before me in a cloud of white and gray. She beckoned to me with arms that became beautiful swan's wings. I reached out to her and felt one of her wings flutter across my hands. They felt so soft, like powder sprinkled on my skin. When I awoke, I noticed the skin on the back of my hands had become mottled with brown spots. I didn't dare show them to my wife.

My longing for Shirley became so strong then. That is when I felt the pain in my chest. It felt as though my heart were breaking. But I know that is silly. If a heart could actually break like a china cup, mine would have shattered many years ago.

I feel it will be time soon. It will be time for me to come home. This is what she whispered to me before she touched me. This is what I eagerly await. This is what I wish so hard to believe.

20

(Leonard Chang, 1968—)
伦纳德·张

作者简介

伦纳德·张（Leonard Chang，1968— ），美国韩裔小说家、编剧、制片人。他出生于美国纽约，1987至1989年在达特茅斯学院（Dartmouth College）学习哲学，后又在哈佛大学继续深造，获得文学学士学位。1994年，他在加州大学欧文分校（UC Irvine）获得艺术硕士学位。伦纳德·张曾任安迪亚克大学（Antioch University）艺术硕士项目的教师、米尔斯学院的杰出客座作家，还是FX美剧《白粉飞》（Snowfall）等电视节目的编剧。

伦纳德·张的代表作包括聚焦美国韩裔私家侦探的神秘小说三部曲《回头》（Over the Shoulder，2001）、《未杀死》（Underkill，2003）、《褪色到透明》（Fade to Clear，2004）以及《水果与食品》（The Fruit 'N Food，1996）、《十字路口》（Crossings，2009）、《触发线》（Triplines，2014）、《撬锁者》（The Lockpicker，2017）等。其作品不仅展示了韩国移民的爱情与家庭故事，还揭露了非法移民、人口贩运等严酷的社会境况，曾入围夏姆斯奖（Shamus Award），并多次发表在《新月评论》（The Crescent Review）、《文学评论》（The Literary Review）等权威文学期刊上。相比于其他作家，伦纳德·张具有独特的文学、神学和社会学领域的跨学科视野。他削弱了对族裔、文化属性的书写，追寻包容、开放的世界主义理想。其笔下的主人公多为第二代移民，同化程度较高，与其他种族、民族交往甚密。目前，他的小说已被翻译成韩语、法语、日语等多种语言，并被纳入欧美、亚洲多所学校的课程学习材料。

《触发线》是一部自传体小说，讲述了主人公兰尼（Lenny）在长岛的动荡童年。伦纳德·张通过再现创伤记忆，让读者感受到兰尼在断裂、破碎的生活中寻找自我价值的艰难与曲折。选读部分摘自第三章：酗酒的父亲动辄打骂母亲和外婆，家庭暴力给孩子们幼小的心灵留下难以磨灭的阴影，兰尼试图逃脱这种令人窒息的家庭氛围，并与当地一位大麻经销商建立起非同寻常的友谊。

作品选读

Triplines

Part III Triplines
(excerpt)
By Leonard Chang

Sal seems lonely. Although Lenny occasionally sees him hanging out near the Gables movie theater on Merrick Road with a couple of other older kids, most of the time Lenny finds him either at his house or riding his minibike, and even when he sees Sal with his friends they seem more like people he just happened to run into. Maybe he's selling weed. Lenny wonders if that's why Sal asked for help, because he doesn't have anyone close to trust. Lenny knows that as a kid, he can be bossed and threatened, and ultimately discarded, although he begins to see that Sal has taken a brotherly interest in him. Once, while they tend his crops, he asks Lenny what he wants to be when he grows up. Lenny says he's thinking about being a martial arts instructor or a kung-fu star.

Sal stops checking the leaves. "Can you actually do that?"

"I guess so."

He looks impressed and continues working. Then he says, "What if you get hurt? Isn't that like a professional athlete?"

Lenny didn't think of that.

Sal says, "My uncle played college baseball on scholarship. He wanted to go pro. But he had shoulder injuries that made him lose his scholarship. He didn't have a back-up plan, so now he's working at a gas station."

Sal straightens up and pushes the hair out of his eyes. "You always need to have a back-up plan."

"What's your back-up plan?"

He points to the marijuana plants. "You're looking at it."

"What was your main plan?"

"To be a superhero."

Lenny laughs.

"Seriously. I was going to be a caped crusader. It didn't work out." He bends down and continues checking the leaves. "Besides, it paid shit."

By the time Lenny returns home his mother has prepared Mira's room for Grandma. In a corner of his room sits a small green army cot his father bought at a surplus store. His mother tells him that he has to be a good roommate, because everyone in the family has to work together for her operation. Grandma will be arriving tomorrow. His mother's operation is in two days.

That night, while he gets used to the fact that he and his little sister are sharing a room—every time she moves on the cot it squeaks—he hears his parents arguing quietly. They move from the living room to the kitchen, where their voices are muted, shrouded by the humming of the refrigerator, and after a while it becomes quiet. His father listens to classical music. His mother comes into his room to check on them. Mira is already asleep.

His mother whispers, "I am so happy your grandmother is coming."

"I don't remember her."

"You were too young. But did I ever tell you how she raised four of us by herself?"

"A little."

She tells him that Grandma went to a high school founded by American missionaries, and they nicknamed her "Maria." She learned how to play the piano well enough to be hired at church services and weddings. She wanted to be a professional, but her father had forbidden it. But she encouraged her children to love music and literature.

"What did she end up doing to support you?"

"Everything. She was cheated out of a business deal for a lumber company because she was a woman, so after that she always ran her own businesses. She sold food to the Korean Army. She ran a small sneaker factory. She owned a coal mine. She ran a bus-driving business. She did whatever she had to. My father died from leukemia when I was very young, so it was up to my mother to provide."

"Do you remember your father?"

"Very little. Almost nothing. I was just a baby."

"What's Grandma going to do when she gets here?"

"Cook. Take care of the house. She will help me." She leans forward. "Be good and listen to your *halmonee*. And if anything happens to me…"

Lenny doesn't like hearing this.

His mother notices his expression and says, "Oh, everything will be fine." She kisses him on the forehead and tells him to go to sleep. She takes a deep, slow, unsteady breath, and he realizes that she is terrified.

Short and hunched, Grandma has thinning silver hair and wears a wrinkled beige pantsuit with large black shoes that clunk on the kitchen floor. She arrives late the next evening as they prepare for bed, and the presence of a stranger in the house—since they almost never have guests—throws everyone off balance. Grandma looks around the kitchen as Yul brings in her suitcase from the garage. Umee has on a big smile, her cheeks flushed, as she introduces her children to their halmonee. Grandma claps her gnarled hands together, taking them in, and asks Umee in Korean with an incredulous voice if Lenny is the same boy who used to be so small and skinny. Grandma holds her arms out for him. Lenny hugs her, and she speaks to him in Korean. She smells of mothballs and cigarette smoke, her wool jacket rough and scratchy. Umee explains to Grandma that Lenny can't understand Korean. They have a brief discussion about this, and then Grandma hugs Mira, saying her Korean name, "Won Hee," fondly.

Yul asks Lenny where his brother is, but Lenny doesn't know. They stand around awkwardly for a moment, until Yul picks up the suitcase and carries it out of the kitchen. Grandma says to Lenny, "Not see you since baby."

He nods his head. She looks nothing like his mother, and he finds it odd that this strange old woman is his mother's mother. Grandma pinches Mira's cheek and pats her head. Mira blinks and stares.

Yul returns to the kitchen and tells the children to go to bed.

Umee says, "Let them stay up. They should get to know their *halmonee*."

He shrugs his shoulders and retreats to the living room. Grandma watches him with a cold expression, and she says something to Umee in Korean, her voice low and hard, and Umee shushes her. They sit in the breakfast nook as Umee brings out leftovers and talks to Grandma in Korean while Lenny and Mira nibble on pajun, a seafood pancake, and dried cuttlefish. Umee speaks quickly and excitedly. Lenny hasn't heard her like this before, almost childish. Even her gestures are unusual—quick head movements and leaning forward over the table.

After a while Mira yawns loudly, making Grandma laugh. She pats Mira on the head again, and Umee shoos her off to bed. Yul comes into the kitchen and pours himself a whiskey on ice. Grandma and Umee stop talking.

Once Yul leaves, Grandma says something quietly, and Umee glances at Lenny, who pretends to be preoccupied with the dried cuttlefish, which is chewy and tough, and requires two hands to tear with his teeth. Grandma repeats herself, and Lenny knows it's something serious about his father from the way his mother tenses. Lenny is getting good at reading their body language, hearing the inflections, and he knows Grandma just told his mother she should leave his father.

They talk quietly for another few minutes, and then his mother waves the discussion away. She mentions the surgery tomorrow. With that Grandma stands up, pushing her chair back, and pulls Umee away from the table. Lenny's mother tells him to go to bed, and Grandma says, "Sleep good."

He watches them leave the kitchen, heading for Grandma's new bedroom, and when he sees that they have left all the food out, he begins putting it away.

In the morning Mira wakes Lenny up with her creaking army cot, and he needs a minute to figure out where he is. He hears his father arguing with his mother, and the smell of Korean food carries down the hall, an unusual smell for a weekday morning. When Lenny enters the kitchen he sees pots bubbling over and smoke rising from a frying pan. Grandma wears his mother's apron and mixes something in a bowl.

She waves him to the table. She pours him a bowl of *jook*, a rice porridge, and pats his head. Yul appears in the kitchen in his suit and tie, and looks around, shocked. He speaks to Grandma curtly, who replies in a scolding tone. His father throws up his hands and walks out the back door. The screen door slams shut by itself.

Grandma snorts to herself. Her annoyed expression fades when she glances at Lenny. She points, making an eating motion with her fingers. Mira complains that she just wants cold cereal—Frosted Flakes—but Grandma puts a bowl of *jook* in front of her, with a small container of soy sauce to add as flavor. When their mother appears, she sits down with them. Ed tries to sneak out of the back door, but she calls him over.

Grandma greats Ed warmly, and speaks to him in Korean. He understands most of this and nods his head. He sits at the table, and their mother says, "I go into surgery today."

They wait.

Grandma puts a bowl in front of their mother, who says in Korean that she can't eat before surgery.

"I've got to get to school," Ed says.

"Your father will be coming home from work early to drive me to the hospital, so I won't be here when you get back from school. I need you all to be good."

Ed, Mira and Lenny look at each other, and then they nod their heads to her.

Because the children can't really communicate with Grandma, she tries to connect with them through food, presenting them with platters that they like for the novelty but tire of quickly. She promptly stores these dishes in Tupperware in the freezer. She cleans constantly—scrubbing appliances, vacuuming, waxing furniture—and this is just her first full day. Lenny comes home from school and finds her on her hands and knees, scrubbing the kitchen floor with a rag. She pulls herself up and presents him with a snack: *kim bop*, rice and vegetables in a seaweed wrap. She tries to talk with him, but he can't understand her. She then pushes him out of the kitchen, pointing to the wet floors, and she goes back to cleaning.

When his mother returns home two days later, she has a long, inflamed, smiley-face scar over her throat that she immediately moisturizes with Vitamin E oil. She hugs her children tentatively, then goes to bed. The operation went smoothly, and the only real after-effect is her exhaustion.

Yul grunts a thanks for the dinner Grandma made, the stovetop sizzling non-stop while Umee was at the hospital. The smell of soy sauce and fried batter overwhelms the kitchen, and Yul leaves the windows in the kitchen open all night.

The tension between Yul and Grandma isn't obvious at first, because they are both focused on Umee, but as she recovers over the next few days, her energy returning, delighted at having her mother around, Yul becames curt. He complains about the constant smell and heat in the kitchen. He says that there just isn't room in the house for this many people. He then says that since Umee is feeling better, Grandma must go.

Lenny hears his parents argue quietly in the kitchen while Grandma watches TV with Mira. Everyone hears them clearly. Grandma sighs to herself. Umee raises her voice, saying in Korean something about the two weeks not being over yet, but Yul says she has recovered so there is no need for two weeks.

Mira tries to speak with Grandma, asking about what she did in Korea, but the language gap is too large. Grandma just smiles.

The fight in the kitchen grows louder, with Umee's voice scratchy and hoarse. Lenny glances at Grandma whose expression darkens as she sits tensely on the edge of the sofa. Mira is the only one watching TV, a variety show with a singer, and when Yul breaks a dish and yells something, Grandma stands up and walks quickly to the kitchen.

The voices stop. After a moment Grandma says something sharp, and Yul retorts back in a louder and more threatening tone. Grandma replies, and Umee tries to intervene.

Lenny tells his sister that they should go to their room.

She eyes the TV, weighing her options.

"Want to go back into the church?" Lenny asks.

She perks up, and they throw on their shoes and leave through the front door to avoid the fight.

Lenny and Mira enter the church through the back door again, and this time they go to the small auditorium where there's a stage and an open room that's used for a dining and meeting area. It's dark, but they find the light switch panel by the side door, and after searching behind the stage curtain they turn on one of the spotlights. Mira stands shyly on the stage. Lenny tells her to sing something.

"What should I sing?"

"How about that *Annie* song?"

Although they've never seen the musical, Mira received the record for her birthday, and learned a few of the songs. She steps forward and sings "Tomorrow." Lenny turns off all the lights except for the spotlight, and she squints. Her voice is quiet and nervous, so he yells for her to sing louder, and he moves toward the back, near the kitchen with two large serving windows. Slowly, as she realizes that she's essentially alone in the dark, she raises her voice and belts it out. Unlike Lenny, she has no speech impediment, and because of her constant mimicking, she has a good voice. She pretends to hold a microphone, making Lenny laugh. She raises an arm to the audience, giddy, and her eyes shine in the spotlight.

They return home and find their father sitting in his lounge chair, the coffee table turned upside down and the green ceramic lamp broken on the floor, the bulb lit and sending odd angles of light onto the wall. Broken dishes lay scattered throughout the kitchen. Their mother is crying in the bathroom. Lenny and Mira walk by the bedrooms, expecting to see Grandma sitting on the bed, but she's not there. He tells Mira to play in their room.

"Where's—"

He puts his finger to his lips, shushing her. He walks past the living room, avoiding his father's gaze, and checks the basement. Ed isn't there, but neither is Grandma. When Lenny returns to the kitchen and looks out into the back, he sees her sitting on the brick steps at the door, hunched over, her arms folded tightly, and she stares down at the crab grass. She wears only a thin sweater, and she's shivering.

Lenny opens the door, but then his father yells, "She does not come into my house! This is my house!"

Grandma shakes her head at Lenny, waving her hand to the door, motioning for him to close it. He does. She studies him, her face wrinkling as she stares through the darkness. She gives him a small smile and turns back around.

He hears his mother come out of the bathroom and yell at his father. They continue fighting, and because Lenny doesn't want to walk by them to get to the bedrooms, he hurries downstairs and into the boiler room, the water heater rumbling. He kicks his make-shift punching bag a few times, the tightly-packed rags in the bag exhaling with each hit. Farther in is the storage room, where old, moldy boxes filled with clothes, books, photo albums and his mother's old paintings have lain untouched since they first moved here. Curious, he digs through the books, and finds stacks of large art books—Leonardo da Vinci, Van Gogh, Monet—with colorful prints.

He hears footsteps above thumping quickly across the house.

More yelling, and then the back door opens. Grandma snaps at Yul, who bellows back, and when Umee screams, Lenny jumps. He hasn't heard her scream like that before. He runs to the stairs, unsure if he should go upstairs.

From down here Lenny can see the back door open, and after a minute of more yelling, his father pushes Grandma and Umee to the door. Umee tries to push back, but Yul easily knocks her aside, and shoves Grandma against the screen door. They argue, Umee crying, and she struggles with him. He hits her chest with an open hand that sends her flying back into the wall.

She lets out a strangled cry and collapses.

Everyone stops. Yul peers down at her. He sways drunkenly. Umee, curled up on the floor, holds her throat. Yul says something and walks back into the living room. Grandma kneels down and speaks softly to Umee who is sobbing, shaking her head, repeating something over and over. Grandma takes her head in her arms, cradling her. She coos, and Umee quiets down. Lenny returns to the storage room and leafs through the sketchings of da Vinci, whom his mother once told him was his namesake. His hands shake as he turns the pages, sweaty fingerprints staining the corners.

21

(Min Jin Lee, 1968—)
李敏金

作者简介

李敏金（Min Jin Lee, 1968— ），美国韩裔小说家、记者。她出生于韩国汉城（今首尔），1976年随父母搬到美国纽约皇后区（Queens County），就读于纽约最著名的老牌重点高中之一——布朗士科学高中（Bronx High School of Science），在耶鲁大学学习历史，并在乔治城大学（Georgetown University）学习法律，于1993年至1995年从事律师行业。后来身患慢性肝病的她辞去了律师的工作，决定专注于写作。

李敏金曾连续三季担任《朝鲜日报》"早间论坛"的英文专栏作家，在哥伦比亚大学、斯坦福大学、早稻田大学（Waseda University）等十余所高校发表有关文学写作的演讲。她受到纽约艺术基金会（New York Foundation for the Arts）、古根海姆基金会（Guggenheim Foundation）、哈佛大学拉德克利夫高级研究院（Radcliffe Institute for Advanced Study at Harvard University）的奖金资助，并入选纽约艺术基金会名人堂，获得蒙莫斯学院（Monmouth College）文学荣誉博士学位。目前，李敏金是马萨诸塞州阿默斯特学院（Amherst College）常驻作家、美国笔会（PEN America）受托人、美国作家协会（Authors Guild）理事。

作为新生代作家的杰出代表，李敏金屡获殊荣，潜力巨大。其短篇小说《幸福之轴》（*Axis of Happiness*, 2004）获得《叙事杂志》（*Narrative Magazine*）2004年度叙事奖（Narrative Prize）；《祖国》（*Motherland*, 2002）聚焦在日本生活的韩国家庭，获得《密苏里评论》（*Missouri Review*）佩登奖（Peden Prize）；长篇小说《百万富翁的免费食物》（*Free Food for Millionaires*, 2007）在美国、

英国、意大利、韩国等多国出版，被《伦敦时报》（*The Times of London*）、《今日美国》（*USA Today*）等评为"年度十大小说"之一。

　　史诗般的历史小说《柏青哥》（*Pachinko*, 2017）分为三大部分，时间跨度近八十年，是第一部为成人读者创作的关于日韩文化的英语小说，具有厚重的历史沉淀与深刻的现实关怀，一经出版就受到《卫报》、美国国家公共广播电台（National Public Radio）、《悉尼先驱晨报》（*The Sydney Morning Herald*）等诸多媒体的好评，位列《纽约时报》2017年度十佳图书（10 Best Books of 2017），入围国家图书奖，获得代顿文学和平奖、美国美第奇读书俱乐部奖（Medici Book Club Prize）等。选读部分摘自《柏青哥》的第二部分《故乡》（"Hometown"）：未婚先孕的金善慈（Kim Sunja）走投无路，不得不嫁给体弱多病的白以撒（Beak Isak），并将随他一起前往日本。两人结婚当日，善慈的母亲来到米店请求老板能破例卖给韩国人些许白米，因为她想为女儿做一顿"佳肴"。在小说人物跌宕起伏的命运中，读者可以感受到战争年代的风雨沉浮、弱势群体的飘零凄苦以及移民在新世界安家立业所面临的牺牲。

作品选读

Pachinko

Hometown
(excerpt)
By Min Jin Lee

Pastor Shin got on bended knees and placed his right hand on her shoulder. He prayed at length for her and Isak. When he finished, he got up and made the couple rise and married them. The ceremony was over in minutes.

While Pastor Shin went with Isak and Sunja to the municipal offices and the local police station to register their marriage, Yangjin made her way to the shopping street, her steps rapid and deliberate. She felt like running. At the wedding ceremony, there were many words she had not understood. It was preposterous and ungrateful for her to have wished for a better outcome under the circumstances, but Yangjin, no matter how practical her nature, had hoped for something nicer for her only child. Although it made sense to marry at once, she hadn't known that the wedding would take place today. Her own perfunctory wedding had taken minutes, also. Perhaps it didn't matter, she told herself.

When Yangjin reached the sliding door of the rice shop, she knocked on the wide frame of the entrance prior to entering. The store was empty of customers. A striped cat was slinking about the rice seller's straw shoes and purring happily.

"*Ajumoni,* it's been a long time," Cho greeted her. The rice seller smiled at Hoonie's widow. There was more gray in her bun than he remembered.

"*Ajeossi*, hello. I hope your wife and girls are well."

He nodded.

"Could you sell me some white rice?"

"*Waaaaah,* you must have an important guest staying with you. I'm sorry, but I don't have any to sell. You know where it all goes," he said.

"I have money to pay," she said, putting down the drawstring purse on the counter between them. It was Sunja who had embroidered the yellow butterflies on the blue canvas fabric of the purse—a birthday present from two years back. The blue purse was half full, and Yangjin hoped it was enough.

Cho grimaced. He didn't want to sell her the rice, because he had no choice but to charge her the same price he would charge a Japanese.

"I have so little stock, and when the Japanese customers come in and there isn't any, I get into very hot water. You understand. Believe me, it's not that I don't want to sell it to you."

"*Ajeossi,* my daughter married today," Yangjin said, trying not to cry.

"Sunja? Who? Who did she marry?" He could picture the little girl holding her crippled father's hand. "I didn't know she was betrothed! Today?"

"The guest from the North."

"The one with tuberculosis? That's crazy! Why would you let your daughter marry a man who has such a thing. He's going to drop dead any minute."

"He'll take her to Osaka. Her life will be less difficult for her than living at a boarding house with so many men," she said, hoping this would be the end of it.

She wasn't telling him the truth, and Cho knew it. The girl must have been sixteen or seventeen. Sunja was a few years younger than his second daughter; it was a good time for a girl to marry, but why would he marry her? Jun, the coal man, had said he was a fancy sort from a rich family. She also had diseases in her blood. Who wanted that?

Though there weren't as many girls in Osaka, he supposed.

"Did he make a good offer?" Cho asked, frowning at the little purse. Kim Yangjin couldn't have given a man like that any kind of decent dowry; the boarding house woman would barely have a few brass coins left after she fed those hungry fishermen and the two poor sisters she shouldn't have taken in.

His own daughters had married years ago. Last year, the younger one's husband had run away to Manchuria because the police were after him for organizing demonstrations, so now Cho fed this great patriot's children by selling his finest inventory to rich Japanese customers whom his son-in-law had been so passionate about expelling from the nation. If his Japanese customers refused to patronize him, Cho's shop would shut down tomorrow and his family would starve.

"Do you need enough rice for a wedding party?" he asked, unable to fathom how the woman would pay for such a thing.

"No. Just enough for the two of them."

Cho nodded at the small, tired woman standing in front of him who wouldn't meet his eyes.

"I don't have much to sell," he repeated.

"I want only enough for the bride and groom's dinner—for them to taste white rice again before they leave home." Yangjin's eyes welled up in tears, and the rice seller looked away. Cho hated seeing women cry. His grandmother, mother, wife, and daughters—all of them cried endlessly. Women cried too much, he thought.

His older daughter lived on the other side of town with a man who worked as a printer, and his younger one and her three children lived at home with him and his wife. As much as the rice seller complained about the expense of upkeep of his daughter and grandchildren, he worked hard and did the bidding of any Japanese customer who'd pay the top price because he could not imagine not providing for his family; he could not imagine having his girls live far away—in a nation where Koreans were treated no better than barn animals. He couldn't imagine losing his flesh and blood to the sons of ....

Yangjin counted out the yen notes and placed them on the wooden tray on the counter beside the abacus.

"A small bag if you have it. I want them to eat their fill. Whatever's left over, I'll make them some sweet cake."

Yangjin pushed the tray of money toward him. If he still said no, then she would march into every rice shop in Busan so her daughter could have white rice for her wedding dinner.

"Cakes?" Cho crossed his arms and laughed out loud; how long had it been since he heard women talking of cakes made of white rice? Such days felt so distant. "I suppose you'll bring me a piece."

She wiped her eyes as the rice seller went to the storeroom to find the bit he'd squirreled away for occasions such as these.

22

(Nami Mun, 1968—)
娜美·文

作者简介

娜美·文（Nami Mun, 1968—），美国韩裔小说家，出生于韩国汉城（今首尔），之后移居纽约布朗克斯（Bronx）。她毕业于加州大学伯克利分校，又在密歇根大学（University of Michigan）获得艺术硕士学位，目前在美国西北大学（Northwestern University）任教。娜美·文的人生阅历丰富，曾做过新闻摄影记者、刑事辩护调查员、养老院活动协调员、街头小贩、服务员等，这些经历为其小说创作提供了翔实的素材。

虽然年纪尚轻，娜美·文已经凭借其杰出的写作才能与独到的跨文化视野赢得了读者与文坛的肯定与青睐。她著有长篇小说《远方》(*Miles from Nowhere*, 2009）与短篇小说《纪念日》("The Anniversary", 2011），定期为《纽约时报》的"星期日书评"撰稿，并在《格兰塔》(*Granta*)、《爱荷华评论》(*The Iowa Review*)、《常绿译论》(*Evergreen Review*) 等多个期刊上发表文章，荣获怀丁奖、手推车奖、芝加哥公共图书馆21世纪奖（Chicago Public Library 21st Century Award)、密西根大学霍普伍德奖（Hopwood Award），并被提名奥兰治新人奖（The Orange Award for New Writers）与美国亚裔文学奖。

《远方》的主人公俊（Joon）是一位未成年韩裔移民，父母长期不和的家庭氛围使她萌生了离家出走的念头。误入歧途的俊经历了被忽视、被压榨的悲惨与痛苦，最终决定与自我、与母亲和解，重新审视人生的意义。"麦康芒先生"（"Mr. McCommon"）选自《远方》，通过借助往日邻居的感人经历，讲述了俊重回童年住处探寻母亲痕迹、回顾昔日温情的故事。

作品选读

Mr. McCommon

(excerpt)

By Nami Mun

Long before I moved out to California. Long before I caught Wink on the evening news, talking about how glad he was for having finally contracted HIV so he could be hospitalized and cared for like the people he'd seen on the news. Long before Knowledge got clean and got work as a counselor in a teen shelter, only to be shot by a kid she was trying to help out.

Long before all this.

I returned to my mother's house in the Bronx. I wanted proof that she had not been a ghost, that she had been as real as blood.

On my way there I pictured our place—a two-story tract home that held down the corner before the ground swelled to a small, grassy hill that lipped the expressway. Cars were always leaving us. Only a few trickled down the exit ramp, and I could hear the sputtering of engines from my bedroom, late at night, when the silence after my parents fought kept me numb and awake. I figured that another family might be living there now, lounging around as if the living room, the vegetable garden, and the front windows bleached by the three o'clock sun had always been theirs. But when I stood at the end of my block I saw no family. And I barely recognized the house. In all the years of reimagining my childhood home, not once had I pictured it boarded up and abandoned.

All the windows were nailed with plywood, and the screen door lay crooked on top of a sagging hedge. Bands of graffiti blackened the aluminum siding, even the dead, brittle lawn, and someone had spray-painted NZONE on the front door, vertically, one letter stacked neatly on top of the other. I couldn't help but take all of it personally. I was being punished for having left without looking back. Five years had gone by, though judging by the sickly roof, the derailed gutters, and the detached emptiness I felt about my mother's death, it might as well have been five light-years.

I walked to the rear, where the kitchen door stood unfazed by all the garbage surrounding it—beer cans, a single flip-flop, a plastic grocery bag trapped under a can of Valvoline. Without much hope I jiggled the brassy doorknob. Nothing. I even tried the back basement door, the one my father had used to escape in the middle of the night to see his mistress, until my mother suddenly took an interest in carpentry and nailed the door shut with two-by-fours, from both inside and out. In return, my father nailed up her dresser drawer, just the top one, where she kept her Bible and brown photos of herself as a ponytailed girl in Korea. This was how my parents talked. They used nails, hammers, dinner plates, and knives, and when those didn't work, they used leaving.

I circled the house. The plank on the side kitchen window—the same one I had once peeked through to see my mother rising from the ground—looked especially warped. I marked a mental X in the center, backed up a few steps, braced my arm and charged, leading with a shoulder and channeling all the TV cops I'd seen doing this very maneuver. The cops were the size of a duplex and I was all of 105 pounds, but I hurled my body into the wood anyway—one, two, three times too many. A strong breeze had a better chance. Without screaming, I held the pain in my shoulder and understood what it was trying to tell me: that I was a stupid girl, that I wasn't getting into the house unless I got rid of my stupidity, and that I would never understand my mother.

"Joon, is that you?"

I was startled to find a man behind me. He was in his mid-fifties and nearly bald, with a few scraggly curls frizzying the sides. I had barely known Mr. McCommon when I was growing up, but he came in for a hug, which would've been fine except that I hadn't expected it. Our clumsy dance led to a sideways embrace, ending with a stutter of pats on the back. His tracksuit, a neon-green, felt both scratchy and smooth.

"I can't believe you're back," he said, and I kept my head down so he could study me without feeling awkward. "I thought you were dead."

A fly landed on his fresh white sneaker. "I thought I was dead, too," I told him.

The boys in the neighborhood had always made fun of his name—Mr. McCommon. Mr. McAverage. Mr. Mc-Usual. It didn't help that he'd worn a boring gray suit and tie almost every day and drove a car the color of masking tape. He was short and thin with narrow shoulders and a long forehead. The expression on his face, which was also long, reminded me of chalkboard that had just been erased—you knew something had lived there once but you never knew what. I'd always felt a little sympathy for him, maybe because the kids who made fun of him had also changed my name to Joon Ching-chong, Joon Ah-so, Joon Chow-mein. None of the kids cracked jokes about his wife, though, a woman everyone thought was the life of the neighborhood, with her frilly voice and large, blond hair. But to me, she was worse than the kids. Whenever my parents battled, I could always count on seeing Mrs. McCommon by her kitchen window, talking into the phone with a hand cupping her mouth, squinting at our house to get the play-by-play.

"Is Mrs. McCommon home?" I asked.

We were in his garage, looking for tools to pry open the plywood.

"No," he said, rummaging through a metal chest. "She had cancer."

He spoke casually, as if reading off a grocery list. I didn't know what to say.

"It's okay," he added. "She's not dead."

I halfheartedly sifted through an open cardboard box. "Is she all right?"

From the chest he pulled out a hammer and pondered its dimensions. "She's probably fine," was all he said, and I let his answer be.

The front half of the garage was a jumble of boxes, laundry baskets, and crates. Some mounds reached my waist and none were labeled or in any way organized. The rear of the garage was a different story. A skyline of neatly stacked items almost eclipsed the entire back wall—items I didn't think anyone collected. Like the white foam trays that come with supermarket meat. Or bundles of old newspaper, every single one wrapped in the Sunday comics. Or empty boxes of Kleenex. Slouching in a corner were roughly twenty paper bags, all of them labeled and brimming with throwaways, like lightbulbs, blue plastic razors, curled tubes of toothpaste, and—maybe the most confusing—clumps of used tissue. That every item was categorized and kept so tidy was what stunned me.

I turned around. Mr. McCommon was still on his knees, now leaning over a different box. His jacket was open, and poking up from an interior pocket was a pudgy cream-colored envelope, the return address inked in calligraphy. It seemed on the verge of falling out, not that he noticed. An orange work light hooked to a beam tanned the crown of his head while blurring his face in shadow, but I could still make out the absolute determination in his eyes. And in his arms, which were elbow-deep in the box, swirling items around in a mad search. Why he was so set on helping me I didn't know. Maybe he didn't, either. I picked a crate and started digging. I wanted to ask why he saved the things he saved but figured that if I felt uneasy asking, then he'd feel uneasy answering. I instead asked if he knew what had happened to all of our stuff.

"The bank foreclosed on your house. I'm guessing they sold everything."

I flipped through an old magazine. "I wonder what they got for my junior-high yearbook."

He laughed through his teeth.

"What am I looking for again?" I asked.

"A crowbar, or anything that behaves like a crowbar."

My hands touched tangled stockings, tubes of lipstick, a blond wig, empty tubs of Noxzema, and other remains, but nothing resembling a tool.

"Mr. McCommon?"

"Yes."

"Can I ask you a question?"

"Here, slide that over," he said, pointing to a laundry basket filled with a hodgepodge of blankets and batteries and music boxes. I nudged it over with my foot.

"How do you remember us?"

"What do you mean?"

"My mother and me. What did we look like to you?"

Without looking up he said, "Troubled. Just like everybody else."

"You and Mrs. McCommon always seemed—"

"Goddamn it!" He chucked something back into the basket and stood up. "I know I have a crowbar somewhere in here." With hands on hips, he looked down the driveway and shook his head as if disagreeing with the trash cans sitting by the curb. The clouds hung low, and the sun was failing. Across the street, a porch light blinked twice before coming on, and that slight hesitation made me wonder if I should leave. The dust in the garage powdered my throat, and plus, I didn't think I needed to see the dying insides of my childhood home. Some things were best kept in the dark. Like my past. Like Mr. McCommon's collections.

"Try over there." Mr. McCommon pointed to a skinny workbench that stood against the right side of the garage. Blue milk crates took up most of the counter. One was filled with kitchen utensils. Another a mayhem of hair-brushes, combs, a blow-dryer, leather gloves, and a pocket-sized Bible, the same kind my mother had kept in her purse. A lime-green pleather cover with *The New Testament* inscribed in gold. The color matched Mr. McCommon's tracksuit, and it came to me then that I'd never seen him in anything but gray. I picked up the mini Bible, opened to a page to smell it but the scent didn't remind me of my mother's hand cream.

"Finally." Mr. McCommon stood behind me, holding a crowbar as if it were a torch. "Come on. Let's go break into your house."

The moon was full, its light widening the sky around it. Mr. McCommon carried the hammer and the crowbar. I carried a flashlight. The neighborhood was quiet; *he* was quiet. I could hear the scrapes of his tracksuit and the long, distant sighs of the expressway as we drifted across my mother's driveway, her yard, and faced the kitchen window.

"Stand back," he said, pushing up his sleeves. At the lower right side of the plywood, he wedged in the flat end of the crowbar and started hammering it in. "I can't see," he said, and I aimed the flashlight at his hands. With a third of the rod now jammed behind the wood, he dropped the hammer, gripped and re-gripped the crook of the crowbar, braced his foot against the aluminum siding, and pulled. "I remember when the workers boarded up the house," he said, grunting with every effort.

"Do you want some help?"

"They didn't mess around." He looked like he was being strangled, the flesh around his eyes and mouth ballooning.

"I can pull with you, if you want."

"Big... guys, with big... nail guns." He changed to an underhanded grip and planted his foot higher on the siding. "But this crowbar... should do the trick." He growled and pulled with renewed strength but the plywood budged less than an inch.

"Maybe we shouldn't be doing this," I said.

"Why not." He hammered in the crowbar farther. "Sometimes it's good to break the rules. Let the neighbors call the cops, I don't care." He yanked harder, and this time his arms began to tremble. I thought they might pop off.

I hadn't even thought about the neighbors. "Don't hurt yourself."

He gritted his teeth, his face frozen in pain, and then as if the sound had been boiling in his stomach for years, he let out a scream so loud and so long, I was sure he'd grown another vocal cord.

"Goddamn it!" he screamed, and picked up the hammer, held it like an ax, and for reasons unclear to me, he began clobbering the wood.

"Mr. McCommon?"

"Not now!" he barked. He was exploding. His arms swung wildly above his head though his face appeared to be doing all the work. Deep, guttural sounds spilled from his crooked lips with every slam, but as wild as his strokes were, the plywood didn't give. "Son of a bitch," he mumbled, and swung harder, out of control. The sound of metal whacking wood struck my temples.

"We really don't have to do this," I told him.

"—Yes

"—I

"—do," he said, and delivered maybe five more swings, each one making a crescent-shaped dimple, each one slowing the next one down, until he finally and simply released the hammer, the head thudding the ground. He folded his body, his palms clutched his thighs, and with every gasp his chest whistled.

"Are you okay?"

"Am I okay?" He laughed, maybe for too long, and the sheer frustration of his laughter clung to my skin. He slumped to the ground, leaned back against the aluminum siding, and closed his eyes. "She said I was boring."

I turned the flashlight off and sidled up next to him.

"I'm the one who watched her going bald. I changed her sheets when she couldn't get to the bathroom in time. I fed her Jell-O, I drained her bedsores. I'm the one who gave her sponge baths. Me. And after all that, she says I'm too dull."

From where we sat, we could see the orange, square glow that came from his garage.

"She didn't want to die married to me."

"But she didn't die," I said.

"Now she's marrying some merchant marine."

"But she's still alive," I said, as loud as I had intended. When the words left me, all I wanted was to run to his garage, pull down the door, bury myself under batteries and blankets and lipsticks and rubber bands, and sleep inside his city of remains.

"I'm sorry about your mother," he whispered.

I felt a tiny collapsing in my chest and it took me a moment to correctly identify the pang, not as grief, but as jealousy. I hadn't loved my mother the way he had loved his wife. I had left her when she needed me most, and in the end, she died, in a car, completely alone with nothing but the sound of metal crushing her. I couldn't grieve for her, not because I didn't want to, but because I didn't deserve to. I looked at Mr. McCommon, his hands smothering his face, his chest flinching. He had no idea that grief was a reward. That it only came to those who were loyal, to those who loved more than they were capable of. He had a garage, full of her belongings, and all I had was my guilt. It took on its own shape and smell and nestled in the pit of my body, and it would sleep and play and walk with me for decades to come.

For a long while we stayed just as we were, listening to the air, letting the expressway mourn our loss. I asked if I could take the green pocket-sized Bible.

"I still miss her," he said, like he was breathing, and I didn't have the heart to repeat myself.

And then, without discussion, we both stood up and tried the window again. Between the two of us, it took just a few minutes to pry off a corner of the wood, only to discover that another plank was boarding up the window from the inside. We never got in, and somehow that seemed appropriate. On our way back to his garage, Mr. McCommon looked up at his bedroom window, which was dark like the rest of his house. "I even miss seeing her sick," he said, and that seemed to me a truth I could hold on to about my mother, a place to begin.

23

(Suji Kwock Kim, 1968—)
苏吉·克沃克·金

作者简介

苏吉·克沃克·金（Suji Kwock Kim，1968—），美国韩裔诗人、剧作家。她曾在耶鲁大学和爱荷华大学作家工作坊学习，还是首尔大学和延世大学的富布赖特学者、斯坦福大学的斯特格纳研究员（Stegner Fellow），目前主要活跃于旧金山与纽约。

她著有诗集《来自分裂国家的笔记》（*Notes from a Divided Country*，2003）与《来自北方的笔记》（*Notes from the North*，2020），荣获国家/发现奖（The Nation/ Discovery Award）、沃尔特·惠特曼奖（Walt Whitman Award）、阿迪生·梅特卡弗奖（Addison Metcalf Award）、怀丁作家奖（Whiting Writers' Award）等奖项。苏吉·克沃克·金的作品流传度很广，不仅发表在《民族周刊》（*The Nation*）、《美国最佳诗歌》（*The Best American Poetry*）、《纽约时报》、《卫报》等权威选本与报纸上，而且被美国国家公共广播电台、英国广播公司电台（BBC Radio）、加拿大广播公司（Canadian Broadcasting Corporation）等官方电台收录，还被翻译成俄语、德语、西班牙语、意大利语、韩语、日语等近十种语言，拥有广大的读者群。此外，她参与合著的多媒体剧《私有财产》（*Private Property*）曾在剧作家视野剧院（Playwrights Horizons）展出，并在英国广播公司电视台（BBC-TV）播出。

《来自分裂国家的笔记》是苏吉·克沃克·金的处女作，其背景跨越纽约、旧金山、首尔多个城市，聚焦殖民主义、战争、移民、种族主义等主题，思考家园共同体的意义，探寻在城市、城镇、战场中"是什么将我们的生活联结在一起"。诗人追踪了从曾祖父母至父母几代人的痛苦，也不乏众多无名之辈的凄惨历史，交织着对往日灾难的恐惧和对未来光明的期待。

"裂口"（"The Chasm"）与"被遗忘的战争碎片"（"Fragments of the Forgotten War"）均摘自诗集《来自分裂国家的笔记》。两首诗歌以朝鲜半岛战争为大背景，描述了普通民众背井离乡、家破人亡、马革裹尸的悲壮场景，看似用语平淡，实则触目惊心。

作品选读（一）

The Chasm

By Suji Kwock Kim

(AUGUST, 1950)
In the dream vultures circle above my mothers cousin.
Eye the gash blown in his belly

by Soviet T-34 tanks or U.S. rocket-launchers
shooting at each other blind across the Naktong River—

a million refugees caught in the crossfire,
crossing far as the eye can see.

Vultures smell the kill.
My mother screams when one drops

on his chest, thrashing for foothold,
his small body shaking beneath its wings,

talons ripping away strips
of flesh like bandages.

She beats it with her walking stick

until it flies hissing to another corpse.

Then another one lands, then another, then another,
her beating the stick until they fly away too,

not for good, swarming again and again to his half-gnawed body,
wave after wave.

Her mother shouts at her to *leave him.*
Digs her nails into her arm and drags her on.

My mother can't see his face anymore
for their jaws, chewing on twisted entrails,

insides pulled out like ropes unlashed from the mast of the spine,
all the bleeding sinews and nerves, strange jellies,

all the hieroglyphs of generation.
Why won't they speak.

I know you were real, even if I can only see you
in dreams, I see

we'll never meet.
It's humiliating to wake up

alive, fifty years later, when I couldn't have saved you.
I couldn't have saved a dog.

For the birds change their faces
and wear the faces of soldiers.

作品选读（二）

Fragments of the Forgotten War

By Suji Kwock Kim

FOR MY FATHER
You whom I could not protect,
                                      when will I forget you:
when will I forget the Northern soldiers who took you away for questioning,
so we never saw you again?

We three sons fled south in January 1951
                                      without you, with a million others
on Shinjangno, the old Imperial Highway between P'yongyang and Seoul—
I felt artillery crash miles away in the soles of my feet, the ground shuddering.
I heard the drone and snarl of engines as B-29 bombers swarmed toward us
like a war in heaven but not heaven,
                                      a war between gods who weren't gods,
now missiles whistling on their search-and-destroy,
now the endless columns of refugees screaming in terror,
now delayed-fuse demolition bombs exploding all around us,
blowing craters larger than houses,
                                    now firing white phosphorus flares 3000 feet high,
while we knelt like beggars before the blasts,
                                    using the dead as shields, corpse-greaved,
covering our faces from the blizzard of shrapnel,
blizzard of limbs and flaming skin,
                                  of all who left this world in a grave of smoke.
I'll never forget the smell of burning flesh.
I'll never forget the stench of open sores, pus, gangrene;
                                    the smell of people rotting
                                        who hadn't died yet:

or the cries of the wounded moaning without morphine,
a boy sinking his teeth into his arm
                              to take his mind off the gash that ripped his stomach,
biting down and down until you saw bone glinting through
                                        like teeth in a mass grave.

At night we fought for the few standing barns, shacks, outhouses.
Without fuel we burned shit for heat
                              until the light from our fires drew bombers.
We caught fever and frostbite from walking hundreds of miles
through snow,
                    walking through Taejon, the Chollas, Taegu, Chinju.
When food ran out we ate cattle feed,
                              ate bark, ate lice from our own bodies
until our gums bled,
                    until we could only shit water by the time we got to Pusan.
What I wouldn't give to bring back that miserable village I hated as a boy.

Sometimes in my dreams you hoot like a soul-owl,
What have you done with your life,
                              who will you become, who, who, who?

I can only speak to you in broken things,
I can only speak in bullets, grenade-shards, mortar casings and ROKA barricades:

I know I'm orphaned,
I know you suffered, but I'll never know how.
I think of the loneliness of the dying,
                    the bodies I saw along the way, rotting separately:
I think of that boy biting his arm
                              who didn't live through the night,
wild dogs gnawing at his skull in the morning, his whole face an "exit wound":
I think of a carcass foaming with maggots, the bone black with hatching flies.

24

(Susan Choi, 1969—)
苏珊·崔

作者简介

苏珊·崔（Susan Choi，1969—），美国韩裔小说家，出生于美国印第安纳州北部城市南本德（South Bend, Indiana）。苏珊·崔九岁时，其韩裔父亲与犹太裔母亲离异，她随母亲搬至得克萨斯州休斯敦生活。她在耶鲁大学获得文学学士学位，并在康奈尔大学获得艺术硕士学位，之后在《纽约客》（*The New Yorker*）工作。目前，她在耶鲁大学教授创意写作。

苏珊·崔是一位多产的作家，主要作品包括：小说《留学生》（*The Foreign Student*，1998）、《美国女人》（*American Woman*，2003）、《嫌疑犯》（*A Person of Interest*，2008）、《我的教育》（*My Education*，2013）、《信任练习》（*Trust Exercise*，2019）；儿童插画读物《老虎营》（*Camp Tiger*，2019）以及与大卫·雷姆尼克合作完成的短篇小说选集《精彩小镇：选自〈纽约客〉的关于纽约的故事》（*Wonderful Town: New York Stories from The New Yorker*，2000）。其中《美国女人》入围 2004 年普利策奖，《嫌疑犯》入围 2009 年笔会/福克纳小说奖（PEN/Faulkner Award），《我的教育》荣获 2014 年浪达文学奖（Lambda Literary Awards）。

《留学生》是苏珊·崔的第一部小说，斩获了美国亚裔文学小说奖（Asian American Literary Award for Fiction）与斯蒂芬·特纳奖（Steven Turner Award）。该小说的背景设在 20 世纪中叶，围绕韩国留学生恰克（Chuck）与美国南部女孩凯瑟琳（Katherine）的朦胧情愫展开，穿插讲述当时美国、韩国的战争局势与社会现实。早年被残酷战争与畸形情感经历所困扰的两人性格孤僻冷峻，机缘巧合之下，这两个异邦人在对方身上感觉到了救赎与觉醒的可能性。第一篇选文摘自

《留学生》第十三章：主人公因涉嫌从事间谍活动而被警察逮捕，在此期间他遭到严刑逼供等非人待遇，对人生、生死、信仰产生了新的感悟。

《信任练习》是她的最新小说，曾获2019年美国国家图书奖，评委称这部小说"融合了后现代技法的严谨思想性，以及一个适时的、令人着迷的故事，并且有一个令人不安的结尾"。小说讲述了20世纪八十年代的戏剧学校学生的懵懂恋爱故事，与"我也是"（Me Too）运动遥相呼应，反映了阶级隔阂与女性权力等深层社会问题。第二篇选文摘自《信任练习》的开篇，介绍了表演艺术学院的由来、学生们的享乐主义生活方式以及金教员所提倡的摸黑爬行、信任练习等病态授课模式。

作品选读（一）

The Foreign Student

Chapter Thirteen
(excerpt)
By Susan Choi

Cheju's villages were emptied of all their remaining boys, young men, older men who had no trouble walking, all of them rounded up by the American MPs and the National Police and gathered into blinking, silent crowds, straw sleeping mats or wool army-issue blankets rolled up and tied to their backs. Small children and women and the very old gathered in a crowd opposite and also stood wordlessly, a strange reflection, to watch them walk away in motley columns, without looking back. No one expected them to return. Their departure was a funeral, every man wearing or carrying his most cherished item of clothing, the thing he was willing to enter the next world attired in. Their best clothes: some owned real wool coats, aviator-style sunglasses, hats with bills or ear flaps, felt fedoras. Some had leather bags slung across their chests, fragile wire-rimmed glasses, American-made combat boots. Others wore only loose pajama-style shirts and pants, dark vests, canvas slippers, with lengths of cotton tied around their heads to warm their ears. If you were a man walking through one of these villages from which every man had been taken, then you were a ghost, or a beast. Women dropped bowls of rice on the ground and withdrew quickly, slamming their doors, as he leaped on the food. Thinking of finding Kim had been a way to mark time, but time stopped for him. He only wanted to gorge his body on hot food, slake his thirst, fall asleep overcome with the drunken sensation of having been fed. He excreted solid waste with tremendous pleasure and regret. When he was not dizzy and amnesiac from hunger he moved through the village streets deliriously, enthralled with his body's continuance, forgetting more and more often to withdraw to the woods until twilight, falling asleep curled like a lover against the warm flank of a building, his hands squeezed between his legs, dreaming of food, shit, flesh, liquid. Preparing. At last he woke howling in pain; his hand had been yanked from its ardent embrace with his body and stamped into meat. There was still the boot on his hand, still stamping its heel, his flesh shredded back to the cool blue knuckle. When a second officer stepped forward and doused the wound with gasoline he fainted. He had been arrested by the National Police on suspicion of espionage. He woke up in the back of a bouncing jeep, screamed, and was clocked in the side of the head with the butt of a rifle.

He was put on a boat and sent to Pusan, to a detention center that had been made from a converted school building. While he was conscious he argued so strenuously for his release that he was repeatedly knocked out again. When he came to he would resume the litany, listing every superior he had ever had during his employment by the United States Army, naming Police Chief Ho, his uncle Lee, his father. "My father is in Pusan," he sobbed, as his head snapped back. And then, the black mist moving aside again, he lunged forward, trying to butt the driver of the jeep. "Minister Su is a friend of my family," he gibbered, "My father is a famous professor, my uncle is Congressman Lee," rushing the words out before he was struck. He threatened his captors with jail. A used bandage was stuffed into his mouth, gooey with fluids. By the time he arrived at the school building both his eyes were swollen to slits. He wove when he walked. The ground seemed to be bucking up toward him. Inside the school building there were still maps on the walls, but scrolled up, and the windows were covered with tar paper. He was taken into a classroom that had been cut in half with a thin wood partition. At first he thought the classroom would be his cell. Later he understood that this never could have been the case, because the classroom had to be periodically withdrawn from him, so that he would live in fear of seeing it again.

On his first day he was beaten with a sawed-off length of wood left from the construction of the partition, and a baseball bat found leaning in a closet. Two soldiers beat him while an officer watched. The officer said, "Avoid his head." When he fell to his knees he was kicked in the stomach, ribs, and buttocks. He bent his face into the cage of his forearms and went sliding back and forth across the floor. A boot tip hit his scrotum and he vomited a clear splash of liquid. "You're a spy," the officer said. "No," he gasped. "First the lies come out," the officer said, as if he were a doctor calmly talking his patient through a procedure. "Stand him up."

The two soldiers stood him up and he crumpled. They stood him up again and one pushed the end of a rifle into the soft pocket of flesh beneath his jaw. Unknown reservoirs of strength opened in him and he continued to stand.

Now his body would fail him by enduring, to be damaged further, and by failing to endure, for which he would be damaged further. There was an exposed pipe bending into the room near the ceiling, covered with blisters of rust, steadily leaking dark rust-thickened water that looked like clotting blood. "Do you see that pipe?" the officer asked him. He nodded. "Point to it." His arm lifted, jerking violently. "Salute the pipe," suggested the officer. "Say, I salute you, pipe." He said it, gurgling. A fire spread from the center of his back up the ropes of his arm, and down the backs of his legs. His kneecaps popped. One of the soldiers was dismissed. The other came and punched him in the sternum with his gun. He doubled over but did not fall. "Louder," said the officer. He shouted again. He was made to stand perfectly still with his arm extended, shouting his salute to the pipe. He did not know how many times he shouted. He could not adjust his body, accommodate its pangs which quickly turned to blinding, unrememberable, voiding black pain. He fainted, waking as he struck the floor.

The officer stood over him. "Are you a spy?"

"No," he said.

He was made to stand up again, immobile, with the arm extended, shouting his salute at the pipe. He could not endure the posture for more than a few minutes at a time without collapsing. Each time he did the officer told him he could remain lying down if he admitted that he was a spy. The soldier kicked him idly. He rose again, stood, saluted, fell, was questioned, kicked idly, made to stand. At the end of the day he was taken to a cell in the basement of the school building, on an empty hallway. The cell might have once been a cement shower stall, a few feet square, with a drain in the center of the floor and a stub of pipe extending out of the wall just beyond his reach, about a foot below the ceiling, with a threaded bolt set like a bar across its mouth. His right arm was handcuffed to this. He had to stand on his toes to keep the cuff from dislocating his wrist, but in spite of this he plunged into a deep sleep, and broke his wrist with the weight of his body.

The next morning he tried again. His wrist had swollen so astonishingly that the guard who retrieved him called a doctor.

"My father is here in Pusan, my uncle is a congressman, I'm not a spy," he told the doctor. His face was washing itself with tears, but these tears were like the tears the eye always produces to roll in its socket, they meant nothing to him. His purpose was to communicate his point to this doctor, who was a good man, an educated man, and must have taken some kind of oath to protect human life. The doctor said, gazing past him with mild surprise. "I think that is your father coming now," and when he whirled to look the doctor squeezed the wrist, snapping the bone into place. His voice tore out of him unbelievingly. "Haaaaaaaaaaah…" He was taken back to the classroom, with the wrist bound. He begged the officer to call Eighth Army headquarters, USIS, his father, the government. "What?" the officer said. "Are you talking? All I hear is blah blah blah blah!" Nothing he said was ever audible. "What?" the officer shouted, striking him across the face. He hadn't been heard. He saluted the pipe until his voice was so strained he was nauseous. He was stood beneath the pipe, and made to throw his head all the way back, so that it screamed on its hinge, and then to swallow the rust-thickened drip. When he fell backwards he was punched in the sternum with the butt of the rifle, or the baseball bat, which stood in the corner when not in use, at an impudent angle, observing him. He would be allowed to stop swallowing if he admitted that he was a spy. When he screamed his own name, the name of his father, the name of his uncle, the two soldiers kicked his scrotum and buttocks, slapped him across the face with their gloves, stood him up, and pulled his head backwards by his hair until he thought his neck would break, while the officer said, "What? I don't understand you. What language is this?" He was stood beneath the drip again and made to swallow, with his head thrown all the way back. The rusty water filled his mouth and ran in streams down his neck. He vomited again, like his gut being withdrawn through his throat. The officer strolled the perimeter of the room, dangling the baseball bat thoughtfully. "Are you a spy?" he asked. He wanted to know where the Communists were hiding on Cheju. The soldier's rifle was resting against the soft pocket of flesh under his jaw and he was made to swallow his vomit, and the rust-thickened water. The sound the pipe made as it dripped was like a kind of incontinence.

That night he was given a piece of putrefying meat to eat; the next morning, when the guard found a pool of feces quivering on the floor of his cell he said, "Make that disappear," and stood over him with his gun cocked while he pushed the waste through the grate of the drain. He was shackled by his left hand now. He learned to haul himself up by it, to gash the inside of his right forearm against the sharp end of the bolt. He made a new gash every night. The marks spread across his arm, crisscrossing sometimes, but still readable, like the lines on his palm. He did not know how else to keep track of time, and he was determined to control at least the passage of his body through time. He could not control anything else. He could not control what his body expelled, or even what it ingested. He was given cattle feed, and ridiculed as he wolfed it down. He was so hungry he ate whatever was given to him, no matter how rotten or inorganic. His body suffered from the lack of everything, and it convulsively took in material, in the same way it convulsively vomited. Five marks on his arm, then eight. Looking at them, he did not experience the duration they represented. He only felt the pain in his body and even this became a dome he lived inside of.

On the ninth day his jaws were held open, and the officer took a straight razor and made small cuts all over his tongue; then he was given a bowl of salt. He ate it, weeping. "Are you a spy?" the officer asked. He said he was. He could have said, so long ago, I am a spy. The officer unfolded a piece of paper in front of his face. There were words coursing across it. He was only watching them, not trying to read them. Words came from a world which did not exist. His face washed itself with tears that were made in the same unfeeling place where his urine was made, and his blood. It meant nothing to him. The officer gave him a pen but his hand couldn't grasp it. His swollen wrist was numb and bound, and his fingers were broken. The officer placed the pen carefully between his fingers and it fell out again. The soldiers laughed. Although they couldn't have said why, this seemed very funny. The officer had to hold his hand, with the pen in it, so that he could sign. They performed the maneuver together, painstakingly. When they had finished, the officer sat down across from him, without releasing the hand. He held it lightly, with a regard for its injuries. "Thank you," the officer said. He nodded gratefully. He was so glad to have done it at last. His hopes kindled. He was being spoken to. The officer watched him with interest and he watched back, enraptured, his breathing quick from his exertion. Then the officer asked, "Where are the caves on Cheju?" He was returned to his cell.

After this there was very little left of him. He mimicked his torturers, making himself deaf to his body's cries for help. His knowledge of his body propagated in chains, telephone lines, bridges between a limb and his love for it, coursing braids of communication wire. He sliced through lines and wires, exploded bridges, excised his mouth and his groin, amputated his limbs. He no longer knew when he urinated. Cast outside the boundary of itself, his body had ceased to obey any boundary between itself and the world. He was always damp and acrid with urine, trickling out of him the way blood trickled out of his various wounds. His terror at the mangling of his fingers had evaporated, and the memory of that terror was as unrecognizable as any of his other possessions. He watched his hand being mangled from a great distance. He had already sawed it off. He had thrown away his body as if it were ballast, not to speed his death, but to survive. It was his body that would kill him.

 He stopped keeping track of the days, and his torturers grew tired of him. Truckloads of captured guerrillas and other prisoners of war from all across the peninsula were arriving at the school, naked from the waist up, roped together at the ankles. They filled the school yard, squatting on their stringy haunches in the cold, falling asleep on top of each other. They were too unwieldy with their arms bound behind them, unable to pick themselves up when they fell over, and bringing the whole column down, and so they were allowed to keep their hands and arms, holding them clasped against their chests as if in prayer. Their shaved heads and bare shoulders shingled together like the scales of a single, ailing creature. In the classroom he was made to stand on a wooden chair that was set on top of a desk, beneath the pipe, with his hands cuffed behind him. The cuffs were attached to the pipe with a short length of chain; he had to double over as his arms were pulled up. He dropped his head and swayed dangerously on the chair, his toes grabbing ineffectually. He was left alone.

作品选读（二）

Trust Exercise

(excerpt)

By Susan Choi

 NEITHER CAN DRIVE. David turns sixteen the following March, Sarah the following April. It is early July, neither one within sight of sixteen and the keys to a car. Eight weeks remain of the summer, a span that seems endless, but with the intuitive parts of themselves they also sense it is not a long time and will go very quickly. The intuitive parts of themselves are always highly aggravated when they are together. Intuition only tells them what they want, not how to achieve it, and this is intolerable.

Their romance has started in earnest this summer, but the prologue took up the whole previous year. All fall and spring of the previous year they lived with exclusive reference to each other, and were viewed as an unspoken duo by everyone else. Little remarked, universally felt, this taut, even dangerous energy running between them. When that began, it was harder to say. They were both experienced—neither was a virgin—and this might have both sped and slowed what took place. That first year, in the fall, each had started at school with a boy or girlfriend who was going to some other, more regular place. Their own school was special, intended to cream off the most talented at selected pursuits from the regular places all over the city and even beyond, to the outlying desolate towns. It had been a daring experiment ten years before and was now an elite institution, recently moved to an expensive new building full of "world class," "professional" facilities. The school was meant to set apart, to break bonds that were better off broken, confined to childhood. Sarah and David accepted this as the sort of poignant rite their exceptional lives would require. Lavished, perhaps, extra tenderness on the vestigial boyfriend and girlfriend in the process of casting them off. The school was named the Citywide Academy for the Performing Arts, but they and all the students and their teachers called it, rather pompously, CAPA.

At CAPA, the first-year Theatre Arts students studied Stagecraft, Shakespeare, the Sight-Reading of music, and, in their acting class, Trust Exercises, all terms they were taught should be capitalized as befitted their connection to Art. Of the Trust Exercises there were seemingly infinite variations. Some involved talking and resembled group therapy. Some required silence, blindfolds, falling backward off tables or ladders and into the latticework of classmates' arms. Almost daily they lay on their backs on the cold tile floor in what Sarah, much later in life, would be taught was called corpse pose in yoga. Mr. Kingsley, their teacher, would pad like a cat among them in his narrow-toed soft leather slippers, intoning a mantra of muscle awareness. *Let your awareness pour into your shins, filling them slowly, from ankle to knee. Allow them to grow liquid and heavy. Even as you can feel every cell, cradle it with your sharpened awareness, you are letting it go. Let it go. Let it go.* Sarah had won admission to the school with a monologue from the Carson McCullers play *The Member of the Wedding*. David, who had attended a theatre camp, had done Willy Loman from *Death of a Salesman*. Their first day, Mr. Kingsley slid into the room like a knife—he had a noiseless and ambushing style of movement—and once they'd fallen silent, which was almost immediately, had cast a look on them that Sarah still saw in the back of her mind. It seemed to mix scorn with a challenge. *You look pretty nothing to me*, the look flashed onto them like a spray of ice water. And then, like a tease, it amended:… or *maybe I'm wrong*? THEATRE, Mr. Kingsley had written in tall slashing letters of chalk on the board. "That's the way it is spelled," he had said. "If you ever spell this with 'ER' at the end you will fail the assignment." These words were the actual first he had spoken to them, not the scornful "you look pretty nothing to me" Sarah had imagined.

Sarah wore a signature pair of blue jeans. Though she had bought them at a mall she would never see anyone else wearing them: they were specific to her, very snug, with elaborate stitching. The stitching went in whorls and patterns spreading over the ass, down the fronts and the backs of the thighs. No one else even had textured jeans; all the girls wore five-pocket Levi's or leggings, the boys the same five-pocket Levi's or, for a brief time, Michael-Jackson-style parachute pants. In Trust Exercises one day, perhaps late in the fall—David and Sarah were never quite sure; they would not speak of it until summer—Mr. Kingsley turned off all the lights in the windowless rehearsal room, plunged them into a locked lightless vault. At one end of the rectangular room was a raised platform stage, thirty inches or so off the floor. Once the lights were turned off, in the absolute silence, they heard Mr. Kingsley skim the length of the opposite wall and step onto the stage, the edge of which they faintly discerned from bits of luminescent tape that hovered in a broken line like a thin constellation. Long after their eyes had adjusted, they saw nothing but this: a darkness like that of the womb or the grave. From the stage came his stern, quiet voice, voiding them of all previous time. Stripping them of all knowledge. They were blind newborn babes and must venture themselves through the darkness and see what they found.

Crawling, then, which would help prevent injury, and also keep them well off the stage where he sat listening. They listened keenly also, as, both inhibited by the darkness and disinhibited by it, by the concealment it gave, they ventured to venture. A spreading aural disturbance of shifting and rustling. The room was not large; immediately, bodies encountered each other and startled away. He heard this, or presumed it. "Is that some other creature with me, in the darkness?" he whispered, ventriloquizing their apprehension. "What does it have—what do *I* have? Four limbs that carry me forward, and back. Skin that can sense cold and hot. Rough and smooth. What is *it*. What am *I*. What are *we*."

In addition to crawling, then: touching. Not tolerated but encouraged. Maybe even required.

David was surprised to find how much he could identify by smell, a sense to which he never gave thought; now he found it assailed him with information. Like a bloodhound or Indian scout, he assessed and avoided. The five guys apart from him, starting with William, superficially his most obvious rival but no rival at all. William gave off a deodorant scent, manly and industrial, like an excess of laundry detergent. William was handsome, blond, slender, graceful, could dance, possessed some sort of race memory of the conventions of courteousness like how to put a girl's coat on, hand her out of a car, hold a door open for her, that William's rigid crazy mother could never have taught him as she was absent from his house for twenty hours at a stretch working two full-time jobs and in the time she was home, locked herself in her bedroom and refused to help her children, William and his two sisters, with meals or housekeeping let alone finer things like their homework; these were such things as one learned about one's fellow fourteen-year-old classmates, within just a few weeks, if a Theatre student at CAPA. William was the heartthrob of Christian Julietta, fat Pammie, Taniqua who could dance, and her adjuncts Chantal and Angie, who screamed with pleasure when William swung and dipped Taniqua, when he spun her like a top across the room. For his part William exhibited no desire except to tango with Taniqua; his energy had no sexual heat like his sweat had no smell. David steered clear of William, not even brushing his heel. Next was Norbert: oily scent of his pimples. Colin: scalp scent of his ludicrous clownfro of hair. Ellery, in whom oil-scent and scalp-scent combined in a way that was palatable, almost appealing. Finally Manuel, as the forms said "Hispanic," of which there were almost no others at CAPA despite the apparent vast numbers of them in the city. Perhaps that explained Manuel's presence, perhaps he was some sort of token required for the school to get funding. Stiff, silent, with no discernible talent, a heavy accent about which he was clearly self-conscious. Friendless, even in this hothouse of oft-elicited, eagerly yielded intimacies. Manuel's scent, the dust-steeped unwashed scent of his artificial-sheep's-wool-lined corduroy jacket.

David was on the move now, crawling quickly, deftly, ignoring the shufflings and scufflings and intakes of breath. A knot of whispers and perfumey hair products: Chantal and Taniqua and Angie. As he passed, one of them grabbed his ass, but he didn't slow down.

25

(Patti Kim, 1970—)
帕蒂·金

作者简介

帕蒂·金（Patti Kim, 1970—），美国韩裔作家，戴安娜·克莱弗（Diane Cleaver）研究员。她出生于韩国釜山，四岁时随家人移民美国，从小就显示出对于创作的极大热情与缜密的观察力。金在马里兰大学（University of Maryland）学习创意写作，于1992年与1995年分别获得英语学士学位与艺术硕士学位。她在本科时崭露头角，获得杰出青年校友奖（Outstanding Young Alumnus Award），并在硕士期间着手创作《"可靠的"的士》（*A Cab Called Reliable*, 1998），小说的部分章节曾在本科生文学杂志《一号路线》（*Route One*）上发表。作为一名年轻的美国韩裔移民，金善于观察并敏锐捕捉周围环境的多元文化因素以及这些差异带来的影响。她的小说围绕家庭关系、文化适应、同理心建构和身份找寻等主题，用诚恳而又不失幽默的风格讲述复杂的故事。

除了处女作《"可靠的"的士》，金还出版了儿童画册《我在这里》（*Here I Am*, 2013）和针对青少年读者群的小说《我是欧克》（*I'm Ok*, 2018）、《米奇你这样的女孩》（*It's Girls Like You, Mickey*, 2020），荣获亚裔/太平洋美国文学奖、国家家庭教育出版金奖（National Parenting Publications Award）、陶森大学文学奖（Towson University Prize for Literature）以及威尔艾斯纳漫画产业奖（Will Eisner Comic Industry Award）提名、每月读书会斯蒂芬·克莱恩奖（Stephen Crane Award for First Fiction）提名等。

《"可靠的"的士》塑造了一位试图跨越现实与理想鸿沟的年轻女性形象。主人公安珠（Ahn Joo）七岁时随家人移民弗吉尼亚，两年后一辆标着"可靠"字样的出租车接走了母亲与弟弟。面对残破的家庭与暴躁的父亲，她从创作中获得慰藉与力量。第一段选文摘自《"可靠的"的士》结尾，讲述了成年的主人公无意发现了自己身世的秘密，最终决定挣脱家庭束缚重构自己的精神家园，此部分的回忆具有意识流特点，语言朴实却直击人心、催人泪下。

《米奇你这样的女孩》是《我是欧克》的姊妹篇，围绕着白人女孩米奇（Mickey）与韩国移民孙珠文（Sun Joo Moon）的友谊展开。第二段选文摘自《米奇你这样的女孩》第七章。金凭借敏锐的洞察力与细腻的心思，巧妙捕捉并刻画出主人公对朋友的渴望与珍惜；选文语言幽默，充满真情实感，使读者重返纯真美好的校园时光。

作品选读（一）

A Cab Called Reliable

(excerpt)
By Patti Kim

Weeping into his pillow, my father begged me not to leave him. He said none of it was his fault. The doctors said she couldn't have any children, and then Min Joo came along, my crying Min Joo; he said he wanted to see his son, his own flesh and blood.

That night, I returned to my room, stuffed my mouth with a corner of my blanket, and wept because my father, in his stupor, had confessed that the mother who had left me, and whom I had waited and longed for, was not mine.

You liked anchovy soup, so I stunk up my hair and the house to cook it for you. You wanted eel, I almost burned down the house smoking it for you. You liked live squid, so I fought with its tentacles to dump them in the kimch't for you. I cut them up, dumped them in the stinging red sauce, and they were still moving. You wanted to listen to old Korean songs, so I bought a tape of "Barley Field," "When We Depart," "The Waiting Heart," and "The Wild Chrysanthemum" at Korean Korner for you. For weeks I heard, "Above the sky a thousand feet high, there are some wild geese crying," "Where, along the endless road are you going away from me like a cloud? like a cloud? like a cloud?"

"Lonesome with the thoughts of my old days." I had to eat my corn flakes with crying geese and rivers that flowed with the blood of twenty lovers. You wanted to read a story about rabbits, so I borrowed *The Tales of Peter Rabbit* for you. You liked cowboy movies, so I bought John Wayne videos for you. You liked to garden, so I stole Mrs. Lee's perilla seeds for you. Your help quit on you, so I skipped two weeks' worth of classes to fry shrimp, steam cabbage, boil col-lard greens, and bake biscuits for you. You liked Angela's mother, so I drove to her store in Southeast D.C. to set up a dinner date for you. You thought you were losing your hearing, so I laid your head on my thigh and removed the wax out of your ears for you.

You sat on the couch. Your feet rested on top of the table. Your gray eyebrows fell over your drooping lids. On top of your heaving stomach, your hands were folded, and the remote control was balanced on your left thigh. You flipped through the channels when I told you I had grilled the croaker and that my car was up to 9,000 miles. You flipped through the channels when I asked you to show me how to change my oil. Without turning your head to look at me, you said that I had to get under the car, that I would crush my head, that I would die. Too dangerous. You told me to get it done and that it was cheap, as you handed me a twenty-dollar bill from your shorts pocket and walked to the kitchen table to eat your grilled croaker. But it was a Sunday evening. Everything was closed on Sunday evenings, and I could already hear the knocking.

"I can hear the knocking."

You broke off the tail end of the croaker and bit into it, leaving the fin between your thumb and middle finger. You chewed the bones and spit them out. "Knocking? That's something else. Not oil problem."

"Anyway, I need to know how to change my oil."

You sunk your spoon into the rice. "You write anything?"

I lied to you and told you I had written two stories.

"That's it? When you write something big? Write something big for me."

"I am not going to write something big for you. That's impossible."

"What about?"

"What about what?"

"Your stories." Your chopsticks poked the middle of the croaker. The skin sHd off. You'll save the skin for last, right after you've slurped its brains out, after you've sucked its eyes out. Makes you smarter. Makes you see good.

"One's about that woman you told me about. You know, the one who lived on Hae

Un Dae Beach with her daughter. And the daughter always wore that black-and-white knit dress with the snowflake patterns?"

"What about them?"

"Well, the daughter grows up and finds a job at a bakery and leaves her mother on the beach."

"That's not true."

"I know. I'm still working on it."

You looked at me, but I stared at the thin layer of grease floating on top of your water. You wanted to call me a liar, but instead you asked, "What about other?"

"It's about your friend who had the two wives. The first one was a little crazy, so he brought in the good-looking second one who sold cosmetics?"

"What about them?"

"The crazy one ends up jumping out of their apartment window on the eleventh floor."

"Didn't happen like that. But sounds good. Second one sell better than first one. Dying at end is good."

"Just show me how to change my oil."

"The first story, that kind don't sell. You need violence. America likes violence." You spit out your bones. "Like this story. I know. Robber breaks into doctor's house with gun. 'Give me your watch, jewelry, money. Give me everything.' Doctor's not home. but doctor daughter's home. She gives him fake diamond ring, fake ruby ring, fake everything. Robber's happy and goes. Robber tries to make money, sees everything's fake and gets mad and goes back to doctor's house, kidnaps doctor's daughter, and puts tattoo snakes on all over her body. So no one marry her because of tattoos."

"People with tattoos get married."

"Not all over body. Korean man don't like tattoos."

"Then they shouldn't get tattoos."

"Man don't get tattoo. Girl gets tattoo because robber puts on her."

"And he thought she would never get married because of the tattoos?"

"Oh yeah. That's true story." The spinach in your teeth moved.

"Here, you've got spinach in your teeth." You waved your hand at the toothpick and dislodged the spinach with your tongue.

"You buy part and oil?"

"Bought part and oil." You pushed yourself away from the table. "Fry croaker next time. Not enough beans in rice. And you boil spinach too long. Too long. Nothing to chew."

I followed you outside to the driveway with my oil filter and bottles of oil.

The crickets started making their noise, and you told me to turn on the porch light. I turned on the porch light. You told me to turn on the driveway light. I turned on the driveway light. The moths and gnats flew in circles above your flat top azalea shrubs like they wanted to drill holes in the air.

You told me to get the lightbulb with the hook and the long extension cord on it. From basement, not back there. From basement. You hung it on the hood of my car. You told me to get, you know, car has to go up. The red metal things where the car goes up. And brown carpet in garage. Rags in shed. Bucket behind shed. Not that bucket, stupid.

Flat bucket to go under car.

"There is no flat bucket behind the shed."

"What's this?"

"It's a triangular basin. It's not a bucket. Buckets are cylinders and have handles on them."

You threw the bucket under the deck, slapped your right calf, and mumbled something about hell and the mosquitos that surrounded you.

You stood in front of my car. The armholes of your tank top were stretched out showing your chest. Your plaid shorts hung underneath your round hard belly, and your socks were pulled to your knees. You waved the four fingers of your right hand to come. Come. Come. Stop. Your head jerked back, and your chin formed another fold of skin, as you burped. Tasting the croaker again, you licked your lips and swallowed. The crickets screamed from your garden. The streetlights came on, and the mosquitos gathered underneath their light. Slowly, you kneeled and pushed yourself with your slippered feet underneath my car.

Your back rested on the piece of the brown carpet that used to cover the family room, wall to wall. One inch padding underneath. Every step, our feet used to sink in, and our toes would grip the standing fibers. You used to yell, "Take off shoes! Take off shoes!" at my friends, and they would run across the carpet with embarrassment, cheeks turning pink, and leave their shoes at the front door.

The lilac bush collared the driveway light, making it look like a groomed poodle standing still in an angle of your triangular garden. In front of the light, a rock with the glowing "3309" in white paint. The left side was lined with azalea bushes like four green basketballs growing out of white pebbles. The right side was lined with pine trees that looked like four green miniature teepees. And the side that lined the edge of our front porch, more azalea bushes, but with flat tops like coffins. In the center of it all, the stump of the magnolia tree you chopped down because its leaves were clogging up our gutter. The Spanish moss you had planted surrounded the stump and began to climb the rotting bark.

You placed the basin underneath the spout and unscrewed the blue filter. The black oil poured out onto your fingers, then into the basin. You wiped your hand with an old sock.

"Where you drive your car? Oil is so black."

"Let me do it. I'll catch the oil."

"Don't touch anything. Your hands get dirty. Keep clean hands."

"I don't care if my hands get dirty."

"Keep clean hands."

"What do I need clean hands for?"

"Keep clean hands to write."

The oil dripped into the basin. Standing up and wiping your hands on the sock, you told me about Miryang. Miryang. Miryang. Miryang. I know. That was the village you grew up in and in that village was a bridge you had to cross to get to school in your bare feet even during the winter because your father bought you only one pair of shoes on New Year's Day, which you stuffed in your pocket so that the soles wouldn't wear out. And when the soles wore out, you nailed wood to the bottom of your shoes, but the wood gave you splinters, so you poured soil in your shoes; it felt just like walking in a fertilized field.

I know about the tree that stood next to the well. The tree that you climbed and napped on. The tree from which you saw the well holding the floating village virgin. The tree under which the village grandmothers peeled potatoes. You've already told me about the man with three teeth and eight and a half fingers who ran the village grocery. Who would get so drunk by early afternoon that he'd give you a bottle of soju rather than the bottle of vinegar your mother was waiting for at home. I've already seen the soybean woman rolling her cart along the dirt road through the village. The chestnut woman who strung her roasted nuts on strands of her own hair. The cows bumping into each other within the fence. The stink of manure in your mother's garden. The stink of sewage when it rained. The rice-grinding factory where you met your mother-in-law. You've already told me about the girl with no eyes marrying the man with no ears. About hiding from your father when school tuition day came around because he'd make you work in the field. Yes, I can hear him yelling, "What good is school? What good is school? Go work in the field." I know about how he broke your watch on your wedding day trying to strike you across the face. It was your engagement watch from Mother. You didn't know then, did you? That she would leave us. Why don't you tell me the truth? Is she my mother or isn't she? How else could she have so easily left me? Why don't you just tell me the truth? I already know about your brother reading books by candlelight underneath a quilt that caught on fire. You don't have to tell me about your sister who was knuckled by your mother so often that she had a dent on the right side of her head and lost her mind and is now steaming rice and boiling potato roots for Buddhist monks. Don't you think I remember the apples, eggs, chestnuts, persimmons you stole and hid in the hole you dug and lined with rocks next to the village manure pile? You don't have to start singing about trying to forget, trying to forget. About walking to the sea sands from day to day. About how summer has gone; fall has gone; now the cold winter in the sea. Abba, I know the women divers searching for clams have disappeared. Stop it. Stop singing about trying to forget, trying to forget by walking to the sea sands from day to day.

You closed my hood, and I drove my car down. You picked weeds out of your garden while I put everything back in its place. You waited for me. When I walked to the door, you followed me in, saying, "Joo-yah, remember when you sing Bbo gook hho gook hho seh?"

"Abba, I don't remember that song."

"You remember."

"I don't."

"Bbo gook bbo gook bbo gook seh..."

"Abba, I told you I don't remember. Stop it." You saw me roll my eyes. Your shoulders jerked back. Three folds of skin formed on your chin. You removed your gray hat and scratched your bald head. Your belly grew as you took your breath.

When I walked upstairs, I heard you say, "No matter how bad my father treat me, I never talk like that. Never walk away like that."

作品选读（二）

It's Girls Like You, Mickey

(excerpt)
By Patti Kim

First thing in the morning, I go to my locker and find me a surprise. It's a note. A rainbow envelope with my name on it. In Korean. A box and a stick next to a backward *F* and a stick. This makes me hop like a bunny, smile so big, and feel so happy, I nearly hug Kevin McDaniel, who's trying to open his locker next to me.

"Look what I got," I say, waving the envelope at him.

He don't even look up, but I don't care. I open the note. On matching rainbow paper, it says:

Dear Mickey,

Thank you for helping me. You are my good friend. Here is the present for you. Can you come to my home? We have the harvest celebration. It is so fun. My family say you can come. Please come if you like to.

Your friend,
Sun Joo

Folded inside the note, there's something bumpy wrapped in tissue paper. I'm so excited. No one's ever done nothing special like this for me. I open the present, and there it is. I gasp. It's a matching rainbow friendship bracelet, same as the one that Sun Joo has on. It's so pretty. The colors beam so bright, it's glowing up the entire hallway.

My eyes tear up, and you know how I feel about crying at school. I put the bracelet on my wrist, but I can't tie it by myself. I look around to see if anyone might help me. At the end of the hall around the corner, I see Sun Joo's little head peeping out. I wave to her. *Come here. Come here.*

She weaves her way through the hall, trying not to bump into anyone. Once she's close enough, I grab and pull her over to my locker. I hug and lift her up, shaking her.

She feels light and flimsy like a rag doll. Her legs swing back and forth like the tail of a My Little Pony.

"Thank you so much," I say, putting her down. "This is so special to me. I'm going to treasure this so much for the rest of my life. This feels better than biting into a warm apple pie with a scoop of vanilla ice cream. You really made my day, Sun Joo."

"Okay," she says, clapping and bobbing.

"Here. Tie it for me," I say, holding out my wrist.

She double knots it nice and tight. I close my locker. We head down the hall together side by side. I bump her. She rubs her shoulder and says, "Owwww. That hurt."

"It did not," I say.

She smiles and bumps me back, to which I throw myself against the wall and say, "Owwwwww!"

She laughs. I love making her laugh. I keep remembering how sad she was under those stairs all by herself, and look at her now. I put my arm around Sun Joo and ask her about this harvest celebration at her place.

"It's the Chuseok."

"The chew what?"

"Chuseok."

"You mean like chew, as in 'chew the fat,' and suck, as in 'suck it up'?"

"Huh?"

"Chew the fat? You never heard of that? It means gabbing. You know, like talking on and on and on, blah, blah, blah, sit around and chitchat, yappity-yap, shoot the breeze."

"Like you do?"

"Ha-ha. Yeah, like I do. And suck it up means, like, 'stop belly aching and stop whining like a baby and keep on trucking,'" I say.

"That make sense. I like it," she says.

"'Chuseok' is easy to remember. So Chuseok's like a party? Is there going to be games and dancing and all that fun stuff? What do you do there?"

"You can just come. Is fun. You eat food, and you meet everyone, and you chew the fat," she says.

"That's my girl," I say, and give her a high five.

"So you come?"

"I'd love to. It's my honor. Wouldn't miss it for all the tea in China, and don't go telling me you ain't Chinese 'cause I know you ain't. I know you're from Korea, from

South Korea, not the North, which is run by a dictator who's starving people to death. I know my Koreas."

"Mickey?"

"Yeah?"

"Shhh."

26
(Chris McKinney, 1973—)
克里斯·麦金尼

作者简介

克里斯·麦金尼(Chris McKinney, 1973—),美国韩裔作家,出生于美国夏威夷首府檀香山,在卡哈卢(Kahalu'u)长大,母亲来自韩国,父亲来自夏威夷。麦金尼就读于夏威夷中太平洋学院(Mid-Pacific Institute),在夏威夷大学马诺阿分校(University of Hawaii at Manoa)先后获得英语学士、硕士学位。他曾是夏威夷大学马诺阿分校的杰出访问作家,目前在檀香山社区学院(Honolulu Community College)教授语言艺术。

麦金尼的小说多以夏威夷为背景,关注弱势群体在社会风云变化之中的困境。其代表作包括《刺青》(*The Tattoo*, 1999)、《泪女王》(*The Queen of Tears*, 2001)、《波洛黑德街》(*Bolohead Row*, 2005)、《午夜,水城》(*Midnight, Water City*, 2021)以及剧本《破乐园》(*Paradise Broken*, 2011)。

《刺青》荣获夏威夷图书出版商协会颁发的优秀文学奖和优秀文学创作奖一等奖(first place awards for Excellence in Literature and Excellence in Writing Literature)。第一段选文摘自《刺青》第三章。小说主人公肯·秀吉(Ken Hideyoshi)从小缺乏父母的关爱,在十几岁时误入歧途加入黑社会,沉溺于灯红酒绿,克劳迪娅·蔡(Claudia Choy)的出现给他颓废的生活带来一束光。通过两人关于克劳迪娅母亲的交谈,读者得以了解这位有权有势、看似风光的韩国女士所经历的悲惨过往,并进而理解战争给个体带来的不可磨灭的创伤。

《午夜,水城》是麦金尼的最新小说,被《出版者周刊》(*Publisher's Weekly*)评为"2021最佳谜团"(Best Mystery of 2021),并被犯罪阅读网站(CrimeReads)

评为"2021最佳推理谜团"(Best Speculative Mystery of 2021)。这部神秘科幻悬疑小说的场景设置在22世纪的水下城市，书中关于未来世界的构想新奇而独特，对于科技发展的剖析鞭辟入里，极具讽刺意味。第二段选文摘自《午夜，水城》第一章：科学家阿基拉木村（Akira Kimura）曾以一己之力避免了地球与小行星的毁灭性撞击，被奉为人类的功臣，但却离奇死在家中。叙述者阴差阳错卷入这场凶杀案，开启了探寻真相之旅。

作品选读（一）

The Tattoo

Chapter 3

(excerpt)

By Chris McKinney

I told her that her mother, despite her flaws, was a great, tough lady. She was someone I respected. She told me about her mother, things I didn't know, like how her mother's mother was forced into the role of comfort woman for the Japanese soldiers during the occupation before the end of WWII. Raped by hundreds of soldiers. Though she never said it, Mama-san was probably half Japanese. Claude told me how as this woman's daughter, her mother kind of became the same thing. Except Americans replaced the Japanese. After her youth was swallowed by the appetites of young men, she'd fled from Korea poor, pregnant, and disgraced. She was raped by an American soldier when she lived in a brothel by the thirty-eighth parallel. Though most called her "whore," she, like her mother, was more of a slave.

Claude told me that she, too, respected her mother greatly, how sometimes when she thought about her mother's past, she was in awe. But then she told me how she thought her mother let the ugliness of her past rule her. How money became her god, how she'd do anything to get it. She couldn't believe that after all her mother had seen, knowing where she came from, she exploited women whose situations were similar to hers when she was young.

When we were lying together in bed one night, Claude spoke over the hum of the air conditioner. "These women from Korea and Vietnam, these women who my mother employs as hostesses, masseuses, and strippers, they need the money and will get it any way possible, even whore themselves. My mother knows the lifestyle sucks, and yet she perpetuates it for her own profit. I don't get it."

"Hey," I said, "another thing I don't get is why is it that it's mostly Koreans and Vietnamese who are in these businesses?"

'You don't know? What were the last two major wars the U.S. fought in?"

"Korea and Vietnam?"

"The natives were trained. These were the businesses they ran for the soldiers during the war. So some of them, when they came here afterwards, knew it was a money-maker and just continued doing it."

"That makes sense," I said. "I guess Koreans get a bad rap for it, you know, peddling sin and all."

"I know, it pisses me off. Koreans get a bad rap for a bunch of stuff. You notice every bad driver in Hawai'i is a Korean lady? Every little grocery store, the ones that sell porno behind the counter, is owned by a Korean. A bar on Ke'eaumoku or Kapi'olani isn't called a 'bar,' it's called a 'Korean bar.'. All of us aren't bad-driving bar and grocery store owners. But people like my mother perpetuate it."

I sighed. "But like you said, maybe it's all she knows."

"I totally respect my mother and I understand why she is how she is, but sometimes I hate her for trying to push her obsessions on me. For her, life is all status. Mercedes and Gucci. Shit. I was almost named Mercedes. She wanted me to go to a 'name' school, get a 'name' job, and marry a 'name' kind of guy. When I was a kid, she was an absolute tyrant. Watched over me like a hawk or something, making sure I was doing all my homework. Sending me to Punahou with the rich kids. Didn't let me go out on weekends. She saw no present for me, she just wanted me to see the future. What is the future, anyway? It's just something that's going to happen no matter what we do."

I looked at her and smiled. "It must be hard, though. To do what she doesn't want you to do considering she's done so much for you."

She pulled the covers closer to her neck. "That's the worst part about it. Sometimes when she's on me about something I can practically see the love and hope pouring out of her. She loves me so much sometimes I hate her for it. It makes me feel guilty and ungrateful."

I touched her face. "So what do you do?"

"I used to fold all the time. When she was unhappy with something I was doing, I'd correct it, no questions asked. But then after a while I got worn down. I used to look in the mirror and not see much, you know. I'd see me, but I couldn't see anything inside. I felt like this non-person, destined to be a doctor and to marry one, destined to have kids, destined to die a grandma. My future lacked imagination. It lacked substance. That's when I found the ocean. I started to surf. I told her I was going to college here at UH. It was a horrible scene. I told her the day she got my acceptance letter from Stanford. That's another thing about her, she always used to open my mail. Sometimes I wanted to report her to the feds."

"What happened?"

"She threw a fit. She even threatened to disown me, can you imagine that? But she calmed down after giving me the silent treatment for a few days. For me, for her too maybe, those were the most horrible few days. I felt so guilty. I'd lie up at night just imagining my mother working in that brothel in Korea, fucking GIs left and right. About her crammed in some boat being shipped illegally to Hawai'i. Can you imagine? She didn't even come here by boat. Her uncle sent her money for a ticket and she flew over. But there I was, imagining her pregnant in some barge, stuffed in a room with a hundred other Koreans, standing in puddles of piss, shit, and vomit. When she finally talked to me, I think she asked if I was hungry or something. I just burst into tears. She hugged me and called me a silly girl. She's still pissed that I didn't go to Stanford, but she accepted that I stayed."

"So what about when you told her you were majoring in Art History?"

She laughed. "That one wasn't as bad. She just called me 'pabo,' you know, 'stupid' in Korean, and it kind of blew over. I think someone told her I could become a professor in the field and it cheered her up. It's like she figured there was a chance for me to become a doctor yet. She told me intellectuals are greatly respected in South Korea and it would be just fine with her if I got my doctorate and became a professor. Can you imagine? A PhD was like the last thing on my mind."

"Pabo, ah. She was calling me stupid all these years and I didn't even know it."

We laughed together. "So what about it?" I asked her. "Are you going for a PhD?"

"I don't know. Maybe. I'd have to go to the mainland for it, though. I mean, if I wanted to teach here. UH doesn't hire UH students."

作品选读（二）

Midnight, Water City

Chapter 1
(excerpt)
By Chris McKinney

Forty years ago, in the year 2102, the asteroid Sessho-seki hurled toward Earth at nineteen miles per second. Only one person could spot it: Akira Kimura. Scientist, savior, hero of the goddamn human race. She did so with the largest telescope ever built, atop the tallest mountain on Earth, to map its trajectory and engineer a weapon to counter it: Ascalon, the cosmic ray that saved the world. It fired with so much energy that its path remains visible, a permanent slash across the sky. People call it Ascalon's Scar.

One in every four girls born in the last decade is named Ascalon, including my youngest daughter, who's nearing eighteen months. Irritating, but my wife insisted. At least the name's popularity is down from one in two, which it was after those world-saving events. I'd guess that by now, only half of the population can recall the name Sessho-seki—The Killing Rock—but everybody remembers Ascalon. Probably doesn't help that Akira gave the asteroid a Japanese name. But being Japanese is coming to mean less and less anyway. Being white, Black, Latino, too.

177 atmospheres below sea level in Volcano Vista, the world's largest seascraper, is where I'm heading. That used to be the crush depth of a super-sub, but we beat crush depth like we beat global warming, Sessho-seki, and sixty being old. I'm eighty now, finally the right age to collect Social Security, but I'll need to grind away another five to ten years. I'm on my fourth marriage and quite a few kids, but Ascalon is the most like me—can't sit still, never sleeps, loves to walk backward. It's probably deluded and egomaniacal to *like* that she takes after me. I'm basically old enough to be her ancestor.

The older I get, the more I care about numbers. I think about them too damn much, which is funny because I'm getting worse at running calculations in my head. At least my iE can do that for me.

The elevator opens, and a boy, maybe sixteen and completely tat-dyed blue, steps out. He's got the indifferent swagger of a teenager and androgynous pink hair draped over the right half of his face. He's trying hard to look like a cartoon. Maybe that's all we ever wanted from the beginning, to look like cartoons. Well, we're certainly succeeding. We all wear the same snug, temp-controlled foam fits spun from synthetic yarn coated with conductive metal. It's like an old-school wetsuit, except it's got a scaly metallic sheen to it that can change pattern and color. Some people, like my wife, like to wear a thin overcoat over theirs. Kids nowadays, they like to retract the sleeves and midriffs, while us older folk constrict it to take advantage of its girdling abilities. Either way, adjust the temp with your iE, and you're good to go for rain, shine, or a frolic in the ocean. This boy, he's wearing one, too, of course. He scratches his mechanical blue tail with an unusually long pinky finger as he walks past me, diving into his uncanny valley, a synthetic form of natural reality that looks plain creepy. Maybe fake tails, like the slang "hemo" and "semi," are in with the kids now? Who knows or even wants to. A weary-looking couple steps into the elevator with me, the woman fighting to re-convert her umbrella-style skirt back into a stiff, conical one. The skirt's clearly winning, and I get it. As the door closes, I look in its mirrored surface at my own reflection. I'm fighting age so hard, I look like a ventriloquist's doll.

This couple has the look of twelve-volt-intellect renters who could never really afford this place. Working their hardest the last decade but not breaking even. They get off at atmosphere five, and I'm alone in the gorilla-glass tube as I continue down. I look out onto a Volcano Vista feed observation platform. A cloud of plankton, freshly released. A school of fish swoops in, mouths wide open, constantly moving, constantly feeding. Then marlin and sharks come for the small fish to keep the food chain spectacle going. Down deeper still, darkness. The sprinkle of marine snow. Bioluminescent jellyfish and creatures that drip instead of swim. I find myself half-wishing the glass would web and shatter, killing this old man by drowning or water pressure imploding my skull. I feel like I'm drowning anyway, and everyone around me is trying to throw me anchors.

This building I'm descending is in essence a buoy, and the life drawn to it gets weirder and weirder-looking as I go. At atmosphere ninety-nine, a vampire squid with glowing blue eyes swims by slowly. Always slowly—the absence of heat and light from the sun forces them to conserve energy. This species is older than dinosaurs. The creature turns itself inside out. Something must be coming for it. Ah, no, it's just spooked by the giant cubes of trash being parachuted up by massive, billowing mechanical jellyfish. Now we're getting close to where The Money lives. The deeper you go, the more primo the real estate.

At 177 atmospheres, the bottom of the ocean, the elevator slows to a stop. Outside are black volcanic chimneys, one source of our geothermal energy. Zombie worms also live out there, grinding whale bones to dust. I spot the hull of a passenger jet from that day, decades ago, that the Great Sun Storm knocked all the planes out of the sky. Oh, and a cannonball from an old pirate ship—there's no way that's the same one I dropped from above the surface all those years ago?

27

(Young Jean Lee, 1974—)
扬·吉恩·李

作者简介

扬·吉恩·李（Young Jean Lee，1974— ），美国韩裔剧作家、导演、电影制作人，出生于韩国大丘（Deagu），两岁时移居美国，在华盛顿州普尔曼（Pullman）长大。她本科毕业于加州大学伯克利分校英语专业，并于布鲁克林学院（Brooklyn College）获得艺术硕士学位。在担任扬·吉恩·李剧院公司的艺术总监期间，她创作并指导了十场演出，并在世界近四十个城市巡回表演。她目前在斯坦福大学教授戏剧和表演课程。

扬·吉恩·李的第一部电影短片《女孩们来了》（Here Come the Girls）在洛迦诺国际电影节（Locarno International Film Festival）进行了全球首映，其戏剧《飞天龙之歌》（Songs of the Dragons Flying to Heaven，2006）、《教堂》（Church，2007）、《吸引》（Appeal，2009）、《装船》（Shipment，2009）、《李尔王》（Lear，2010）、《无题的女性主义者舞台剧》（Untitled Feminist Show，2011）、《异性恋白人男性》（Straight White Men，2014）等曾在纽约公共剧院（The Public Theater）、巴里什尼科夫艺术中心（Baryshnikov Arts Center）等多地放映。2018年，《异性恋白人男性》在海丝剧院（Hayes Theatre）上映，她由此成为第一位在百老汇上演戏剧的美国亚裔女性。她曾获古根海姆奖学金、美国戏剧奥比奖（Obie Awards）、多丽丝·杜克表演艺术家奖（Doris Duke Performing Artist Award）、苏黎世艺术节奖（ZKB Patronage Prize）、美国国家艺术基金会奖金、当代艺术资助基金（Foundation for Contemporary Arts Grants to Artists）等多项荣誉，并于2016年获得笔会和劳拉佩尔斯戏剧奖（PEN/Laura Pels Theater Award），于2019年获

得温德姆·坎贝尔文学奖（Windham-Campbell Literature Prize in Drama）。

　　选读部分摘自《装船》与《李尔王》，两部戏剧是扬·吉恩·李的代表作，分别于2009年和2010年在纽约首演。《装船》采用全黑人的演员阵容，通过舞蹈、歌曲、单口喜剧、滑稽小品等形式，展示了黑人演员们长久以来被强加的刻板印象，通过融合常规娱乐形式和荒诞怪异行为使观众产生陌生感。比如，演员们身着不合身的娃娃衣服，并用小布条固定，这让观众一时不知作何反应，并对此保持警惕。《李尔王》吸纳了莎士比亚同名悲剧的相关情节，并增加了荒诞离奇的后现代元素，着眼于子辈在驱逐谋害父亲后的灵魂挣扎。

作品选读（一）

Shipment

(excerpt)
By Young Jean Lee

Author's Note

　　The show is divided into two parts. The first half is structured like a minstrel show—dance, stand-up routine, sketches, and a song—and I wrote it to address the stereotypes my cast members felt they had to deal with as black performers. Our goal was to walk the line between stock forms of black entertainment and some unidentifiable weirdness to the point where the audience wasn't sure what they were watching or how they were supposed to respond. The performers wore stereotypes like ill-fitting paper-doll outfits held on by two tabs, which denied the audience easy responses (illicit pleasure or self-righteous indignation) to racial clichés and created a kind of uncomfortable, paranoid watchfulness in everyone. The second half of the show is a relatively straight naturalistic comedy. I asked the actors to come up with roles they'd always wanted to play and wrote the second half of the show in response to their requests.

A bare stage. Stark lights. Ominous white noise in the background.
　　Sudden lights down.

Sound of footsteps.

Sound of shoes clattering against the floor as Dancer 1 begins his dance in the dark. A rock song—Semisonic's "F.N.T."—begins.

Lights up on Dancer 1 mid-jump, his arms and legs sprawling. He is wearing a black tuxedo with a white shirt, black suspenders, black cummerbund, and black bow tie.

Dancer 1 performs a series of bordering-on-goofy choreographed moves that are unidentifiable in genre. Occasionally we'll see a flash of possible minstrel reference—a gesture, a bit of footwork. Sometimes Dancer 1 is smiling, sometimes not. It's difficult to tell what his relationship is to what he's doing and to the audience.

Dancer 2 enters and watches Dancer 1, looking bemused. He is wearing a black suit, white shirt, flowered vest, red tie, black flower lapel brooch, and white shoes.

He starts to shake violently, still smiling. The two Dancers take turns doing herky-jerky movements and then flail wildly back and forth across the stage, sometimes syncing up to flail in unison. It's reminiscent of a tap routine, except that neither of them has any coordination and they look as if they are about to fall.

They break out of the flailing and walk in a square pattern around the perimeter of the stage, stopping downstage to stare at the audience. Then they move upstage to do a partner dance that involves Dancer 2 shaking violently in place while Dancer 1 twirls around him, grabbing hold of Dancer 2's stiff, jerking hands as he dips and spins.

For the big finish, both Dancers take turns doing fancy spins with their arms out. Dancer 1 breaks the pattern to do a goofy little jump. Dancer 2 does an even goofier move. Dancer 1 runs up to the back wall and touches it with his butt. Dancer 2 follows suit. Both Dancers push themselves off the back wall and collapse onto the floor downstage, standing up crookedly to do a little half-smiling hat-tip to the audience before walking offstage.

"F.N.T." lyrics:

Fascinating new thing
You delight me
And I know you're speaking of me

Fascinating new thing
Get beside me,
I want you to love me

I'm surprised that you've never been told before
That you're lovely and you're perfect
And that somebody wants you

Fascinating new thing
The scene makin'
Want a temporary savior

Fascinating new thing
Don't betray them
By becoming familiar

I'm surprised that you've never been told before
That you're lovely and you're perfect
And that somebody wants you

I'm surprised that you've never been told before
That you're priceless and you're precious
Even when you are not new.

I'm surprised that you've never been told before
That you're lovely and you're perfect
And that somebody wants you

I'm surprised that you've never been told before
That you're priceless
Yeah, you're holy
Even when you are not new

Fascinating new thing (fascinating new thing)
Fascinating new thing (fascinating new thing)
Fascinating new thing (fascinating new thing)
Fascinating new thing (fascinating new thing).

作品选读（二）

Lear

(excerpt)

By Young Jean Lee

Author's Note

The following synopsis is handed out to the audience along with their programs: "A Partial and Approximately Accurate Synopsis of Shakespeare's *King Lear*"

King Lear was an old man who ruled England for many years. He had three grown daughters named Goneril, Regan and Cordelia. One day, Lear decided to retire from the burdens of ruling. He intended to divide his kingdom among all of his daughters, until he began to suspect that his youngest daughter Cordelia did not love him. Enraged, he disinherited her and sentenced her to banishment. At the time, two kings, France and Burgundy, were in Lear's court vying for Cordelia's hand. Lear tried to humiliate his daughter by presenting her to them, banished and without a dowry. France chose to marry her anyway and took her to France. In her absence, Regan and Goneril shared their father's lands between them. Soon they fell out with Lear. They barred him from his former castles, leaving him out in a storm, where he began to go mad.

Lear's closest advisor was another old man named Gloucester. Gloucester had two sons, Edgar and Edmund (a bastard). Gloucester tried to aid the old king behind Goneril and Regan's backs, but was exposed by Edmund. Goneril and Regan seized Gloucester, blinded him (Regan did the actual blinding), and sent him into the storm to join their father.

Our show begins roughly at this point in the story. Nothing else that happens in Shakespeare's text is necessarily relevant to what you are about to see.

Note on Casting

Goneril, Regan and Cordelia should be played by women of color.

There is a Gothic-arched proscenium with ornate bas-relief detail: rosettes, trefoils, and diamond latticework in golds and copper with scarlet accents and hints of lapis lazuli. There is also an elaborately patterned red-and-gold curtain with heavy gold fringe.

An ominous, pulsating rumbling sound plays continuously as the audience enters.

The curtain rises on Goneril and Regan in a throne room, doing a stately, measured Elizabethan court dance to consort music ("Mistresse Nichols Almand" by John Dowland). They smile with real pleasure as they dance.

The side walls of the throne room consist of mahogany panels in the shape of columns, between which are recessed panels filled with red damask. There are twin-armed candelabra sconces mounted on each column, backed by gold sun-shaped mirrors. Above the panels are diamond-pane windows made of clear, red, and yellow leaded glass. There are two benches of dark paneled wood and red upholstery downstage left and right, and two entrances, midstage left and right, through Gothic archways.

A huge gilded throne, intricately carved with winged-lion armrests and upholstered in tufted red velvet, sits on a large, two-tiered dais upstage center. The throne is flanked by two smaller, but equally baroque, red-and-gold armchairs. Red Persian rugs cover the floor and dais.

There is an arched back wall covered in Gothic tracery with ornate medallions at the intersections, all in gold woodwork on a red field covered with gold-leaf sunbursts. The tracery radiates out around the throne like a peacock or explosion.

Goneril and Regan wear sumptuous Elizabethan gowns with full skirts—Goneril in royal purple, Regan in emerald. The dresses are made of velvet, satin, and metallic jacquards with standing white lace collars, open bustlines, and gold trimmings and beltings. The women wear necklaces, pendants, rings, and bracelets, as well as elaborate wigs with bejeweled hair ornaments.

Edgar and Edmund enter and join in the dance, creating more intricate patterns. Everyone smiles and dances with real pleasure.

The men wear Elizabethan doublets and pumpkin breeches made from rich black fabrics with metallic accents in the cloth and trimmings—gold for Edgar and silver for Edmund. They have stiffly tailored ruffs and lace cuffs, elaborate chains-of-office, necklaces, rings, and lavishly trimmed capes. Ornate swords carried in scabbards hang from their belts. Edgar wears a fake mustache and goatee that he will later remove.

The dance ends with all four dancers holding hands with their bodies facing *outward, skipping in a circle. As the music ends, they break the circle to assume their positions for the following scene. Regan sits on the stage-right bench, Goneril sits on the stage-left bench, Edgar sits on the dais upstage left, and Edmund stands upstage right.*

Blackout with lit candles and loud, ominous rumbling.

Lights up. Faint consort music ("Semper Dowland semper dolens" by John Dowland) plays.

Goneril reads a book, Regan does needlepoint, and Edgar polishes his sword. Edmund is deep in tortured thought.

Pause.

Edmund makes a noise of anguish. Everyone ignores him.

Pause.

Edmund makes a louder noise of anguish and is once again ignored.

EDGAR: Edmund and I just enjoyed the most wonderful meal.

REGAN: What did you have?

EDGAR: Six different roasted meats and fowls, new potatoes, spring sausage, onion soup, and gooseberry tart with country cream.

GONERIL: Lovely.

EDGAR: The soup was covered by nearly an *inch* of baked cheese.

GONERIL: Goodness, Edgar. How did you—

EDMUND: I'm a bad person!

(Pause.)

EDGAR: Why.

EDMUND: I only care about myself.

REGAN: Everyone is selfish.

EDMUND: I betrayed my father. He's out in the storm with his eyes gouged out!

EDGAR: Our father was a traitor!

(Pause.)

EDMUND: Plus, everyone is starting to look fat to me.

EDGAR: What do you mean?

EDMUND: Everyone looks fat. Regan looks fat, you look fat. Unless someone is completely skeletal with no muscle or anything, I think they look fat.

GONERIL: That's really evil.

EDMUND: I know!

REGAN: But you're not a bad person.

EDMUND: Then who is?

REGAN: Torturers working in a torture center.

EDMUND: But what would I do if I was in that position, I'm not... I want to win, to fit the pattern... would I have taken babies by their legs and smashed them against trees? I don't know! If the torture center is getting too full and your superiors tell you to kill people off in a less expensive way... people always manage to justify doing horrible things.

EDGAR: What is wrong with you today, Edmund?

EDMUND: Nothing.

(Pause.)

I suck!

EDGAR: But you have the raw material to become something great. If only you could see your own value as I do, buried beneath your excess weight.

EDMUND: Everything sucks!

REGAN: The world is full of things, and you just fight them off. Because what are you going to do? Nothing. So you have to accept them.

EDMUND: But the pain.

EDGAR: I have to say that I believe the true answer lies in Buddhism.

REGAN: Buddhism is great.

GONERIL: I really like Buddhism, and all the psychology that comes out of that, with that influence.

EDMUND: What do you mean by Buddhism?

EDGAR: You know, like with... like you just accept everything. If something bad happens then you just accept it.

REGAN: When a thought comes into your head you just label it "thinking" and it helps.

GONERIL: And also, another thing about Buddhism is that... I don't know, I just like it.

(Pause.)

EDMUND: I'm losing my hair.

REGAN: How awful.

GONERIL: How can people stand to be bald.

REGAN: I don't know. I think most people think they look pretty good. I don't think they would leave the house otherwise.

EDGAR: I think most people have that body and face dysmorphia, you know, only in the opposite direction. Like, they think they look better than they do.

REGAN: People's bodies are just tragic.

EDGAR: Maybe some day modern technology will be able to cure that, you know?

GONERIL: Yeah, how do old people, how can they even bear to touch each other?

EDGAR: Some day modern technology is going to advance to the point where that really helps us out a lot.

GONERIL: Do you ever play that game where you're... it's called "Who Won?" and you're looking at couples on the street and you ask yourself, "Who won?"

EDGAR: That game doesn't work unless you know what the guy does for a living.

REGAN: People are such... and people have such mean personalities.

28

(Cathy Park Hong, 1976—)
卡西·朴·洪

作者简介

卡西·朴·洪（Cathy Park Hong, 1976— ），美国韩裔诗人、作家，洪在美国加州洛杉矶长大，毕业于欧柏林学院，之后于爱荷华大学作家工作坊深造，获得艺术硕士学位。目前她在罗格斯大学（Rutgers University）教授创意写作，并担任《新共和》（*The New Republic*）的诗歌编辑。

卡西·朴·洪共著有三部诗集：《翻译元音》（*Translating Mo'um*, 2002）、《跳舞跳舞革命》（*Dance Dance Revolution*, 2007）、《发动机帝国》（*Engine Empire: Poems*, 2012）以及一部自传《微妙之感：美国亚裔的清算》（*Minor Feelings: An Asian American Reckoning*, 2020）。其中，《翻译元音》荣获2002年手推车奖。《跳舞跳舞革命》混杂了英语、西班牙语、法语、韩语等多语种以及非正式俚语，打破了严格的书面语规范。在与历史学家的互动中，叙述者将她对于韩国光州革命的回忆与搬至沙漠后的生活娓娓道来。2006年，她凭借此部诗集荣获伯纳德女诗人奖（Barnard Woman Poets Prize）。此外，她曾在《公共空间》（*A Public Space*）、《巴黎评论》（*The Paris Review*）、《诗歌》（*Poetry*）等期刊上发表诗歌，还为《村声》（*The Village Voice*）、《卫报》等出版物撰写文章，广泛关注美国亚裔女性的权益与诉求，获得2018年温德姆·坎贝尔文学奖、2020年美国国家图书评论奖、古根海姆奖学金、富布赖特奖金、美国全国艺术基金会奖金、纽约艺术基金会奖金等荣誉，并被提名2021《时代》100人物（*Time 100 list*）。

《微妙之感：美国亚裔的清算》是卡西·朴·洪出版的第一本非虚构类书籍，作者将亲身经历与宏观历史结合，兼顾文化批评，揭示了美国猖獗的种族歧视行为，与2021年"停止对亚裔的仇恨"（Stop Asian Hate）运动相得益彰。《教育》（"An Education"）节选自《微妙之感：美国亚裔的清算》。叙述者与艾琳（Erin）、海伦（Helen）因为对艺术的追求而结交，她们处在边缘化移民社区，都曾面临被忽视、被失语的困境。节选部分对于家庭和友谊、艺术和政治、身份和个性等话题的阐释别具一格，具有启发意义。

作品选读

Minor Feelings: An Asian American Reckoning

An Education

(excerpt)

By Cathy Park Hong

The artist liberates the art object from the rules of mastery, then from content, then frees the art object from what Martin Heidegger calls its very *thingliness*, until it becomes enfolded into life itself. Stripped of the artwork, all we are left with is the artist's activities. The problem is that history has to recognize the artist's transgressions as "art," which is then dependent on the artist's access to power. A female artist rarely "gets away with it." A black artist rarely "gets away with it." Like the rich boarding school kid who gets away with a hit-and-run, getting away with it doesn't mean that you're lawless but that you are above the law. The bad-boy artist can do whatever he wants because of who he is. Transgressive bad-boy art is, in fact, the most risk-averse, an endless loop of warmed-over stunts for an audience of one: the banker collector.

Art movements have been built on the bromances of bad white boys. Their exploits are exhaustively catalogued: boys who were "fizzy with collaboration" and boys on "their decade-long benders" in bars that are now hallowed landmarks. From a young age, these boys speculated on their own legacy and critics eagerly bought their stock before they matured. But the importance of women is recognized belatedly. The female artist is given a retrospective postmodern. Archaeologists must unearth the crypt and announce they have discovered another underrecognized genius.

As I read about the friendships between Kelley, Shaw, and McCarthy, or de Kooning and Pollock, or Verlaine and Rimbaud, or Breton and Éluard, I craved to read about the friendships where women, and more urgently women of color, came of age as artists and writers. The last few decades have ushered in legions of feminist writers and artists, but it's still fairly uncommon to read about female friendships founded on their aesthetic principles. The deeper I dug into the annals of literary and art history, the more alone I felt. But in life, I was not alone. I realized that I had already experienced that kind of bond through my own friendships with Erin and Helen.

By chance, Erin and I ended up at Oberlin together, but we didn't become close until our second year because Erin, to my disappointment, arrived at orientation with her tattoo artist boyfriend from Long Island. When I first saw her on campus, Erin was even more baroquely goth, with new chin and septum piercings and a battalion of spiny arm tattoos. Her boyfriend was equally pierced and tattooed. He was also so white he had white dreads.

This boyfriend spent all hours of the day in their closet-sized dorm room. Because of him, I thought, Erin was antisocial, microwaving vegan curry with him in the tiny dormitory kitchen instead of eating with the rest of us at the dining hall. When she wasn't making art or studying, she slept at all hours under her black velvet blanket that looked about as snug as a dust cover. Thinking back, it's hard to reconcile that drowsy soft-spoken Erin with the loud and opinionated Erin I know now.

I thought her passivity had something to do with her boyfriend, who I suspected was controlling and probably psychotic. Maybe I was a little possessive of her too. Erin attracted that in her friends, this envy, this sense of proprietariness, especially later from Helen, but though her boyfriend was kind of a jerk, it wasn't because of him she was so narcoleptic and passive. Her boyfriend was actually the only one there for her while she grieved.

Helen said she first noticed me in our sophomore year, in a gut course called Chemistry and Crime, where the professor droned on endlessly about the O. J. Simpson trial. She observed, "You were that girl who snuck out of class to do coke every morning." This was a curious take on my habit of going to the bathroom and sitting in the stall for five minutes because I was so bored in class. I said that I didn't know she was in that class even though I did. She had long, yellowy dyed hair and wore a beige Burberry scarf, the required status accessory for all Korean international students. Her look was confused. A preppy music conservatory student trying to look arty.

I can't recall how Helen came into my and Erin's lives, only that as soon we met her, it was as if we'd known one another forever. Over the years, she began to resemble Erin, with her black wardrobe, chunky shoes, and glasses with aggressive black frames, until senior year when Helen came into her own glamorously butch look. Because her father had a career that required him to work overseas, she lived in six different countries before arriving at the Oberlin conservatory to train as a classical violinist. Then, burnt out from the pressure of performance, she transferred to the college to study religion and fine arts. She threw herself into every discipline with passion before abandoning it completely. She did this with friends and lovers, and with countries she'd lived in. Helen spoke five languages and had an ear for accents as well. After living in London, her family moved to Baltimore and Helen switched to an American accent within a week.

Nothing stuck to her. Only God and art stuck. That, and her body, which she tried to starve down to nothing. She stopped taking her lithium because it made her gain weight. One Easter week, on a cold, bright, and glittering day, she drove her father's powder-blue Lincoln around campus, pelting friends she loved with pink marshmallow Peeps and those she detested with her lithium pills.

The greatest gift my parents granted me was making it possible for me to choose my education and career, which I can't say for the kids I knew in Koreatown who felt bound to lift their parents out of debt and grueling seven-day workweeks. The wealthier Korean parents had no such excuse, ruthlessly managing the careers and marriages of their children, and as a result ruining their children's lives, all because they wanted bragging rights. I was lucky because my father too wanted to be a poet, which he never revealed to me until I began taking a poetry class at Oberlin.

My father's business did so well that by the time I was a teenager, we lived in a house with a pool in a white suburban neighborhood. From my window, I used to watch sparrows swoop down to sip a teardrop of chlorinated water before swooping back up. The move did not erase the unhappiness in our family but threw it into sharp relief because of our isolation. To unpack the source of my adolescent unhappiness would be to write about my mother, which I have struggled with in this book: How deep can I dig into myself without talking about my mother? Does an Asian American narrative *always* have to return to the mother? When I met the poet Hoa Nguyen, the first question she asked me was, "Tell me about your mother."

"Okay," I said. "That's an icebreaker."

"You have an Asian mother," she said. "She has to be interesting."

I must defer, at least for now. I'd rather write about my friendship with Asian women first. My mother would take over, breaching the walls of these essays, until it is only her. I have some scores to settle first—with this country, with how we have been scripted. I will only say that my mother was broken then, though I don't know how. When illness is unnamed, the blame for it is displaced onto the child, the way I used to feel at fault just for sitting there in the passenger seat when my mother, without warning, jerked the car into the other lane, nearly crashing into another car while threatening she was going to kill us both.

Back then, my mind was a dial tone. I hid from my mother and hid from the horrible rich kids in the high school I attended. I hid in art, and if I wasn't in the art studio at school, I willed myself invisible on the school bus that was hotboxed with the cruelty of a bully who daily reminded my friends and me that we were ugly as dogs. No matter our income, my family could not cough up the thorn embedded in our chests. That stain of violence followed us everywhere. I thought I could escape it by moving to Ohio, but it followed me there too.

Erin, Helen, and I used to go to J. R. Valentine's, a freestanding diner that always advertised a fried perch special on Tuesdays. The diner had an alpine green roof and a parking lot that collected more brown humps of snow than cars. We were invariably the only college students there, because it was a few miles outside of campus. We stayed for hours as we asked for endless refills of bad coffee or ordered odd dishes off the menu. I wish I'd had a stenographer who followed me so I had transcripts of these quotidian moments that as a whole were more lifechanging than losing your virginity or having your heart broken. Freud said, in his correspondence with Josef Breuer, that "creativity was most powerfully released in heated male colloquy." The foundation of our friendship was a heated colloquy that became absorbed into our art and poetry. When I made art alone, it was a fantasy, but shared with Erin and Helen, art became a mission.

Helen made you think like the world would end without your art. But while she lavished you with praise, it wasn't just flattery. She was also learning from you until she surpassed you. Helen was curious about poetry, so I lent her my phonebook-sized twentieth-century poetry anthology, thinking she'd boredly flip through it, and then I was annoyed when I found the book in her room with every other page dog-eared and underlined. Another time, I took her to the gym and showed her how to use the treadmill. While I jogged lightly for two miles, Helen cranked her treadmill up and sprinted as if she were running for her life. "Take it easy! You're going to be sore," I said when I was done, but Helen, drenched in sweat, wheezed on for another ten miles.

She never slept. What did she do all night when everyone was asleep? She couldn't sleep in her own bed and regularly crashed with friends. One night, a friend woke up in the middle of the night and was freaked out to find Helen in her room, sitting in a chair, smoking her menthols in the dark.

When Helen was happy, she was both childlike and maternal. In the mornings, she'd jump into bed with me and say in a childlike voice, "Let's go to breakfast." Sometimes she'd also sniff my blanket, yank it away, roll it up, and throw it in the washer. Still groggy, I'd always succumb to going to breakfast with her. Eventually, I noticed that she did this more with Erin. Wake her up. Enjoin her to come out and experience the day.

By her sophomore year, Erin was the star of the art department. Her sculptures and installations were always the most imaginative and original. Helen was still new to art and she imitated everything that Erin did at first. She used soil in her installation after Erin used soil, made artist books after Erin made artist books—but Erin never minded, finding it flattering.

Eventually, they both became indomitable forces in the art department. They were a blitzkrieg during art crit, tearing down their classmates' ugly sculptures with daunting acumen. Famous guest artists were not immune. One guest photographer presented loving photographs of his nude pregnant wife, and Erin and Helen dressed the photographer down for objectifying the female subject as a biologically determined object. The professors adored them. My classmates feared them. But they also resented them. Without caring that it was racially insensitive, everyone passive-aggressively mixed up Erin for Helen or Helen for Erin. They had a nickname: the Twins.

I once taught a poetry workshop with three female Persian students enrolled in the class. When I called out one of their names during attendance the first day, the student responded in a voice that was both embarrassed and defiant, "Yeah, hi, I'm the *other* Persian." Half the class was white but none of the other white kids felt self-conscious about the fact that there were so many of them. But I knew how she felt. I always know when there are too many people like me, because the restaurant is no longer cool, the school no longer well rounded. A space is *overrun* when there are too many Asians, and "too many" can be as few as three. With Erin and Helen, I could feel my selfhood being slurred into *them*, but Erin and Helen didn't care. They dressed to be aggressively present. They wore big clomping shoes. They wanted to be intimidating.

Erin and Helen were an invasion in the art department, previously dominated by white boys in ironic death metal bands who silkscreened posters for off-campus parties and moved to Chicago for the music scene. Art was a pose, an underachieving lifestyle. Erin and Helen, on the other hand, were unapologetically ambitious. Art had to have a stake.

Erin was influenced by land artists like Robert Smithson and yet her style was all her own in its brooding minimalism. She made earthworks, forming perfect miniature dirt cubes, marking each one with a dissection pin, and arranging them in patterns on the gallery floor. Another time, Erin dragged an old chair into the arboretum, sat on the chair, and spent the night digging a hole into the soil with her shoes. At the time, I made fun of her for that piece (That's *it*? A *hole*?), but in retrospect, I can imagine its beauty during a morning walk along the marsh, seeing, in the white fog, the golden elms surrounding a lone abandoned chair and a barely perceptible depression.

During the year between the summer I met Erin in art camp and when I saw her again at Oberlin, she experienced a family tragedy that she is still private about to this day. I had mentioned what happened to her in this book until its final edit, when Erin intervened while we were having dinner on the Lower East Side. I was telling her about a dream I had where Helen was in my life again. I was so happy to see Helen until it dawned on me that I had to tell her that I'd been writing about her.

"By the way, you're not writing about my family, are you?" Erin asked.

"I mention what happened," I said. "One sentence, that's all."

"Off limits. We discussed it."

"You said I could mention it but not to go into detail!"

"That's an optimistic interpretation."

"It was a core part of your artwork in college. I don't see how I could not talk about it at all, since I write about your artwork."

"Let me tell you something. When I was in Shanghai this summer, there were so many rules. Every time I asked permission to gain access to a site or equipment, the people in charge would say no. They didn't even know what the rules were, but they didn't want to get in trouble, so it was easier to say no to everything. I had no idea how anyone got anything done until an artist told me that China is a culture of forgiveness and not permission. You break the rule and then ask for forgiveness later."

"Are you saying that I can write about it and ask for forgiveness later?"

"No, what I'm saying is that we're not in China. You can't ask for forgiveness. I won't forgive you. Our friendship is on the line here."

"Okay. I'll take it out."

"Thank you."

"It's just—"

"What?"

"I'm taking it out—and I swear this is not a justification to keep it in—but I think it's a problem how Asians are so private about their own traumas, you know, which is why no one ever thinks we suffer any injustices. They think we're just these—robots."

"My need for privacy is not an Asian thing—it's an artist thing."

"How is it an artist thing?"

"All artists are private about their lives. They do it to protect their careers."

"That's a *huge* generalization."

"And your comment about Asians isn't? What I'm saying is true, especially if you're a female artist of color. If you reveal anything, they collapse your art with your life—and I don't want my autobiography hijacking my art. Maybe back then, my loss was a deep part of me but I have worked really hard to separate my work and my identity from that loss, and I will not be knocked back down."

"You understand that I'm not using your real name."

"Doesn't matter," Erin said.

"I guess it's a good thing I'm not friends with Helen anymore."

"That's something to think about. What if you were? What would she think? Where's the care in the essay? Why is it necessary to take from other people's lives?"

"Erin, you haven't read the essay. There's plenty of care. And it's unrealistic for me as a writer *not* to take from other people's lives. I'm not some friendless orphan. My life overlaps with the lives of others so I have no choice but to take from others, which is why writers are full of care, but also—if they're at all truthful—a bit cruel."

"As I said, our friendship's on the line."

"I'm taking it out!"

29

(Catherine Chung, 1979—)
凯瑟琳·钟

作者简介

凯瑟琳·钟（Catherine Chung, 1979— ），美国韩裔作家，出生于美国伊利诺伊州埃文斯顿（Evanston, Illinois），在纽约、新泽西（New Jersey）和密歇根（Michigan）长大。凯瑟琳·钟本科期间在芝加哥大学（The University of Chicago）学习数学，这一经历对其文学创作影响颇深。此外，她还在美国兰德公司（RAND Corporation）工作，之后进入康奈尔大学深造并获得艺术硕士学位。她是莱比锡大学（Leipzig University）的客座教授，也是阿德菲大学（Adelphi University）的创意写作助理教授。

凯瑟琳·钟多次在《纽约时报》、《兰普斯》(*The Rumpus*)、《格兰塔》上发表短篇小说和散文，并被《格兰塔》杂志评为2010年度"新声音"，荣获多萝西·萨金特·罗森伯格诗歌奖（Dorothy Sargent Rosenberg Prize in Poetry）、2014年美国全国艺术基金会创意写作奖金等。她的处女作《遗忘的国度》(*Forgotten Country*, 2012)问世不久即入选当年《书目杂志》(*Booklist*)十佳小说以及《旧金山纪事报》(*San Francisco Chronicle*)和《书页》(*Bookpage*)的年度最佳图书，并获得2013年海明威笔会奖（PEN/Hemingway Award）荣誉提名。她的第二本书《第十缪斯》(*The Tenth Muse*, 2019)同样好评如潮，获得当年美国国家犹太人书奖（National Jewish Book Award）提名。

《遗忘的国度》中萦绕着一个跨越几代人的诅咒：自日本占领朝鲜半岛以来，珍妮（Janie）家族的每一代都会失去一个女儿。在妹妹汉娜（Hannah）不辞而别、离奇消失后，珍妮被迫踏上寻亲之旅。她逐渐揭开父母二十年前突然搬到美国的真相，并且正视家人沉默的痛苦以及她与汉娜的矛盾关系。对家庭与爱的审视、对背叛与宽恕的思索为这部小说注入独特的情感内核。凯瑟琳·钟不仅向读者展示了韩国移民家庭中紧张的代际关系，而且让读者意识到，对于移民而言，他们在母国与移入国都难以拥有真正的家。选读部分摘自《遗忘的国度》第五章：珍妮的父亲身患癌症亟须回韩国救治，熟悉的搬家场景触发了主人公对于往日举家迁往美国的记忆。此部分哀伤与愤怒交织，隐晦地反映了光州大屠杀的残酷社会历史背景，具有极强的渲染力与时移性。

作品选读

Forgotten Country

Chapter 5

(excerpt)

By Catherine Chung

There was something familiar about packing up our house and getting ready to move: nearly twenty years ago we had dismantled everything and come to America, and now my parents were leaving everything again to rush back. I had been eight years old that first time, and though no one would explain the circumstances, I knew we were running away. While my parents never used the words "blacklist," or "exile," or "enemy of the state," these were words I learned in the months before our move, though I never spoke them aloud.

I knew they were linked, however, to our leaving, and to the night my uncle came to our apartment and stood in our living room in tears. That year, President Choi had been assassinated and General Han had taken power through a military coup. Ever since, there had been pro-democracy demonstrations, and crowds in the streets, with soldiers and policemen and roadblocks and air horns. General Han tried to shut down criticism by closing all the universities and arresting all his opponents, but the demonstrations continued all over the country: so many citizens demanding democracy.

During all this, my uncle was deployed to Kwangju to put down an uprising there.

He was doing his year of mandatory military service, and when he left Seoul, none of us knew much about what was happening out there. Several student demonstrations had been staged throughout the country on the same day urging democracy. In Kwangju, when some students were fired upon and killed, the city rose up and armed itself. Many of the protesting students had themselves just served their mandatory military service, so they were able to fight. When the military was sent in to contain them, they were told that it wasn't a student demonstration at all, but a communist uprising.

There were rumors of another civil war. There was talk of a massacre. My parents and I sat in my grandmother's living room, watching the news. No one believed the official number of two hundred casualties. Everyone knew more people had died. In front of the television, my grandmother prayed. We sat all evening, and then Hannah was packed off to sleep, but my grandmother insisted I stay up and watch.

"This isn't for children," my parents said. "She'll have nightmares."

But my grandmother ignored them. "She is old enough," she said. "This is not the first time such a thing has happened." All her life in Korea, people had been killed for their ideas. Students had died asking for change.

Long ago, when she was a child, families of dissidents had been driven to churches and town halls and burned into piles of ash. You breathed in that ash, my grandmother told me. It covered your skin. You held that ash inside you: it coated your lungs. It clung to your eyelashes and settled on your hair.

"Mother," my mother interrupted. "Things are different now." She covered my ears with her hands, even though I had already heard it, and could hear through her fingers anyway. When I shook my head, she stroked my hair. "Don't listen," she said. "All that was a long time ago."

"It was not so long ago," my grandmother said. To my father she said, "Your parents died in the war." He looked startled. I saw his jaw clench, but he did not respond.

"Mother," my mother said again, a warning in her voice, but my grandmother ignored it. Water in her village, she told me, had run red. It had tasted like iron. For years, she said, skulls would rise out of the ground during heavy rain, so that human bones were discovered along the fields and then reburied, as if they were seeds. "And now it is happening again," she said.

My father shook his head. "Things have changed. But be careful what you say," he said. "You still never know who is listening."

My parents were in the habit of cutting off conversation when it became most interesting.

Even though the massacre in Kwangju was important, outside of that night we spent watching the news in the living room, we never talked of it openly again. I stayed quiet, too, but without understanding. I did not know that the massacre had become a censored topic, and even bringing up the town's name could be considered a suspicious act. At the time I thought my parents were the source of the silence around the event. I had not yet learned that any powers beyond them existed.

Weeks later, my uncle returned, and I knew then that he'd been diminished somehow. Injured, perhaps. Grieved. But my parents seemed not to notice. When he finally came home they ushered him into our living room, and punished him. They pushed him for information. How many innocent victims had been killed? He did not know. Hundreds? Thousands? He could not say. The dead were mostly college students. They were young men, barely grown out of boyhood, his age. Had he killed anyone? my mother asked. Had he fired into the crowd of students? Had he any blood on his hands? He stood in the center of the room, facing my parents, our summer fans whirring around them and blurring all their voices. He was not supposed to tell. He was not supposed to talk about these things, but my parents would not relent.

My grandmother should have stepped in and stopped them then, out of love or pity, but I think they were punishing him for their own relief at his safety. They had worried about him ever since the first reports of the conflict. In any case, my grandmother left: she left my uncle in my parents' hands.

He responded haltingly to their questions. He'd been told the students were communist sympathizers. He'd been told the students had declared war on their current government. He'd been given direct orders to do what he did. "I had no choice," he said.

"Everyone has a choice," my father said. "Even if the choice is between honor or death, you can still choose not to kill innocent victims." This comment terrified and exhilarated me. He sounded so heroic, so willing to bear anything.

Then I looked at my uncle's bent head, and I wanted to run into the room and take his hand. But I stayed put. It probably wouldn't have made a difference if I had gone to him. I probably would have been sent back to my room and put to bed. Still, I have always wished I had gone and stood by his side.

He stood with his head down, and his shoulders shaking. My parents did not touch him, but stood, watching him. It wasn't until much later that they would come to regret the work they did that night.

When I woke up the next day, my uncle was gone, and my parents were grim and tense, and would say nothing about it. Something happened in the following weeks: one day they just turned against each other. My father had written a pamphlet about the details they had been able to glean from my uncle, and published it under the pen name of Eun Po. This man had been a famous poet and scholar and advisor to the king in the fourteenth century, and had been murdered for refusing to betray his king. Only my mother and two of his close friends knew my father had written this pamphlet, but my mother was furious at the danger she believed he'd put us all in.

For the next several days, they fought. They argued over the dishes, on the way to the grocery store, everywhere they went that we were alone. In public they were silent, but they stopped taking us to the playground, they didn't go to the store. They stayed at home and fought. They shouted at the table between bites of food.

"You're a mathematician," my mother said. "This isn't for you to do."

"I'm a citizen and a patriot. I did the right thing, the honorable thing."

"You did nothing but put us at risk. And no one will notice if something happens to you, or us."

"I thought you would support me," my father said. "When we met, you felt differently."

"That was before we had children."

"Someone has to protest. We can't always yield."

"You're risking the lives of our children."

"You used to believe in things."

"I believe in new things now. We have a family."

"You used to be brave."

"You call yourself brave?" My mother drew in her breath. "I should never have married you," she said. "I should never have given you children."

Then my father was silent. Perhaps my mother's words had lodged in his heart, as they had in mine. She was wishing her marriage to my father undone, Hannah and myself unmade.

Several days later, my parents called us into the living room. At first neither spoke. Then, "We are leaving," my father said. "We are moving away."

He didn't say more. After a moment I asked, "When are we going?" and Hannah let out a whimper, and puckered herself up to cry.

My father turned to her. "Come here," he said, opening his arms. She crawled over me to get to him and leaned her head against his shoulder. She was comforted so easily.

"We've been thinking of moving for a long time." His sister, my Komo, who had lived in America since before I was born, had found him a job. Both he and my mother thought it'd be best if he took it. He said this with a sideways look at my mother. He sat up a little straighter and shifted Hannah in his arms. He held out his hand to me. "Shake," he said.

I reached out and shook his hand. In school we had learned that this was how they greeted each other in the West. This was how they made a deal.

When my father let go of my hand, I turned to my mother. She had fixed her eyes on the building across from us, her whole body angled away. "Umma?" I asked. "Will you come, too?"

She tapped her foot against the ground, but she didn't answer. She didn't even turn to look at me.

"Umma?" I asked.

She stopped tapping her foot and touched her forehead as if to clear away a stray hair.

"Are you coming?" I repeated.

Her laugh was brittle. "I have no choice, since your Komo says to do it. Your father listens to his sister when she tells him he's in danger, but not to his wife."

I looked from her to my father and back. "So you're coming?" I repeated in a small voice.

My mother looked back at me, her face hard to read. Then she shook her head and said, "Oh, you little fool," and her voice was unexpectedly warm. She stood up and reached down for me, picking me up off the ground and hugging me hard. The relief of her touch was miraculous. I let it wash over me and was silent, as if I had asked the only question that mattered.

30
(Paul Yoon, 1980—)
保罗·尹

作者简介

保罗·尹（Paul Yoon，1980—），美国韩裔小说家，出生于美国纽约。他于1998年毕业于菲利普艾斯特中学，2002年毕业于卫斯理大学（Wesleyan University）。目前，他是本宁顿写作班（The Bennington Writing Seminars）的教员，并在哈佛大学任教。

保罗·尹著有短篇小说集《昔日的岸边》（Once the Shore，2009）、《大山》（The Mountain，2017），长篇小说《猎雪人》（Snow Hunters，2013）、《带我到地球》（Run Me to Earth，2020）。其中，《昔日的岸边》当选《纽约时报》年度优良图书，被评为《洛杉矶时报》（Los Angeles Times）、《旧金山纪事报》、《出版人周刊》（Publishers Weekly）、《明尼阿波利斯星坛报》（Minneapolis Star Tribune）的年度最佳图书以及美国国家公共广播电台的年度最佳处女作；小说《雪猎人》同样好评如潮，荣获2014年纽约公共图书馆幼狮小说奖（Young Lions Fiction Award）；小说《带我到地球》入围2021年卡内基文学奖（Andrew Carnegie Medal for Excellence in Fiction）。此外，其作品还被编入亨利奖故事集（PEN/O. Henry Prize Stories）。2010年，美国国家图书基金会推选他为"5位35岁以下最值得期待的作家"（5 Under 35 honoree）之一。

《带我到地球》是保罗·尹的最新作品，讲述了老挝内战期间三名孤儿的故事，追寻了他们分离后的生活轨迹。小说采用第三人称全知叙事视角，时间跨度六十余年，地域涉及老挝、纽约、西班牙、法国，兼具高超的艺术性与厚重的历史感，在语言迷宫中微妙还原历史真相。选读部分摘自小说首章《阿利萨克

（1969）》（"ALISAK (1969)"）：阿利萨克（Alisak）、普兰尼（Prany）和诺伊（Noi）三人被招入一所临时战地医院，他们冒着空袭和待引爆集束炸弹的威胁运送医疗物品，见证了无数平民百姓被战争荼毒的悲惨场面。

作品选读

Run Me to Earth

ALISAK (1969)

(excerpt)

By Paul Yoon

They were around the same age, Alisak, Prany, and Noi, and they had once lived next door to each other on a different hill, in a small settlement on the outskirts of the town, where the space between their houses was the width of a motorbike's handlebars. Where they were aware of the sound of each other behind the perpetually damp walls—the sound of their bodies, the clatter of their makeshift kitchens in the corner, their voices calling to play, calling for help—aware of each other's shadows outside their wooden doors long before they had a sense of a greater world beyond that slope, that river.

Then they had cared for each other when there was no one else to care for them. Alisak's parents eventually succumbed to the opium they were lured to farm; the siblings, who had no memory of their mother, lost their father early on in the war, when he was hired by the government to fix a bombed road two days' journey south but was caught by the Pathet Lao. He was told to walk the road as the soldiers took bets on whether he would step on a bomb, grew bored when nothing happened, and shot him. Neither Prany nor Noi was certain of anything for weeks—their father was often gone—until the peddler who passed through every season came to the hill, asking for them.

It was when the fighting intensified, after that encounter with the Tobacco Captain, that they began to wander the country, always staying together, sleeping where they could, finding work where they could, avoiding the armies where they could. They spent three years surviving the rainy seasons, the sudden approach of strangers, and a war where the boundaries shifted endlessly, where they often jolted awake from the sound of bombers or the sudden appearance of an army in a town or a village they were staying in.

When a jeep appeared that day to recruit them for the hospital, they had only recently returned to their own town. They hadn't meant to. It was just that there didn't seem to be anywhere else they could go anymore.

Alisak and Prany were now seventeen, Noi a year younger. It was the early fall of 1969. Their last season together here. Or at least that was what Vang told them. That they would in all likelihood be evacuating soon.

Alisak never said this out loud, but he felt as though he could stay here with them in the madness of this house forever. He thought there would be nothing better. Paintings, mirrors, pillows, and tall windows. A kitchen and a piano upstairs. The three of them always together. The great motorbikes.

Their answers to the question of where they went to in the evenings, in their dreams or when they were awake, as they tried to keep their minds off the denotation flashes coming closer and getting louder, and the steady flood of the maimed and the wounded, were always different.

Where did they go at nights?

A museum or Paris. The moon. A cave, an endless beach. They had been doing this since they were children.

No one ever said home.

Some days, Alisak thought he would miss the bikes more than he would any of the people they worked for at this field hospital. By his count there were about twelve personnel he could recognize and whom he had grown accustomed to helping. Some of them were Thai, others were Hmong and from the mountains, and many of them were from the lowlands, south. All of them were allies of the Royal Lao Government and spoke some mix of Lao, Thai, Hmong, English, and French, always adding hand gestures.

Save for Vang, however, Alisak's interactions with everyone had been brief and in the orbit of chaos. A nurse shouting at him, *Hurry up, boy, hurry and bring the tray over. Dammit, don't spill, that's the last we have of it. Shove the bit between his teeth and hold it down, harder, believe me, he won't feel his teeth breaking.*

So Alisak did, standing behind the injured boy whom he thought he recognized from the town, and talking to him. He pointed up with his chin toward that corner of the roof that had fallen from the concussion of a bomb one month ago in order to give the boy something for his pale eyes to focus on instead of his own body.

It was the rainy season. The rain came in furious bursts, never lasting for more than a minute, but it felt as though the roof wouldn't be able to hold the force of weather. They watched the miniature waterfall in the ward that lasted long enough for Vang to amputate a leg above the knee. They would use the pooling rainwater to mop the floors.

Sometimes, as the rain kept falling, Vang walked over to that corner, slipped off his gloves postsurgery, and washed his forearms and his hands. Then, like the flip of a coin, the sun returned. As though it never rained at all, catching the rim of Van's eyeglasses. And Alisak, not realizing he was still holding the ends of the wooden bit, woke from where he was, felt a nurse unlocking his fingers as she told him he could go.

The truth was that this Lao doctor, Vang, seemed different from the others. He was the only one, Alisak thought, who had the ability, when he addressed them, to pull them out of the world that was consuming them. If that were possible in the panic that never seemed to end, in the voices and the detonations across the valley that always caused another bit of the house to collapse.

Once, a wounded farmer tried to flee, having no memory of the cause of his injuries, shouting at everyone that he had entered some kind of war prison and had been tortured. He had run down that hall of mirrors straight past the kitchen and grabbed Noi by the hair, assuring her that he would help her, that it was all right, that he was here now as he tried to drag her out of the house.

He took her as far as the entrance hall. Then, for unknown reasons, he let her go and ran across the tobacco fields entering the valley. They waited for a buried bombie to go off but nothing happened. They never saw him again.

The ceaseless sound of the house, the people, the bombs. Alisak had learned to almost think of it all as the rain. Or that was what Vang had once told him, snapping his fingers and ordering him, in French, to repeat the phrases as though he were no longer in this country but somewhere foreign and far.

(They had all gotten better at conjugating verbs—*Coudre! Couds! Coud! Cousons!*—and listing Parisian landmarks as Vang took them along on a quick tour around the city in his mind. How did he know Paris? They would never find out.)

Other days, he played the piano for them. It was upstairs, in the corner room where they—the three lost orphans, as Vang called them affectionately, referring to an ancient children's story everyone knew—took turns as lookout, panning across the valley for movement with a pair of binoculars and a rifle as their ears were invaded suddenly by the foreignness of a few bars of Bach.

Wild, reckless notes that Alisak felt under his ribs. Spaces of quiet.

When Vang wasn't there, Alisak would flip through the stack of music sheets that had been left behind, trying to decipher the coded symbols for himself.

Vang was never able to finish what he was playing. He adjusted his glasses that almost always slid down his nose as he ran out to answer another doctor shouting for him. Or, he rushed into the room where they had brought in a radio so that they could communicate with the government or with the Hmong fighters who, if they could, relayed back the advancing positions of the Pathet Lao and the North Vietnamese.

Mostly, though, Alisak, Prany, and Noi kept to themselves, performing the tasks they were assigned. Or they were away, riding the motorcycles, following each other and the route they made into Phonsavan, where there was another hospital that had been set up.

There was also the river where they could pick up supplies that were delivered by an old woman operating a boat. They had known this boat woman since they were children, and their parents had known the woman because they used to buy food from her. It had also been a way for them to travel. They rarely ever spoke to her—Prany was convinced she was actually a mute—but when they were younger, she used to let them ride with her upriver past the villages. If they helped her sell, she gave them extra food or some money and brought them to the riverbank, where they jumped off the boat without her ever stopping.

She was still alive, still with her boat, and still silent, though she didn't have any extra food now. There was instead a rifle in a basket by her legs, Alisak not knowing if she had ever had the reason to use it.

They carried pistols when they were on their missions but they rarely had the chance to fire them. Here, the fighting on the ground had for the most part ceased after the majority of the roads had been bombed, and because of the rain, so they had in the recent months encountered very little of the armies. Instead, there was the new landscape the fighting had left behind: abandoned tanks in the fields, trucks split in half in a muddy crater, clothing, unidentifiable bones that were bright as steel, weapons, cases of ammunition they quickly loaded onto their bikes, and empty shell casings they could bring back to collect rainwater.

Now, in this corner of the country, everything happened from the air, from the side that was supposedly theirs. There had been times when they were forced to outrun jets flying low, the pilots unsure of who they were, whether they were enemies, the three of them with their faces wrapped in bandannas like bandits as they sped quickly into the woods and vanished under its thick canopy.

They stayed a full night once in the woods, sitting on the ground by their bikes and listening not to the rain, which fell silently, but to the endless torrent of bombers somewhere above the canopy that seemed so close they kept expecting one to crash down on them, cutting off the tops of the trees. They had never seen an airplane up close before and a part of Alisak wished one would come down. He wanted to see where the bombs were stored, how they were released, what a pilot did to release them. What kind of person a pilot was.

In the woods that night, they didn't sleep. They huddled under the thickest canopy and tried to ignore the rain seeping through their clothes. They reached out to soak some stale bread they had found in the kitchen, to soften it, and passed it around, biting off pieces. *Couds, cousons.*

At first light, they returned to the town that had for the most part remained intact, though hardly anyone was there anymore. Yet they continued to raid and scavenge, in case they overlooked places: in the cupboards and closets of the café where there was a half-torn propaganda poster depicting a monk standing beside a soldier, both of them with their fists raised; in the rooms of homes or the guesthouse they would never have dared entered years ago, where an old, blind woman hid behind a door and listened to them walking around. Or in the restaurant behind which they used to loiter with the stray cats, waiting for a cook to give them some leftovers. Alisak remembered how Prany always fed the animals, their teeth sometimes breaking his skin, though Prany never seemed to mind, wiping the blood away with a silk handkerchief he had untied from the collar of a dead dog when they were wandering the south.

What happened to that handkerchief?

In the town the next morning, after scavenging for supplies, they hurried to the other hospital, where a terrified doctor, who appeared as though he had crawled out of a cave from another century, handed them one last box of morphine. He had wrapped it in his doctor's coat because the box was soaked from the rain and about to fall apart.

"Tell Vang there's no more," the doctor said. "Please stop coming. Leave us alone. We can't help anymore. We can't help."

He hurried back inside. He had spoken to them like the beggars they had been. Noi took out her pistol and aimed it at him, at the glass door that was still there, beyond which they watched the man returning down a corridor with some kind of limp. When he was gone, she fired, shattering the glass. A nurse who had appeared in the lobby screamed and ducked behind a man she had been pushing in a wheelchair. Noi would have fired again if Prany didn't remind her they needed to save the bullets.

Noi kicked the hospital door once for good measure. Prany claimed the doctor's coat.

When they drove back to the farmhouse, all the windows dark because the electricity had gone out again, the nurses, even Vang, tried to hide their surprise as they lifted candle flames toward them in the hall, thinking the three of them had run away, or that they had died.

中国人民大学出版社外语出版分社读者信息反馈表

尊敬的读者：

　　感谢您购买和使用中国人民大学出版社外语出版分社的 _____ 一书，我们希望通过这张小小的反馈卡来获得您更多的建议和意见，以改进我们的工作，加强我们双方的沟通和联系。我们期待着能为更多的读者提供更多的好书。

　　请您填妥下表后，寄回或传真回复我们，对您的支持我们不胜感激！

1. 您是从何种途径得知本书的：
   □书店　　　　□网上　　　　□报纸杂志　　　　□朋友推荐
2. 您为什么决定购买本书：
   □工作需要　　□学习参考　　□对本书主题感兴趣　　□随便翻翻
3. 您对本书内容的评价是：
   □很好　　　　□好　　　　□一般　　　　□差　　　　□很差
4. 您在阅读本书的过程中有没有发现明显的专业及编校错误，如果有，它们是：
   _____
   _____
   _____

5. 您对哪些专业的图书信息比较感兴趣：
   _____
   _____
   _____

6. 如果方便，请提供您的个人信息，以便于我们和您联系（您的个人资料我们将严格保密）：
   您供职的单位：_____
   您教授的课程（教师填写）：_____
   您的通信地址：_____
   您的电子邮箱：_____

　　请联系我们：黄婷　程子殊　吴振良　王琼　鞠方安

　　电话：010-62512737，62513265，62515538，62515573，62515576

　　传真：010-62514961

　　E-mail：huangt@crup.com.cn　　chengzsh@crup.com.cn　　wuzl@crup.com.cn
　　　　　　crup_wy@163.com　　jufa@crup.com.cn

　　通信地址：北京市海淀区中关村大街甲59号文化大厦15层　　邮编：100872

　　中国人民大学出版社外语出版分社